D1522333

Honeysuckles

on a Tennessee

Breeze

LeTresa Payne

Printed by Amazon Kindle Direct Publishing, Inc.

ISBN: 9781795286855

Printed in the United States of America

Cover Photo Credit:

Nsey Benajah, Photographer on Unsplash

Acknowledgements

First, as always, I must acknowledge God for allowing me to complete another work of fiction. After not publishing a book in over a year, it's only by His grace and mercy that I am able to publish this work. I thank you, Lord, for all you have done for me and will continue doing for me.

Secondly, I want to thank all of my readers who have been rocking with me since my first published novel. Without all of you, this writing thing would've continued to be just a dream of mine instead of the reality that it is. I am forever grateful to each one of you who give me a chance by reading my works.

A special word of thanks is in order to Bryan Jones. Thank you for your encouragement to continue writing. You've been here for me through some of the toughest times in my life and I am thankful to God for you and for you motivating me to move forward when I didn't have any motivation to even type a single word. You are a blessing to me.

I want to thank Roxie Rhoden, Kimberly Parker and Sonja Chambers for supporting my works. You ladies have been a blessing to me.

A thank you is in order for Johnna Whetstone and Alexandra Thompson of the Chapter Chatter Pub on Facebook for supporting my work. You girls are some amazing friends. I want to also thank Colleen Anthony, Nikki Valdez, Lori Brickey and Mary Possinger for reading my work, as well. You ladies rock!

Darla Obrien, you have been a wonderful friend. You have brought a light into this world that will never be dimmed.

I did this one for my hometown... Stand up Ripley, TN!

Dedication

I'm dedicating this story to my mother, Teresa Harris. You are the queen of my heart and I thank God daily for you. I love you.

Chapter 1

The sound of the wind whistling through the trees above my head were comforting, yet, alarming at the same time. The ever-crunching sound of the fallen leaves and branches beneath my feet as I hastily made my way through the woods represented my urgency to escape the terror that I left behind me. As quickly as I released a breath, I inhaled another as I picked up the speed. *I gotta get home. I gotta get home.* Sweat dripped downwards from my forehead steadily as I moved forward towards home in the sweltering heat of late August. Although the branches overhead offered shade, cloaking me in semi-darkness, the end of summer Tennessee heat was overwhelming. *I gotta get home. I gotta get home.*

Tears stung my eyes as I tried to block out the image I witnessed moments before from my mind. *Why hadn't I just listened to Big Ma and stayed at home?* If I hadn't have been so hard-headed, I wouldn't have seen something so awful that was definitely going to stay with me for the rest of my life. *Shoot!* I should've stayed at home and helped Big Ma shuck the corn like she had asked me to, but naw, I just had to follow Sister to the 5 and 10 store 'cause I wanted to convince her to buy me some penny candy. I knew if I had begged to come along, she would've just said no like she always does. Since Sister was five years older than me and a teenager now, she felt like she didn't have any time for little sisters like me hanging all around her bugging her or being "worrisome" as she claims I am.

Pushing my way through the brush, I stumbled out of the woods and breathed in deeply as I took in the fresh country air which was engulfed in the fragrance of honeysuckles and Big Ma's rose bushes. The warmth of the afternoon sun fell upon my body, wrapping me in its protection. *Had Sister seen me? Did she know I saw her?* Climbing the steps to Big Ma's house two at a time, dirty red tennis shoes heavily stomping the old wooden steps, I pulled opened the screen door and flew past Big Ma who was sitting in her favorite chair next to the wall. Listening to gospel music which came pouring from the floor radio's speakers, she sat shucking corn with my little brother, Isaiah who we affectionately called Junebug, sitting at her feet.

"Cora!" I heard Big Ma cry out as I fled from the front room and into the back bedroom that I shared with Sister in the five room shack we lived in at Big Ma's house. I jumped onto my bed and lay down on top of a quilt Big Ma had made me and my sister.

"Cora Leanne!" came Big Ma's worried voice from the front room again. Burying my head into the down feathered pillow on the bed, huge tears soaked through as the image of Sister and some white boy doing the nasty behind the 5 and 10 entered my mind again. "How could she just let that boy do that to ha'?"

I thought to myself as my shoulders heaved up and down on my body.

The soft shuffling sound of Big Ma's house shoes entering the room made its way to my ears. "Cora?"

I kept my head buried into the pillow. There ain't no way I'm squealing on Sister and telling Big Ma what I saw. Sister would pop me upside my head as soon as Big Ma got finished whipping her. I was sure of it.

Big Ma's presence could be felt next to the bed before I felt her loving hand on my bare shoulder. Her hands always felt so strong and loving. Within her hands held the story of many years of struggle and sacrifice that she has made for her family. Those hands had endured the blistering summer weather of sharecropping and picking cotton for so many years, just so this family could survive. There was no other person on this earth that I loved and respected more, except for my baby brother, Isaiah.

"Cora Leanne Harris, if you don't roll ya' lil' self ova right na' and tell meh what's tha' meaning of ya' comin' in this house like ya' jus' did?"

"Ion wanna..." I mumbled into the pillow. I rarely back talked Big Ma, but there was no way I was telling on Sister.

"Cora!" Big Ma said sternly.

Rolling over on the bed, I sat up straight and wiped my face with the palms of my hands. My long reddish-brown pigtails flopped unto my chest and the ends of them ended up tickling my thighs as I folded my legs on top of the bed. Big Ma eyed me curiously, her dark brown eyes focused on me intently with worry written behind them. Her beautiful, dark face was scrunched up as she watched me and I marveled at the age lines that adorned her face like timeless beauty marks. Big Ma had seen many things in her day and I'm sure something like catching your big sister humping a white boy wouldn't even faze her, but it was killing me on the inside.

"Nothin', Big Ma. Nothin', I swea'," I mumbled, looking down at my wrinkled yellow tank top, that was now more of a dingy yellow, than the bright yellow it had once been when Sister used to wear it. I got all of Sister's hand me downs and it bothered me that I only received new clothes on my birthday or Christmas day because we were too poor for me to get them any other time.

"Stripes, if ya' don't tell meh what's tha' matter wit' ya', I'm sure ta' whip ya' into next week! What's tha' meaning of ya' runnin' up into this house like a bat outta hell? Have ya' surely done lost ya' eva' lastin' mind?" Big Ma fussed as she put her hands on her faded blue, aproned tied hips.

Stripes was the nickname my Uncle Joe gave me when I was a baby. I really hate my nickname because it means "Zebra" or "Cross breed" like the kids at school call me. I don't even like to think of myself as being different from the other kids I know, but I am. I'm the only mulatto kid in my entire school. Everyone else is Negro. It bothers me because the kids make fun of me all the time because I look so different. My hair is different, my skin color is different, and worse of all... My eyes are different. No one has these eyes except for me and well, Sister. We share the same eyes... They're a bluish-green color and I've never seen any other Negro with them, but us. But since Uncle Joe gave me the nickname, I just don't have the heart to tell him I don't like it.

"Well?" Big Ma asked in a huff, impatiently waiting on my response.

I tried to think of a lie quick, but luckily for me we both heard the front screen door slam shut with a bang.

"Junebug?!" Big Ma's eyes grew wide and she hurried out of the room towards the front room. I eased off of the bed and slowly followed her, curious as to who had entered the house so angrily. Big Ma must've thought Isaiah had run out the house, but I knew it couldn't have been him slamming the door. Isaiah never did too much of anything on his own. As I inched my way down the hall towards the front room, I stopped just outside of it, holding on to the flowered wall-papered wall and peeped inside. There stood Sister looking all roughed up with Sheriff Bradford holding her by the wrist.

"Sheriff Bradford, what's tha' meanin' of all this?" Big Ma asked cautiously as she looked back and forth between Sister and the sheriff.

Sheriff Bradford was a big stocky fellow with white skin that was reddened by the harsh summer sun. He had beady black eyes like a hawk's and the skinniest, longest nose I had ever seen on anybody's face in my life. It was known that he didn't like Negroes one bit and I feared for the reason he now had Sister in his possession.

Sister stood slightly in front of the sheriff with her red hair looking messy upon her head as if it were a bird's nest. She tried her best to jerk away from him, but he held his grip firmly on her arm. Sister's pretty polka dotted blue dress was torn at the bottom and I knew that Big Ma was gonna whip her hard tonight because of it. Big Ma always told us to take pride in all of our belongings because they were a gift from God and we never knew when we would be able to get another gift from Him. What I wanted to know was if God gave us gifts, why did we have to always wait so long for another one?

"Virginia, I caught this thieving youngin' of yours behind the store digging through the trash bins. Now, I'm gonna warn ya' just this once and this the only time, ya' hear me? Keep this high yella bitch out from 'round the 5 and 10! If I catch her down there agin', I'll have no choice but ta' lock her up and let the judge deal wit' her!" Sheriff Bradford let go of Sister and pushed her into Big Ma with such force I thought they both would tumble down to the floor.

At the roaring sound of the sheriff's angry voice, Isaiah started wailing and rocking back and forth in the corner he was now sitting in. His tears fell like gum drops and I longed to run into the room and scoop him up into my arms. I hated to see my baby brother cry. His tears caused me a deep pain that was indescribable. Maybe it was because when I looked into his eyes I saw our Mama. Isaiah looked just like her.

Big Ma hugged Sister closely to her body and looked up at the red-faced monster standing before her and nodded. "Yessuh... You won't have any mo' problems outta this chile."

Sheriff Bradford cleared his throat and eyed Sister with disdain before adjusting the holster on his waist underneath his huge, protruding beer belly. Pushing open the screen door, he took his leave. Moments later the sound of his 1961 Chevy police car was heard being cranked and then gravel crunching as he pulled out of the drive.

Big Ma let go of Sister and reared back and slapped her hard across the face.

"What I tells ya' fast tail 'bout goin' down there to that store?"

Sister raised a hand to her face and rubbed the spot where Big Ma had hit her that was now turning as red as a ripe strawberry. Narrowing her eyes, she spoke in the coldest tone I had ever heard come from her lips. "I was jus' down there tryna find work, is all. I'm tied of wearin' all of these old clothes! Tied of not havin' any fancy dresses like those rich gals in my class. I'm prettier than all of them, but you could neva' tell it 'cause I gotta dress like I'm some ole' poor, country hick!"

Big Ma's eyes grew wide and she clucked her tongue. I waited for the slap that was surely coming to Sister once again, but to my surprise it never did.

"You's just like ya' mammy. Just like ha'," Big Ma said shaking her head in disgust. "Always wanting newer and excitin' thangs. Always gotta have the latest dress or shoes or fancy makeup. You must wanna end up like her, too, huh? Is that it? Huh, Billie?"

My hand flew to my lips as I stifled a gasp from escaping. Big Ma never called Sister by her first name because she said it reminded her too much of Sister's daddy who Sister was named after, so I knew she had to be angrier than hornet bees after someone knocked their nest down out of a tree. Sister had been called by her nickname for as long as I could remember because she was so close in age with Big Ma's youngest child.

"I sho'll do! 'Cause at least she was smart enough to get tha' hell outta this backwards ass town!" Sister sassed, eyeing Big Ma down. At this point I was fearing for her very life because none of us had ever cussed in front of Big Ma before.

Big Ma shook her head and wiped her sweaty palms with the tail of her apron before turning away from Sister. Returning to her seat in the big, tattered, sunken in arm chair she loved so much, she picked up an ear of corn and began shucking it.

"Cora?" she called out to me.

I didn't answer at first in fear that she surely was gonna try to lay a whipping in on someone if it wasn't indeed Sister.

"Cora?" Big Ma called again.

"Ye... Yes'm?" I asked quietly from my hiding spot.

"Come on out from behind that wall and tend ta' Junebug ova there. Git' him ta' stop all that cryin'," Big Ma said calmly as she lay down the corn cob she had just shucked into a bowl and reached down into an old paint bucket filled with more ears.

I eased on out of my hiding place and kept my eyes low to the ground as I walked past Sister who was still standing in the middle of the floor watching Big Ma. Sitting down next to Isaiah, I scooped him up into my arms and started rocking him back and forth slowly, shhing him. His cries settled down as soon as he rested his head on my shoulder before sticking his thumb into his mouth.

"So, that's it? You ain't got nothin' else ta' say?" Sister pressed, still eyeing Big Ma defiantly.

"Since yo' tail is all grown now, naw. I sho'll don't. You can git' locked up in that jail downtown if ya' wanna. Just know that when ya' do, I'm not comin' down there wit' no bail money." Big Ma pulled back the leafy green skin of a corn cob before speaking again. "And, I knows what ya' been up to, too... I can just smell ya' from ova here. Ya' fast just like ya' mammy was. Gone in tha' kitchen and boil ya' some water on tha' stove for a bath. Don't forget to get tha' metal washtub from out back on tha' back porch befo' ya' boil that water."

All the color drained from Sister's face at the revelation that Big Ma knew she hadn't been digging in the trash like the sheriff claimed she was. Turning abruptly on her heel, she stomped out of the front room and into the kitchen. The next thing we heard was the sound of the backdoor screen creaking open, then slamming, and creaking open again.

I looked over at Big Ma curiously and wondered how she knew what Sister had been up to. Big Ma was so wise that it seemed as if she always knew what each and every last one of us were up to and it made me wonder that if I lived to be that old would I know everything everybody did, too?

Looking down at Isaiah as he laid in my arms softly sucking on his thumb, I wondered would life ever feel the same for us in Big Ma's house again, because suddenly, almost unknowingly, the world had just shifted right up underneath our feet.

*

As I lay quietly in the full-sized bed I shared with Sister that night, I listened to her soft breathing and watched through the dimly moonlit light in the room as her chest rose and fell. It amazed me how she could easily fall asleep after everything that happened today. Did she really not have a conscience? How could she just do what she did with that scrawny little white boy, be brought home by the sheriff, sass mouth Big Ma and still be living? Let that have been me... I would've been dead twice and not been able to live to tell about it.

Sister sighed in her sleep next to me and repositioned herself in the bed. She had no idea that up until today, I had idolized her. I wanted to be so much like her. In my eyes, she was the most beautiful girl in the entire world. She had breasts and hips and was thick like biscuits in all the right places where I was still stuck in my stick figure of a body. Her gorgeous red hair had been messy when she came home today, but normally she wore it in long loose waves that cascaded down her back like water in a flowing stream. Our eyes were the only thing we still had alike and I hoped to God that they would never change like the rest of her body had. I wanted something about Sister to stay the same at least. Over the past year she had grown up so much that I barely recognized her.

"Stripes?" Sister called out into the darkness and I jumped slightly, startled at the sound of my name.

My jumping had already given away the fact that I wasn't asleep, so it was no use in pretending now. "Yeah?"

Sister took a moment before responding. In a cool voice, she asked, "You followed me out there today, didn't ya'?"

My body froze at her question. She saw me?

"Answer me, Stripes... Did ya'?"

Swallowing hard, I wished on end that my mouth hadn't just went dry. "Uh..."

Sister groaned and rolled over on her side to face me. Her eyes glistened as the moonlight fell upon them through the window. "How many times have I told ya' not to follow up behind me all tha' time?"

"I know, but..."

"No, buts..." Sister said as she looked at me angrily. "I know ya' saw what I was doin' out there with Johnny Ray. I ain't want ya' ta' see that, but I'm glad that we heard ya' when ya' knocked ova' that paint can or we would've been in a whole heap of trouble."

I looked at my sister as her angry eyes grew softer and waited on her to continue.

"If it wasn't for ya', we would've been in some real big trouble for sho'. I'd probably be dead or somethin'. Johnny Ray probably would be locked up for screwin' a Negro."

The thought of Sister dying made my heart skip a couple beats in my chest. I didn't want to think of such a thing and she was scaring me.

"Wh... Why were you doin' that wit' that boy anyways?" I asked in a quiet voice. Up until that moment earlier today, I had never seen anybody doing the nasty. I had only heard about it once from a girl named Betsy Jo at school who had seen her mama and daddy doing it by accident one night when she walked in on them in their bedroom. What she had described that time surely mirrored what I saw Sister doing earlier with that white boy.

"'Cause... Well, you're too little to understand, Stripes..."

Frowning, I sat up slightly in the bed and rested my head in the palm of my hand as my elbow sunk into the mattress. "No, I ain't, Sister!"

"Okay... If ya' ain't, tell me what I was doin' wit' him then."

"You was, uh, um..."

Sister tilted back her head in laughter. "See, ya' can't even git' it out ya' mouth."

Narrowing my eyes at her, I continued gruffly, "Y'all was doin' tha' nasty!"

That stopped her laughter and she looked at me. "How'd ya' kno' that?"

"I just do. I told ya' I ain't that little!" I replied, eyeing her. "Why'd ya' do it anyways?"

Sister rolled back onto her back and gazed up at the ceiling. "'Cause it feels good. That's why. You'll understand when ya' older."

Shaking my head, I looked at her like she was crazy. There was no way in the world I would ever let a boy touch me down there like she had. What she had been doing looked painful and for the life of me I couldn't figure out how it felt good to her.

"Naw, I won't. Ain't no crusty kneed boy finna eva' put his thang in me."

This made Sister laugh aloud again and I was hoping she would shut up, so that Big Ma wouldn't wake up in the other room and come in here to put a whipping on us. Some parts of me still believed that Sister's whipping was still on the way.

"When you git' ta' be my age and them hormones of yours start goin' wild, I swea' you'll change ya' tune, Stripes."

Something was still bugging me about Sister's behavior earlier and I just had to know about it. "Why'd ya' do it wit' that white boy, tho'?"

Sister exhaled deeply and as the moonlight gently kissed her face, I saw a smile as big as the Milky Way spread across it. "'Cause, I love him..."

Love? She loved a white boy? It surprised me because her daddy was white and she hated him. "Huh?"

"Ya' heard me, right. I love Johnny Ray. He swears that when we turn sixteen next year, we gonna catch a train up North and git' hitched! He's the only boy for me."

"Hitched? Ya' gettin' MARRIED?!" I shrieked in disbelief forgetting that Big Ma could walk in at any moment with a switch and whip my behind. I couldn't believe my sister was talking about leaving me and running off with some red neck little white boy.

Sister turned over and covered my mouth with her hand. "Shh! Before ya' wake up Big Ma!" I nodded and she removed her hand from over my mouth. "Yes, we's gettin' married next spring. He said so. He's workin' on gettin' me tha' ring and everythang."

"Ohhh..." I replied softly and closed my eyes, so that I wouldn't show her my emotions.

A lump was forming in my throat and I wanted to cry. I couldn't take it if my sister left me. Was she really just like Mama like Big Ma said she was? Mama had left us behind again right after Isaiah was born. She showed up on a snowy Christmas morning at Big Ma's front door carrying with her a baby wrapped in a thick brown blanket and handed him over to Big Ma like that was her Christmas present to her. She just literally handed him over without a word and took back off down the road in the fancy car of some wealthy Negro she had met. None of us had heard from or seen her since that day nearly six years ago.

"Stripes?" Sister called out in the darkness, but this time I pretended I was sleep and made some slight snoring noises and soft coos to give it the added affect. I felt Sister roll over and kiss me softly on the forehead before turning back over to go to sleep. When I heard soft snoring coming from her side of the bed again, I opened my eyes and stared widely into the darkness as hot, salty tears escaped my eyes, falling one by one onto my pillow. *What was I going to do without her? I had already lost my Mama, now I was gonna lose my big sister, too?*

Chapter 2

"Joe, I tells ya', I just don't know what Imma do 'bout that, gal," I overheard Big Ma saying to her son as she fixed us some breakfast in the kitchen.

Uncle Joe was Big Ma's youngest child out of five children, but he's the only one who still lived at home. Big Ma once had a daughter named Aunt Bertha, but she died when she was 9 from heat exhaustion working in the fields sharecropping. Uncle Sammie, Big Ma's oldest, lived in Chicago with his third wife and had about eight or nine kids, I can't keep up. Aunt Trish lives in Memphis about an hour away from us and is a school teacher who refuses to have any children of her own and last but not least, my Mama, Glory Jean, who ran off from home when she was sixteen and pregnant with Sister just to later bring her back home for Big Ma to raise, just like me and Isaiah.

"She's just like Glory Jean, Mama, and ya' knows it," Uncle Joe said in between sips of his morning coffee. "Ya' sees it just as well as I do. That chile gon' end up knocked up just like she did, too, befo' long."

Big Ma threw the washrag she was holding down on the kitchen table in disgust. "Now, you just hursh ya' mouth right on up, boy! That gal ain't gon' end up like Glory Jean if I got any say in it."

Chuckling, Uncle Joe shook his head. "Mama, now tell meh how you suppose you gonna keep Sister's legs closed? She's hot to trot just like Glory Jean was in her day and probably still is, if she's living. You'd have better luck to place ya' hopes in Stripes. That baby gal ain't nothin' like Glory Jean and I'm so thankful for it. That baby got a good head on her shoulders and barely gives ya' any trouble."

At the mention of my name, I entered the kitchen pretending that I just didn't hear their conversation. Sister was still fast asleep in bed, as she wasn't an early riser like I was. Big Ma once told me that I had an old soul and I believed her, because sometimes I didn't even act like I was my age. I saw things a whole lot differently than most kids I knew.

"Mornin', Big Ma, Uncle Joe," I said quietly as I took a seat next to Isaiah who was busy spinning a cold drink bottle cap on top of the kitchen table.

"Mornin' Stripes," Uncle Joe said with a warm smile that could brighten even the darkest of days.

"Mornin' Cora," Big Ma said as she picked up the discarded washrag and made her way to the gas-powered stove and opened the oven door to retrieve some freshly made buttermilk biscuits. "Where's Sister?"

"Still sleep, I bet," Uncle Joe chuckled as he winked at me before taking a sip of coffee.

"In the bed, Big Ma," I replied, then leaned over in my seat to give Isaiah a hug. He moaned in response and kept right on spinning the bottle top.

Sitting back upright in my seat, I thought about what I had overheard Uncle Joe say. Was my mother still living? If she was, where exactly was she? I was five years old the last time I saw her and my memory of her was foggy. The question that was forever etched into the back of my mind was how could Mama just up and leave us like she did? Didn't she love us?

"That chile, that chile," Big Ma said shaking her head. Putting her hands on her hips she looked my way. "Well, she's just gonna miss out on ha' breakfast befo' church then."

Usually that would be my cue to go and shake Sister awake, but somehow this morning I didn't feel like being bothered with her. My heart still hurt from what I witnessed on yesterday and from what Sister planned to do in the spring.

"Well, Stripes, ain't ya' gonna go wake Sister like ya' always do?" Big Ma asked.

Shaking my head, I reached out and grabbed some bacon from the platter that was sitting in front of me and placed it on my plate. Sister would be her problem this morning as I didn't want to have any dealings with her at all.

Big Ma looked at me curiously, then dusted her hands off on her apron. Untying the apron, she laid it on the kitchen chair at the head of the table where she always sat each morning and headed out of the room, most likely to wake up Sister.

"You okay, Stripes?" Uncle Joe asked watching me in concern.

"Yessuh," I replied in between bites of eggs.

Turning towards Isaiah, I dug a spoon into the eggs on his plate and lifted the spoonful up to his mouth. "Here, eat Junebug," I requested.

Isaiah opened his mouth and I placed the spoon inside. Closing his mouth, I gently removed the spoon and he chewed twice before swallowing. Grinning, he dropped the bottle top onto the table and started clapping his hands and rocking back and forth.

"They's good, huh?" I asked him, smiling.

Isaiah continued smiling and rocking, so I took that as his response that they were. Returning my attention to my own plate, I picked up a biscuit and slapped some butter and some of Big Ma's tasty homemade peach preserves on it. Taking a bite, I closed my eyes as my taste buds relished in the explosive flavor of the biscuit and jam. If there was one thing I loved most in this life, it was the home cooked meals my Big Ma made. I opened my eyes when I heard Sister fussing with Big Ma as they entered the kitchen.

"I don't wanna go ta' church today!" Sister exclaimed as she sat down angrily in the chair opposite of me at the kitchen table. Crust from sleeping so hard were at the corners of her eyes and she had red lines embedded on her cheek from sleeping on her fingers.

"Little gal, if ya' don't hursh up ya' mouth! I've 'bout had it up to my neck wit' ya' sassin'!" Big Ma replied in a huff as she took her seat at the head of the table. "As long as ya' livin' under my roof, you's gonna go up to that church wit' ya' family and praise the Lord!"

Sister rolled her eyes and crossed her arms over her chest. "Well, maybe I should just move then!" she grumbled, irritably.

"And go where, young lady?" Uncle Joe chimed in, eyes flashing angrily as he looked Sister's way. "Yo' gran'ma is tryin' ta' do tha' best she can by you and yo' sister and brother. You ain't that grown where you can't get no whippin', so I suggest you sit down at this here table, eat tha' good ole' breakfast Mama done made, and then go and get ready for church. Do I make myself clear?"

Sister rolled her eyes and uncrossed her arms. "Yeah..."

"What was that?" Uncle Joe demanded.

"Yessuh," Sister replied angrily before picking up her fork and placing some eggs into her mouth.

Uncle Joe was usually a fun-loving man to be around who loved to joke a lot, but he was serious when it came down to it and did not appreciate anyone disrespecting his mother or any other elderly person.

I eyed Sister from my seat, but she kept her head downwards, focusing on the food on her plate. Her fiery red hair enveloped the sides of her face like a curtain. Taking a sip of milk from my drinking glass, I wondered if I would act like her when I turned 15. If this is how hormones made you act, I never wanted to grow up. Ever.

*

"Praise the Lord, saints. Praise the Lord!" Pastor Solomon exclaimed from his position behind the pulpit. The church parishioners responded with a loud, resounding "Praise the Lord!" which resonated off of the small wooden church's four walls.

"Today is indeed a day that the Lord has made and is one that we should all be glad to see. Can I get an Amen?"

"Amen!"

I sat on the second row of the church next to Big Ma and Isaiah. Sister was sitting on the opposite side of Isaiah next to Uncle Joe and she was still upset that she had to come to church. She more than likely wanted to run off into town to meet up with Johnny Ray again.

Isaiah was tightly holding onto my hand causing it to sweat, because it was extremely hot inside the little country church. Big Ma sat proudly in her seat, fanning herself with a church fan that had the town's only Negro owned funeral home printed on the back of it. The large peacock feather in her hat swayed with every blow from the fan.

When prayer time was announced, I held onto Isaiah's hand as we followed Big Ma up to the altar. Usually when prayer time came at church, I just closed my eyes and pretended to pray before opening them back up and scanning the room to see if anybody else was not paying attention like I was, but not this time. This time I was on a mission, because I had a favor to ask God.

Standing at the altar while one of the deacons prayed, holding Big Ma's hand in one hand and Isaiah's in the other, I closed my eyes and prayed earnestly to God.

"Dear Lord, please keep Sister here wit' me. Don't let ha' leave me like my Mama did. I need ha', dear Lord. Please, dear Lord. Make Johnny Ray go far, far away and neva' bother Sister agin'!"

Mind you, I spoke this prayer in my head, because I didn't want anybody to know my business, but I meant every heartfelt word I uttered unto God that morning. I need Sister and I knew she needed me, too.

By the time we made it out of church, the sun was high up in the sky blazing down on us, making it hard to breathe. As soon as Uncle Joe's pickup rolled to a stop in the front yard, Sister took off like a flash into the house. I slowly exited the vehicle and waited for Isaiah to jump down from the seat.

"Atta boy!" I exclaimed jubilantly when he did, kicking up small swells of dust from the gravel driveway with his patent leather church shoes.

Giggling happily, Isaiah held my hand and skipped along as we followed Big Ma and Uncle Joe towards the front porch. I couldn't understand how Sister could just think about up and leaving us behind like she was. When I looked at Isaiah, it made it hard for me to ever believe we would ever part. He was as much a part of me as the very air that I breathed.

When we made it on to the porch, Big Ma stopped us before we could go inside the house. Raising her dark, thin hand in the air, she said, "Stripes, I need you and Junebug ta' stay out 'chere fa' just a lil' bit, okay?"

Frowning, I eyed Big Ma peculiarly, but I knew better than to question her. Steering Isaiah to the two large wooden rocking chairs which sat on the front porch, we sat down and did as we were told.

Turning to Uncle Joe, Big Ma looked at him with a hardened face before saying, "Joe, stay out 'chere wit' tha' youngin's or betta yet, take them fa' a ride."

"Mama, we just got home and it's hot as the devil's tail in that truck. I ain't gettin' back in it. I just wanna get outta this here suit and lay it down."

"Not right now, ya' ain't. I gots some bidness ta' take care of right now."

Uncle Joe nodded, and shed his suit jacket, laying it down on the back of a wooden chair on the porch before sitting down on it. Unbuttoning the top button of his pressed white button-down shirt, he fiddled with the collar as if his neck was steaming from the heat.

Big Ma entered the house and all was quiet for a few moments until we heard Sister screaming and the sound of Big Ma's leather belt hitting bare skin.

A few minutes later Sister came running out the house with fresh tears falling down her face which was now as red as a woodpecker's head. She had a packed bag in one hand and a pair of shoes in the other.

"I hate you! I hate you!" Sister screamed as she bounded down the porch steps.

Big Ma slowly opened the screen door and stepped onto the porch with the belt still held firmly in her hand. Sister stood in the front yard and looked angrily back up on the porch at Big Ma. Her eyes that mirrored mine were full of tears and I wanted to hug her but was afraid to move, so I hugged Isaiah tightly to my body, as he had jumped out of the chair he was sitting in and into my lap when he heard Sister screaming.

"I'll neva' come back here! I see why my Mama left this hellhole! You're a wicked woman, Big Ma! I's 15 now, damn near grown and you sho'll can't tell meh what to do! This will be tha' last time you eva' and I mean eva' lay a whippin' on meh!"

"Lil' gal, I've had it wit' ya' sassin' and fast tail ways. Keep on livin' tha' way ya' do and you gonna end up in one of two places, dead or in tha' jailhouse." Big Ma took a few steps closer towards Sister but remained on the porch. "Do ya' really thank that lil' white boy who got ya' nose wide open finna be wit' ya Nigga self? Do ya' really thank that? Let me tell ya' somethin' from an old woman who done seen many a thangs in mah day. That lil' white boy only usin' ya' fa' what ya' got in 'tween them legs or yours and as soon as he gits tied of ya' he's gonna move on ta' one of his own kind. No matter how light skin ya' is or how long and pretty ya' hair is like them white folks or how pretty them blue eyes of yours is, in his eyes ya' still a Nigga!"

My eyes bucked at the harshness of Big Ma's tone and words. From my seat on the porch, I watched as Sister's already red face reddened even more in anguish. Isaiah started humming loudly to no doubt drown out the argument that was taking place in front of us.

Sister wiped a solitary tear from underneath her eye, then stood up straight, proudly sticking out her chest. Pursing her lips, she said, "Johnny Ray does love me, Big Ma! You'll see. He said he's gonna git' meh away from this damn hick town and take me up North where folks like us who's in love can live peaceably wit'out being judged by whites or even worse by coloreds like you!"

Uncle Joe stirred in his seat who had been surprisingly quiet while watching the entire ordeal take place before our eyes. In his deep, rumbling voice, he spoke in a cool tone which sounded like a warning. "Billie, ya' needs ta' listen closely ta' what ya' gran'ma is tellin' ya'. She's only tellin' ya' what is right 'cause she loves ya' and don't want ya' ta' end up hurt. That white boy ain't gon' give ya' nothin' but heartaches and sorrows. If ya' leave this house today, ya' ain't gon' return tha' same way."

Now, I didn't know exactly what my uncle meant by what he was saying, but his words chilled my soul and brought upon a deep fear within my heart. Sister stood defiantly on the ground and shook her head, long red hair swinging around her like a shawl. She looked so much like her daddy's kin right now and I hated it.

"Uncle Joe, no offense, but you don't know Johnny Ray like I do. He ain't gon' hurt meh."

Turning around, Sister started to take off down the gravel driveway with her bag and shoes in hand. I couldn't believe that God hadn't answered my prayer and was just letting Sister leave me! Pushing Isaiah gently off of my lap, I took off of the porch like a flash and bounded down the stairs after her. Big Ma reached out and tried to grab me, but I was too quick for her. Catching up to Sister, I pulled on her arm.

"Sister! Don't leave me! Please!" I pleaded as huge tears fell from my eyes, soaking the top of my plaid dress.

Sister stopped in her tracks and turned her head to the side to look down at me. I saw fear, hurt, and anger written inside her eyes and I wanted nothing more than to hold her in my arms and take all of her pain away.

"Cora..." Sister said, softly and it alarmed me that she was addressing me by my given name.

"Hmm?"

"I gotta go... I love ya', I do, but I just can't live here anymo'."

"But..."

Sister shook her head softly and gently pulled her arm out of my grasp.

"No, buts... Cora, gon' on back up ta' the house now."

"No!" I cried and threw my arms around her, burying my head into her bosom. "I won't let you go. You can't leave me!"

Sister looked up at the sky blinking back tears before looking back down at me again. Dropping her bag and pair of shoes to the ground, she gave me a tight squeeze and rested her face gently on top of my head.

"Stripes, I love you, but I'm grown now. I gotta leave. Let me do this... You'll understand one day. I swea' ya' will."

Unwrapping my arms from around her waist, she backed me away from her. Bending down, she placed a cool, wet kiss upon my forehead before picking her belongings back up. "I'll write ya' from Chicago..." Without another word or a backwards glance, my big sister walked off down the winding country road and out of my life.

That night as I laid in the bed alone for the first time in my life without Sister, I held myself tightly, curled in the fetal position. I was wrapped up underneath a thin quilt and wondered how I would be able to live a life without my sister being in it. Cicadas chirped in the trees outside the window singing woefully about summer coming to a close and I couldn't help but feel as if a major chapter in my life had just ended, as well. Thoughts plaguing my mind of Sister's well-being kept me from comfortably falling asleep. *Is she okay? Where is she staying? Did that awful, scrawny, pale faced Johnny Ray and his family take her in?*

Tears stung painfully at my eyes and I wallowed in self-pity and anguish at the fact my sister left me just like our mother did so many years ago and at the fact that God did absolutely nothing to stop it. My 10-year-old mind just couldn't conceive how Sister could abandon me without giving an account of how this would affect my life. She didn't even say goodbye to Isaiah of all people! A fresh anger was now boiling up into my chest, bubbling up from the pits of my stomach and suddenly I hated her, just like I hated my mama sometimes for leaving me.

The soft shuffling of feet outside of my room alerted me that I wasn't the only one who was still up. Rolling over on the bed, I saw a shadowy figure standing in the doorway of my room.

"Cora?" Big Ma's voice softly fell upon my ears as she walked over to the middle of the room and pulled down on the long cord hanging from the light in the ceiling. A warm yellow glow instantly clothed the room and I blinked my eyes several times adjusting them to the light.

"Yes'm?" I asked, quietly, not hiding the fact that I had just been crying.

Big Ma's loving eyes softened when she saw my tear stained face. Shuffling over towards the bed, she sat down upon it and pulled me into her arms, sitting me upon her lap, something she hadn't done in years since I was a toddler at least. Rocking back and forth, she brushed down wisps of my hair with one hand and patted my thigh with the other.

"I want ya' ta' know that I neva' meant fa' this ta' happen like it did. I love you and Junebug and Sister very much. Very much. I just won't stand fa' no sassin' like Sister was doin'. I want tha' best fa' y'all chil'ren. I swea's fo' God, I do. Ya' mammy left ya' wit' meh ta' be in mah care and I's plans on raising ya' as if y'all was birthed straight from meh. Sister will be back. Mark mah words. She will be back, so stop all ya' cryin', sweet chile, and get some rest."

I wanted to believe Big Ma's words, I did, but part of me wouldn't believe them to be truth. Wiping the remaining tears from my eyes, I closed them and allowed my mind to fall at rest. Big Ma began humming an old Negro spiritual and I snuggled up closer to her as she lulled me to sleep. I found myself saying a quick prayer to God as I silently asked Him to bring Sister back home and my Mama, too. With Big Ma's loving arms wrapped securely around my body, I drifted off into a peaceful, yet dreamless sleep.

Chapter 3

In the days that followed, Sister's absence from the home was made painfully clear. There was no one to help me fix my hair in the mornings before school, I had to walk with Isaiah to school by myself unless Uncle Joe offered to drop us off before heading to work, and I had to do all of the chores left behind that were normally assigned to Sister.

Sitting in the front room watching Isaiah push one of his big toy trucks around on the floor, I wondered if I would ever see my sister again. I missed her presence awfully and I just wanted things to return to the way they once were before Sister had discovered taking a liking to boys. I was furious with her still for leaving Isaiah and me behind. I wouldn't ever turn my back on my little brother. No matter how much a liking to a boy I got, he would never come before Isaiah. We were a packaged deal and I thought that Sister felt the same way about me, but I was wrong. Horribly and painfully wrong.

The phone rang and Big Ma hurried into the front room from the kitchen to answer it. None of us children were allowed to answer the phone because Big Ma said it was only for "grown folks business". She dusted her flour covered hands that resembled snow covered tree branches off on her apron and picked the receiver up off of the rotary dial phone and spoke into it.

"Hello?"

I pretended to be watching the cowboy and Indians show that was playing on the black and white TV sitting on an old end table next to the wall so that Big Ma wouldn't fuss at me for eavesdropping, but all the while I kept my ears perked up just in case someone was calling with some information about Sister.

"Uh, huh... I heard that... Is that right?"

Big Ma was nodding her head intently while listening to the caller on the other end of the phone. I tried my mightiest to strain my hearing so that I could try to pick up the caller's voice, but unfortunately their voice remained muffled and unrecognizable. Out of the corner of my eyes I watched Big Ma's facial expressions to try to decipher what she was being told over the phone. I just hope that whatever is being said isn't anything bad about Sister... I couldn't take anymore hard blows to the heart right now.

"Alright... I'll have Joe come by and get ha'," Big Ma said, and I turned my head her direction. When she caught me looking at her, I quickly jerked my head back and focused my attention on the show playing on the TV. An Indian had just shot a white cowboy with an arrow and I smiled. Good, he got what he deserves for messing with him and I hope Johnny Ray gets what he deserves, too, for taking my sister away from me.

Big Ma hung up the phone and called out to me. "Stripes, I knows ya' was listenin' ta' what I was sayin'."

I turned towards her and shook my head. I wasn't gonna flat out admit that I had been eavesdropping, that was grounds for a whipping. Big Ma always said that children were to be seen and not heard and that we were always supposed to stay in a child's place. I never really understood why she felt that way because how was I ever supposed to learn how to be an adult when I grew up if I never knew what to expect or how to act like one?

"Stop shakin' that big head or yours. I was watchin' ya' strain ya' neck ta' hear tha' whole time I was on tha' phone." Big Ma walked calmly over to where I was and stopped in front of my seat on the old tattered couch that was probably older than me and Sister combined. Sweat decorated her brow like dew on grass in the morning and I watched in fascination as little drops created their own streams and flowed down the sides of her face like tiny rivers.

"I need ya' ta' run next door ta' Bessie Mae Lee's house and tell ya' uncle ta' go into town and pick Sister up from Carol Ann Taylor's house. She's been stayin' there overnight wit' Carol's daughter Lou Mae and done wore out her welcome. Tell ya' uncle ta' brang that chile home right now." Big Ma looked at me sternly with her hands placed firmly on her hips. "Ya' heard meh, youngin'?"

I nodded my head and replied, "Yes'm", then shot out of the house in a flash. A wide smile crept upon my face as I raced through the fields of dry hay towards Miss Bessie Mae's house. Tiny bristles of dried grass scratched at my bare legs as I combed my way through the field that separated our house from hers. Grasshoppers and crickets hopped and popped up as I disturbed their peace among their homes in the fodder, but I didn't care. I was on my way to get my sister back. Sister was coming home.

Exiting the field, I fought my way through the thicket that aligned the front and side lawn of Miss Bessie Mae's house and jumped into the yard. I spotted Uncle Joe right off the bat in the front yard leaning up against his rusty old truck shooting the breeze with Miss Bessie Mae's fiancé, Leroy Mack. Leroy had just placed a can of Budweiser up to his lips when I sped up to them.

"Damn, Stripes, slow it on down, babe girl. You almost made meh spill my beer," Leroy said with a chuckle and a grin, showing off his deep dimples in his face. He was the color of a paper sack bag kissed gently by the sun which brought out the red undertones in his skin.

"Sorry, Mr. Leroy," I said, blushing under his gaze. He was the most handsome man I had ever seen in my life and I thought that Miss Bessie Mae was certainly a lucky woman to be marrying him.

"What's the rush, Stripes?" Uncle Joe inquired and I tore my eyes from Mr. Leroy's beautiful dimples towards him. The one thing I loved about my uncle was that he never drank. He said he refused to because that's what killed his daddy, God rest his soul, my granddaddy, Willie B. Harris. I hated to see people drink because it turned usually nice folks into horrible creatures when they got full of it, especially some dumb drink called moonshine. Sister had taken a drank of the stuff one night Big Ma had a barbeque for the 4th of July when Big Ma wasn't looking and became a belligerent fool. You can best believe she got her hind parts torn to shreds that night 'cause of it.

Panting, nearly out of breath, I told Uncle Joe that Big Ma said for him to go get Sister from Missus Carol Ann Taylor's house. After hearing that, Uncle Joe shook Mr. Leroy's hand and we both climbed up into his truck and sped down the highway towards town. Pulling up to Missus Carol Ann Taylor's house which was painted a pretty light yellow and was two stories with a wraparound porch, we saw Sister sitting out on the front steps with her bottom lip poked out and a scowl as big as the entire state of Tennessee drawn across her forehead. I didn't care how mad she was, I was just glad she was finally coming home. She had been gone for two whole weeks now and I was miserable without her.

"That damn gal looks like she's angry enuff ta' spit fire," Uncle Joe mumbled as he pulled up into the driveway and put the truck in park. Rolling down his window as far as it could go, he turned to me and said, "I want ya' ta' stay in this truck. Ya' hear meh, Stripes?"

I couldn't understand why he wanted me to sit in a hot truck in Mid-September when any other time I could get out and speak to Missus Carol Ann Taylor, Lou Mae, and the other kids, Bobby, Squirt, Tunk, Mickey, Dimples, Stanley, Mary and Teresa. I crossed my arms defiantly across my flat chest and pouted. "Why for, Uncle Joe? I wanna say hey to Missus Carol Ann Taylor and the kids, 'specially Teresa. Since she's in Missus Brenda Clark's class this year, Ion git' ta' see her much."

Teresa was my best friend and we had been friends since before I could even remember back when her mama and papa them stayed down the road from us in the country before her papa got that good new job helping the white folks down at the cotton gin in town. I cried so hard when their family moved two years ago 'cause Teresa was like a sister to me and it was hard enough making friends with the kids at school when I usually got picked on for being mixed. I got called a cracker so much that I quit eating them. I hated being called out my name for something I couldn't help and I hated that Mama had fallen in love with a white man and made me. Why she couldn't have fallen for a nice colored man like Mr. Leroy? What was so wrong with colored men that Mama had made a mistake and fallen for not just one, but two of those ugly, racist redneck fools?

"'Cause, we ain't stayin' long, that's why," Uncle Joe said, but his words might as well had fallen on deaf ears because Teresa and Squirt (I loved Teresa's baby brother's nickname. He was called that because he was the baby of the family and was so tiny) came bustling down the front porch steps past Sister and raced up to the truck, stopping right outside the passenger side door.

Uncle Joe looked at the kids then looked back towards me. Shaking his head, he said, "Alright, you can git' on out and say hey ta' them, but we ain't stayin' long. I gotta speak wit' Carol Ann and then git' that hardheaded sister of yours and you back home. Ya' hear meh?"

Grinning from ear to ear, I nodded eagerly and pushed open the truck door which squeaked and groaned. It sounded as if it needed to be oiled down badly. Teresa and Squirt stepped back out of the way and I jumped out of the truck. I was excited to see Sister, but it was a real treat to see Teresa and her baby brother, too. Shutting the door, I waved happily to the kids.

"Hey, Teresa! Hey, Squirt!"

Teresa pushed her black, plastic cat eyed shaped glasses up onto the bridge of her nose and smiled warmly before giving me a hug. "Hey, Cora! I missed ya' so bad!" When she stepped back away from me, the sun hit her reddish-brown afro just right so that it looked like a bright ball of fire on top her head.

"Hey, Cora!" Squirt said and looked up at me bashfully from under his thick eyelashes. He had the prettiest eyelashes I had ever seen on a boy before. The kind of eyelashes that a grown woman would die to have so that she could put mascara on them and blink her eyes all pretty like when she flirted with men. Squirt was two years younger than Teresa and me and it was no secret that he had a little crush on me. I thought it was the sweetest thing.

Smiling down at him, I replied, "How ya' doin' today, shorty?"

Squirt giggled and dug the toe of one of his blue sneakers into the soft grass that aligned their paved driveway. One thing I loved about the homes in town was the fact that they all had beautifully paved gray or blacktop driveways. Quite the contrast from the gravel, mud holed driveways in the country like the one we had at Big Ma's house.

"Squirt! Quit digging your shoe into that ground!"

All three of our heads turned towards the direction of their mama's voice coming from off the porch. None of us had noticed that she had emerged from inside of the house and was standing on the porch talking with Uncle Joe while Sister, red faced and all, still sat fuming on the steps. Missus Carol Ann Taylor was one of the most beautiful colored women I had ever come across in my life. She was the color of maple syrup and had light brown eyes with dark hair so long that it came down all the way past her waist when she had it pressed out. She was so loving and motherly that it almost made me wish she was my mama.

Squirt stopped digging his shoe into the dirt and stood upright, stuffing his hands inside his overall's pockets. "Yessum!" he hollered back and then glanced at me shamefaced, no doubt embarrassed about being called out by his mama in my presence, before staring at the ground.

Teresa turned and looked at me and I couldn't help but envy the pretty red dress she was wearing and her pretty, shiny black shoes with bows on the top of them. I wished I could have a dress so pretty, but all my dresses were Sister's once before and by the time they reached me, they were faded and worn. I looked down at my khaki shorts and pink t-shirt and felt like a bum standing in front of her.

"Ya' wanna come inside and play dress up with my new dollies?" Teresa asked with a smile. She was missing one of her side baby teeth which had recently fallen out, but it didn't take away from her un-denying beauty. Her caramel skin, button nose and beautiful brown eyes that were made even bigger by her glasses had all the boys in our grade crushing on her.

As inviting as playing with new dolls sounded, I knew Uncle Joe would say that I couldn't because we had to get back home before nightfall.

Shaking my head, I replied, "Nah. I wish. Uncle Joe said we ain't gon' be here too long. We just came to pick up Sister."

Teresa took a step closer to me and whispered, "Why'd ya' gran'ma kick her out anyways? I overheard Lou Mae and Sister saying that ya' gran'ma tried ta' lay a hurtin' on Sister so bad that Sister snapped and came a runnin' into town. Was it 'bout some white boy?"

I looked from Teresa back up towards the porch and breathed heavily as I saw how pitiful Sister looked. That damn Johnny Ray, he was the talk of much speculation going around, I saw. Turning back towards Teresa, I nodded.

"Yeah... Big Ma said she was tired of Sister's sassin'," I said simply and watched as a swallow-tailed butterfly flounced from one dying rose bush to the next. Soon it would be cold and all the butterflies would be gone. I really didn't want to talk about why Sister had left home, I was just glad she was being made to come back and it made me think that if Sister had been staying with the Taylor's this long, Big Ma had to have known all along.

"Stripes, come on up here and say hello to Missus Carol Ann befo' we go," Uncle Joe hollered out to me. I watched as he said something to Sister and she rose resentfully from her seat on the stairs and picked her bag up.

Teresa, Squirt and I headed towards the porch as Sister brushed past us without a word or even a glance in our direction.

"Hi, Sist…" I started, but she wouldn't even look my way which deflated my spirit in such a way that was almost indescribable. We hadn't seen each other in two weeks and she just walked pass me as if I were a common stranger on the street.

Following Teresa and her baby brother up the porch steps, I stopped in front of Missus Carol Ann Taylor and mumbled, "Hello" with my head down, eyes focused on how pretty her baby doll pink kitten heels were.

"Now, what's the matter with you, sweetheart?" she asked as she reached out and lifted my downward chin, looking me directly in the eyes.

"Nothin', ma'am," I replied, not liking how my upbeat spirit had just been crushed in matter of seconds by my older sister, the only person I knew who could cause my emotions to be twisted in knots. I knew Missus Carol Ann Taylor wouldn't want to hear about my childhood woes or the fact that my only sister meant the world and the sun and moon to me and it didn't appear to me that she even felt remotely the same about my presence in her life as I did about hers in mine.

Missus Carol Ann Taylor was a wise woman, a very wise one. She looked from me out towards the driveway at Sister who was already seated in the cab of the truck and then back at me before saying, "Trouble don't last always, ya' know. Thangs gonna get betta sooner than later. Remember that, sweetheart". Then she kissed me lightly on the cheek and bid Uncle Joe and I farewell.

The ride home was silent. Sister spent the entire time breathing heavily as she kept her eyes focused on the world outside the window which went by in a nauseating blur. She was so heated that I felt the fiery rage going on inside her body radiating from her unfortunately warming the right side of mine. I was seated in between her and Uncle Joe who was chewing loudly on some dipping snuff and spitting in his disgusting spit cup ever so often. This was the quietist ride I think I had ever spent inside that truck because usually Uncle Joe would be cracking a joke or two, but he wouldn't even crack a smile at my attempts to carry on a conversation, so I eventually let it drop.

When we finally arrived home, it was dusk, and all the lights were on making the house appear to be alive as the lights lit up each window like eyes. Sister opened the truck door and slammed it hard before I could even exit the vehicle. Grabbing her bag from the truck bed in the back, she stomped off towards the house leaving Uncle Joe and I sitting in the car watching her in bewilderment. The girl that Sister had become over the past year was someone I barely knew, and it pained me so to even see the type of person she was becoming.

Uncle Joe opened the driver's side door and stepped out, taking one of my hands in his. "C'mon, Stripes, let's go in." He made sure I had safely jumped down and out of the truck before closing the door behind us.

Somewhere off in the distance a wolf howled, and it made my skin crawl. I kept up the pace and stuck to my uncle's side like superglue as we took the journey from the gravel drive towards the house. Crickets chirped loudly serenading us with their end of summer tunes, the rise and fall of their melody was deafening and I couldn't wait to go inside. I hated nighttime with a passion. I was terrified of possible boogeymen and ghosts invading the night.

We entered the house and I exhaled a breath that I didn't even know I had been holding. Isaiah waddled up to me and grinned with a small amount of slobber dripping from the corner of his mouth.

"Mmm... Mmm..." Isaiah said as he grabbed my hand pulling me deeper into the front room. He most likely had missed me because I was never away from his sight for very long except for when we were at school. Although he was turning six soon, he was still in the head start class and would possibly be there for another year. I was working hard every night and on the weekends to teach him how to use words.

"Awww, I missed you, too, Junebug," I said lovingly as I allowed my younger brother to lead me to what he so desperately wanted to show me.

Uncle Joe took off down the hall towards the room besides the kitchen where he slept and I noticed that neither Big Ma nor Sister were anywhere in sight. Isaiah let go of my hand when we stopped in front of a spot on the linoleum floor where I supposed he had been sitting before we arrived home. Bending over, he retrieved a piece of paper off the floor that had been lying on top of more scraps of paper next to bits of broken pieces of crayons, all colors of the rainbow. Standing upright, he thrust the paper out towards me and moaned.

Taking the paper from out of his hand, I looked down at it. Isaiah had scribbled on it with various colors of crayon and it looked as if he tried to draw a picture of a girl and boy. I just assumed it was us. Lowering the paper, I saw that he was gazing up at me expectantly with his huge brown eyes which resembled Mama's so much. Smiling, I pulled him closely to me and gave him a big hug.

"Thanks, Junebug. I love you so, so much!"

Junebug moaned in response then jumped at the sound of arguing coming from my bedroom. The angry voices were none other than Sister's and Big Ma's which explained where they had run off to.

"I never wanted ta' come back here!" Sister shrieked, which startled Junebug so much that he dropped down to the floor and began rocking back and forth, crying huge tears.

Big Ma raised her voice in reply and I heard the sound of something being thrown against the wall. More than likely it was a pair or two of Sister's shoes.

Easing down onto the dusty floor, I sat in front of Isaiah and tried to console him. "It's okay, Junebug. Everything is okay," I offered in the calmest voice that I could while patting him gently on the knee, but truth be told my insides were knotting up like when my fishing line gets accidentally caught up in Big Ma's on the creek bank.

I was tired of Big Ma and Sister arguing even though it had been two weeks of silence since Sister had been gone. *Why couldn't Sister just act right? Be normal for Christ's sake?*

"Now, I ain't gone whip ya', but ya' listen ta' meh closely young lady. I's not gone stand fo' no mo' disrespectin' in mah house! In mah house ya' gonna kno' ya' place! You are a chile and you's gonna behave like a chile! You's gone go ta' school, learn and make sumthin' outta ya'self and become a respectable woman. You's not gone be whorin' 'round town like ya' mammy did befo' ya' was born! You's gon' go ta' church and praise our Holy Father wit' ya' family and you's gone tend ta' ya sister and brother and do ya' chores! Ya' understand meh?!"

The house fell silent, so I didn't hear a response from Sister, so I had no choice but to assume that she had agreed to Big Ma's conditions of living in the house. Isaiah's tears ceased, but he continued to rock back and forth whimpering. I stood from my seat on the floor and walked towards the kitchen to grab a towel to wipe his face. When I returned to the front room, Big Ma was standing in the middle of it with exhaustion displayed on her face. Sweat prints could be seen in the armpits of her blue flowery cotton duster and her green kerchief had slid slightly off of her head.

"You's hungry?" Big Ma asked as I wiped Isaiah's tears away along with drool and snot.

"Yes'm," I replied not looking up, but keeping my attention on cleaning my brother's face.

"Okay, gon' in the kitchen and fix ya' a plate after ya' done there wit' Junebug. We's already ate. I made ya' a pitcher of that good sweet tea ya' like so much."

"Thank ya', Big Ma."

Big Ma walked over to the front door and locked it and let down the dusty, yellowed aged curtain that she raised every morning and secured with a clothespin at the top of the door's window. Then she left the room without another word, going back towards the bedroom she shared with Isaiah.

"You gonna stay in here or follow me?" I asked Isaiah who had finally stopped his rocking which was his way of self-soothing himself in stressful environments. He didn't respond but pushed himself up off of the floor and trailed me into the kitchen. The wonderful fragrance of roast and potatoes and freshly baked sweet cornbread hit my nostrils before we even stepped foot into the kitchen. My mouth began watering immediately in anticipation of the delicious meal I was soon to enjoy.

Isaiah sat down in his normal seat at the table while I fixed myself a plate and poured me a glass of sweet tea out of the icebox. He began humming a sweet little tune resembling, "This Little Light of Mine" and I smiled, loving how in his own way he made the world a better place. He loved Negro spirituals and was able to recall tunes to songs out of the blue. If no one else could understand my baby brother, I could. He was the closest thing to a pure and honest angel I had come to know and no matter what ever happened in my life, just by looking at him I knew I was looking at a miracle itself from Jesus and it gave me hope for the future. Our future.

Chapter 4

Summer ended and along came fall, hurtling its way towards us with its chilly northerly winds that attacked the dying leaves on the trees sending them soaring through the air in an array of wondrous colors. The days were shorter which brought upon much disappointment because now I couldn't remain outside as long as I would like since it grew dark so early. By the time we made it home from school we only had a good hour of sunlight left before it was time to head into the house, eat supper and prepare for the same routine of waking for school the next day.

Sister has calmed down, surprisingly, over the past month she's been home. She doesn't backtalk Big Ma as much anymore, but honestly, she doesn't even carry on conversations with any of us like she used to. She's changed... Again. I couldn't decide which was worse, when Sister was no longer living in the house with us or the girl she's become now, one who was so distant and seemed far away although she lay right next to me every night in our bed.

It was a crisp Saturday morning and I sat in one of the weathered, paint chipped rocking chairs on the front porch wrapped in a soft pink blanket that I've had since I was a baby. I loved this blanket because it was the only thing I had in my possession that came from my mama. Poking some fingers out from their warmth underneath the blanket, I trailed my fingers along on the edge of it, then traced the large cursive C embroidered on the corner. My mama had to have loved me enough to buy me this blanket, but why didn't she love me enough to keep me?

A dove cooed somewhere off in the distance in a faraway tree and I sucked on my teeth. Every time I thought about my mama leaving me behind, my heart would swell and feel as if it would burst from the unshed tears I kept hidden deep inside. My God, how I wished for a mother like Missus Carol Ann Taylor. Teresa didn't know how lucky she was. She had a mother to fuss and worry over her and all I had was Big Ma. I love my grandma with everything in me, but her love isn't the same as having my mama to love on me. I wanted desperately to know how it would feel to have a mother dote over me and everything that I did. I wanted my mama to shower me in hugs and kisses for no reason at all, fix my hair up prettily like hers before church, and praise me for getting an A on my arithmetic test after struggling so hard to understand why multiplication tables were such an important task to learn even though it was extremely boring and tedious.

Rocking back and forth in the chair, it creaked and groaned with every motion on top of the wooden porch. I watched in delight as a red, bushy tailed squirrel hurried along a tree branch and then down the trunk, finally resting upon the cold dirt ground beneath the tree. It perked up its tiny ears listening carefully and closely for sounds of hidden foes before preceding forward into the dying grass to retrieve one of many fallen pecans that lay upon the morning frost covered ground. Its paws rapidly moved as it crunched open the pecan shell and happily ate the meat within before tossing the empty shell to the side and scurrying over to another pecan on the ground before repeating the motions again. How simplistic a squirrel's life must be? How I longed for a life of simplistic happiness.

A gust of wind whipped around my body chilling me to my core. I pulled my legs upward until my feet were planted firmly on the seat of the chair and my knees met the underside of my chin. I could feel chill bumps spring up on my arms, but I wasn't ready to go inside just yet. I enjoyed the feeling of freedom that the outside world gave me. When I went inside I knew I would be met with Sister's cold shoulder and the responsibility of watching Isaiah. There were hardly ever any deviations from my weekend routine.

My eyes fluttered close and I envisioned my mama standing before me with her arms stretched open wide welcoming a hug. Her hair was like black spooled silk resting upon her shoulders. She was wearing an emerald colored dress that stopped just above her knees with black buttons and short sleeves. She had on black stockings with black Maryjane's and looked stunning, like one of those actresses I saw on the television. The most striking thing about her was her beautiful brown eyes that were gazing at me with such intensity, holding within them all the love I had been missing for the past 10 years of my life without her. I could feel myself smiling warmly at her mirroring the smile she held on her face just for me. Hesitatingly, I took a step closer towards her, gingerly, one at a time until I nearly stood face to face with her. Just as I was reaching out to her, to wrap my arms around her waist in an embrace I felt a tap on my shoulder.

My eyes flew open and I turned my head upwards and to the side. To my amazement Sister was standing next to the chair expressionless. I must have dozed off in the chair because now my body ached and I was extremely uncomfortable and cold. My nose felt as if it would fall off at the slightest touch.

"Hmm?" I said to Sister.

Sister was still in her solid white gown that came all the way down to her ankles and her hair was pinned up, but messy at the same time. No matter how unkempt she appeared, she always seemed to hold a natural beauty that defied any form of unattractiveness that anyone else would hold first thing in the morning. I searched her eyes and saw they held a listlessness that wasn't there before she left home all those weeks ago. It almost appeared as if she was dead inside. I shivered at the thought of it.

"Big Ma said to come and git' ya' so ya' can eat breakfast and feed Junebug."

Without another word, Sister opened up the screen door, pushed open the wooden front door leading into the house and shut it tightly behind her. *What had happened to Sister for her to be acting this way?* I knew she was upset that Uncle Joe brought her back here, but was she gonna stay mad at us forever?

I placed my bare feet down on the cold porch floor and stood, gathering up my blanket around me. When I made it inside, Uncle Joe had the wood burning stove blazing, so the house warmed me instantly. I quickly fixed Isaiah and me a plate, fed him and myself, then waited for my turn to use the metal wash tub so that I could take a bath. As I rinsed my body off in the tub, I overheard Big Ma and Uncle Joe talking in hushed voices in his room.

"Joe, that there chile is beginnin' ta' worry meh..." Big Ma said quietly. "She will barely eat and walks around here like some sort of spook... Like she's the walkin' dead."

Uncle Joe's voice was so deep and rumbling that I could barely make out his response, so I stepped out of the wash tub and wrapped myself with a towel before making my way over to the kitchen wall that was on the opposite side of his bedroom. Placing my ear firmly up against the wall, I strained to hear more of their conversation.

"Maybe ya' should have the doc' come out here ta' run a checkup on her. She has been actin' mighty strange. Mighty strange. She won't even say ten words to meh at a time. Won't even look mah way and that gal has barely even carried on wit' Stripes or Junebug. She acts like they don't even exist now."

"Ya' sholl is right, Joe. Ya' sholl is right. I'm real worried 'bout her. I ain't neva seen no chile act like this befo' in all of mah years. Her mama neva' acted like this either. I got some mind ta' thinkin' that she gits this behavior from her white side," Big Ma replied.

There was a brief pause before Uncle Joe replied. "Could be..."

I pulled back from the wall and finished drying off and proceeded to put on my clothes. The morning was cool, but the weatherman on the radio claimed it was going to reach at least 70 degrees today. Unusual weather for the beginning of November. When I entered the front room, Sister sat there on the old tattered couch dressed in blue jean overalls with a teal colored flowered long sleeved button up shirt on. She had pulled her long wavy hair back into a ponytail and it hung low and down her back. Her eyes were fixated upon the television and she didn't acknowledge my presence in the room. Isaiah, however, looked up from his seat on the floor, grinned and reached out to me.

"Co...Co..." he said and my heart darn near stopped beating.

I fell to my knees in front of him and gave him a tight squeeze, then pulled away from him and held onto his shoulders. Looking into his eyes, I said excitedly, "What did you say, Junebug?"

Isaiah looked at me and grinned as a small amount of dribble emerged from the side of his mouth. I subconsciously reached inside of my jeans pocket, removed a handkerchief from it and dabbed the corner of his mouth.

"Say it again, big boy... Say my name," I pressed.

"Co..." Isaiah replied and I squealed.

Glancing over in Sister's direction, I yelled excitedly, "Sister! Did you hear that?! Junebug said my name!"

Sister cut her eyes at me, rolled them, then rose from her seat and stomped off sluggishly towards our room. Frowning I watched her leave. How could she not be excited that our little brother has finally spoken? He literally just said his first word right before his sixth birthday!

Shaking off Sister's aloofness, I returned my attention to Isaiah. "Now you just stay right here, lil' man, while I go grab Big Ma and Uncle Joe. I'm so very proud of you!" I gave him a quick peck on the cheek, then ran through the house towards Uncle Joe's room.

Running up to his open door, I stopped just inside the door frame. Big Ma and Uncle Joe looked up at me from their conversation.

"Stripes, chile, what's the meaning of all this here runnin' in this house?" Big Ma demanded.

Grinning, I boasted proudly, "Junebug just said his first word, y'all!" With my hand, I beckoned them to follow me back to the front room.

"Oh, my word! Praise the Lord, praise the Lord!" Big Ma cried aloud as her hand flew to her duster covered bosom.

"That's mah boy!" Uncle Joe said with a grin and twinkle in his eye.

They followed me back out to the front room where Isaiah was still sitting in the same spot on the floor where I left him. He was now busily pushing a toy car around on the linoleum. He looked up when he saw us standing in front of him.

Bending down next to him, I took one of his hands in mine. "Can you say it again, Junebug? Can you say what you just said ta' me a lil' while ago? Who am I? "

Isaiah grinned and I swear his smile was as pretty as what Heaven must look like. The fresh look of innocence on his sweet face melted my heart.

Isaiah slowly opened his mouth and said with sure conviction, "Co!"

Big Ma clasped her hands together as tears of joy streamed from her eyes. She bent down and scooped Isaiah up into her arms and kissed him lovingly on the cheek. Isaiah was a big boy, but Big Ma's strength was unparalleled and she held him with ease. I watched as Uncle Joe proudly beamed down at his nephew and used the sleeve of his shirt to wipe his damp eyes. Big Ma gazed affectionately down at her grandson then tilted her head back, looking up at the ceiling. "Thank Ya', Jesus! Thank Ya', Jesus! Thank Ya'!"

One of Big Ma's prayers had finally been answered. Isaiah had said his first word and if he could jump that hurdle, I knew with time, patience, and love he would be able to overcome many more. As I watched Big Ma and Uncle Joe love on and praise Isaiah I couldn't help but feel a tug on my heart as I longed for Sister to feel the same way about him. Turning my head in the direction of our room, I exhaled deeply. *Sister... What's going on with you?*

*

Another week had come and gone and so had Isaiah's sixth birthday which meant my 11th one was right around the corner. It was a dreary, cold Friday afternoon when I finally found out what was bothering Sister. I had crept into our room hoping not to disturb her sleeping soundly on the bed when to my surprise she turned her head on the pillow away from the wall and looked at me.

"Stripes..."

I stopped dead in my tracks and turned to face her. I had only come into our room to get my ball and jacks game from out of the closet, so I could play me a game while I waited on Big Ma to finish supper.

"Yeah?"

"Com'ere," she muttered, patting the space on the bed in front of her.

Slowly and steadily, I walked over to my sister, feeling as if it were some sort of dream. I couldn't believe she actually wanted to talk to me. Climbing up on the bed, I sat down cross-legged in front of her.

Sister's eyes were brimmed with tears and I longed to hold her in my arms, but didn't dare move, afraid she may reject my affections.

"I'm sorry I's been so mean and hateful towards ya', Stripes..." Sister pushed herself up on the bed and leaned back against the Maplewood headboard our granddaddy had made with his bare hands back when he was living. Her red hair cascaded down and around her shoulders like waterfalls, stopping right underneath her breasts.

"I've just been in sucha angry place. I's feel like I don't belong here. Like I don't belong anywhere. I'm so mad at Big Ma. Mad at Carol Ann for sending meh home and I'm pissed off at Johnny Ray!"

There we have it, folks. Once again, all trouble boils right back on down to Johnny Ray. What a thorn in Sister's side he was and the sad part about it is that she doesn't even realize it.

I tugged at some lint on one of Big Ma's handmade quilts that lay on top of the bed and looked over at Sister. "Why? Why are ya' so mad for? Big Ma loves you so much. Don't ya' see that?"

Sister nodded, then brushed some fly away hairs from out in front of her eyes. Licking her lips, she then bit the bottom one before speaking.

"Yeah, I know that, Cora... It's not really Big Ma who I'm mad at now. I'm mad at myself."

Her response wasn't one that I was expecting which caused me to frown at her in confusion.

"Huh?"

Sister blew out an exasperated breath and I could tell she was irritated about the fact that I didn't understand what she meant.

"I'm mad at myself 'cause I done went and did exactly what Big Ma and Uncle Joe said I would do."

My mind started back tracking to overheard conversations between Big Ma, Uncle Joe, and Sister but I couldn't pinpoint on one thing that they said Sister would do that would cause her to become upset with herself.

"And what is that?"

Sister rubbed her hand over what used to be her flat, washboard stomach that now had a slight pudge to it. Looking downwards, she said softly, "I's done got knocked up by Johnny Ray."

My mouth gaped open and I swear if anyone could've seen me they would've sworn I looked just like a large mouth bass gasping for air once you had caught them and was trying to pull the hook out their mouth.

Sister looked up at me as tears spilled over onto her face from her steadily reddening eyes. "Well, ain't ya' gonna say sumthin'?"

I didn't really know what to say. I mean, here I am just a kid who doesn't really even know all the specifics behind how babies are made and my big sister is carrying one in her belly.

"Uh... Uh..." I stammered.

Sister pursed her lips and groaned. "I know it's a lot for a lil' kid like you to understand. I just needed ta' tell someone. I haven't even told Lou Mae, yet. I'm 'fraid she'll probably blabber the news ta' tha' whole damn school and then it'll get back to Johnny Ray somehow."

I took a deep breath and then released it, hoping that it would calm the rapid beating of my heart so that I could start thinking clearly.

Clearing my throat, I looked her dead in the eyes. "Well, have ya' told Big Ma, yet?"

Sister tilted back her head and cackled awkwardly. "Are you kiddin', Stripes? Me tell Big Ma that I done got pregnant by a white boy just like her whore of a daughter did at my age? You really think she's gonna wanna hear that shit?"

I frowned. I hated for her to speak ill of our mama. I hated for anyone to bad talk her really. Crossing my arms over my still flat chest, I grit my teeth. "Mama ain't no whore."

Sister narrowed her eyes at me. "Stripes, when are you gonna get yo' fairy tale illusion of Glory Jean out yo' head?" She shook her head and continued. "She ain't nothin' but a common black whore who gave not one, but all three of her damn chil'ren up and left us to be raised by our gran'ma! Mama never loved me, she never loved Junebug, and Mama never loved you!" Anger flashed in her blue eyes as her face flushed with emotion.

My fists balled up at my sides as I watched my sister looking back at me. I had never wanted to hurt someone so badly in my life as I wanted to hurt my big sister right now. *How dare she say my mama didn't love me?* She did and she does. I just know she does. Cutting my eyes at Sister, cheeks flaming, I scrambled off the bed and ran out of the room, forgetting about the ball and jacks. My two pigtails slapped my back like whips as hot, salty tears blurred my vision and I ran smack dab into Uncle Joe.

"Whoa! Lil' lady!" He chuckled at first until he looked down at me.

Placing a firm hand on my shoulder, he asked, "Stripes, what's ta' matter, baby?"

I couldn't have found the words to formulate what I was feeling at the moment if I wanted to. How could my sister have said something so mean, so terribly wretched to me? How could she dare open up her mouth and allow the words, "Mama never loved you" to even escape?

Shrugging my shoulders, I tried to move past him, but he wouldn't let me.

"Cora..."

I wiped the tears from my eyes with my fingers and looked up at him. Uncle Joe's kind face was twisted in concern. I knew he meant no harm by questioning what was wrong with me, but all I wanted to do at the moment was run and hide and go as far away from Sister as I could possibly get.

Trying to move from in front of Uncle Joe without first answering his question was pointless. He would hold me hostage all day if he had to. That was just his personality. No one, and I mean no one, defied him.

"Sis... Sister said... Our Mama..." I could barely get the words out they were cutting me so deeply. I felt as if my air supply was being choked off, I was just that angry.

"Sister said what?"

Taking a deep, shuddering breath, I exhaled slowly, then continued. "That Mama never loved me. She never loved none of her kids." Glancing upwards, I searched his eyes for the truth. Mama was his older sister, he had to know if it were true or not.

Uncle Joe clenched his jaw and I watched as the muscles in his face contracted. Steering me towards the couch, we sat down and he wrapped an arm around me, pulling me closely to him.

I lay my head on his chest and listened to the soothing sound of his heartbeat and wondered if this is what it would feel like if I had a daddy. I'd never met mine because Big Ma said he died in a tractor accident on a farm one county over back in '52, one year after I'd been born. It really didn't matter to me that I had never met him because he probably would've disowned me anyways. I'd never heard of a white man claiming his "nigger" children before.

"Stripes... Baby, I want ya' ta' listen ta' meh good," Uncle Joe said in a quiet voice. "Ya' Mama loves you, Junebug, and Sister. She does. It's just that..." He paused as if there was something he wanted to tell me but really couldn't. "Lordy, Cora, all

I can tell ya' is that Glory Jean loves all her chil'ren. She's just shows it a lil' different is all."

"How? All she does is send money in the mail every month. I haven't seen her since I was five years old. And even then, she didn't come in and kiss meh or hug meh or nothin'. She gave Big Ma Junebug and ran off again."

Uncle Joe closed his eyes and rubbed his temple as if a headache was coming upon him. When he opened his eyes, he gazed down at me lovingly.

"Just know that ya' Mama loves you, okay? I swear one day she's gonna come back and you'll know then why she did what she did by leavin' y'all wit' Mama. I'd rather for Glory Jean tell ya' straight from her mouth what caused her to do what she did than ya' hear it from meh or somebody else." With that Uncle Joe leaned over, kissed me roughly on the forehead and stood from the couch leaving me sitting in the room alone with my thoughts.

I still wasn't convinced that what Sister said wasn't true, but I wanted like all hell for it not to be. Even though our mama had abandoned us, I still loved her and always wanted to think the best of her and that she was gonna come back one day soon and then we would finally be a family like I'd always dreamed we could be.

Chapter 5

"Ahhhhhhh!!!!"

Sister's screams were deafening as she yelled
while sitting in the kitchen across the table from the
town's only colored doctor, Dr. Jones. The doctor eyed
sister as she continued to turn red in the face while
screaming at the top of her lungs. Big Ma stood by
clutching a dishrag in one hand looking disturbed
while my aunt Trish held her other hand. Aunt Trish
had decided to come down for the Thanksgiving
holiday and would be staying with us for a week. I was
glad she was here. She looked as if she could pass for
Mama's twin, at least that's what it seemed like from
looking at old high school photographs of Mama.

I stood just outside of the kitchen doorway
holding onto it for dear life while I watched Dr. Jones
quiz Sister on intimate details about her "woman
parts". Sister didn't even have to end up telling Big Ma
about the baby because Big Ma had a sixth sense
about these types of things. Big Ma said that she
noticed Sister's belly was steadily getting rounder and
that the only time a young lady wanted to sleep all day
and night was when they were expecting. I asked Big
Ma what she meant by that and she told me to stay
outta grown folks' business.

"I wish ya'll would leave meh tha' hell alone!"
Sister spat as she surveyed the room and gave them all

the evil eye. She tapped her foot impatiently on the kitchen floor and grit her teeth. "Ya'll actin' like me havin' this baby is the worse sin since Adam ate that damn apple off the tree! No matter what y'all say, I'm havin' this baby and me and Johnny Ray and our baby gon' go live up North where we won't be frowned upon by uppity Negroes like you!"

Sister's harsh words caused Aunt Trish to suck in her breath hard. Before I knew it and anyone else did either, Aunt Trish made her way over to Sister's seat and backhanded her hard across the mouth. So hard that a tiny drop of blood made its way out of the corner of Sister's mouth and dribbled down her chin.

"How dare you disrespect Mama, me and this fine doctor here with all your sassing?!" Aunt Trish said shaking with anger. Grabbing Sister by the chin, she looked her directly in the eyes. "Mama is just trying to make sure that you aren't too far along whereas you can't get an abortion before you ruin your life!"

Sister jerked her chin out of Aunt Trish's hand, eyes flashing angrily. Wiping the blood off her face, she pushed her chair back from the table with such force it came clanking down on the floor with a loud boom. Placing her hands on her hips, she stood toe to toe with our aunt.

"What? Ruin my life like mah Mama? Or ruin my life like you did?"

Aunt Trish gasped and took a step back, eyes wide with astonishment. Holding a hand up to her mouth, she shook with anger. "Ex... Excuse me?"

"What? Auntie you think yo' saditty self is so self-righteous that nobody knows that you got pregnant in high school, too and did the very same thang ya' want meh ta' do now? Ta' mah baby?"

Dr. Jones sat quietly like a lump on a log and watched the drama unfold before him. A man in his late 60's, I'm quite sure he has seen quite a few scenes like this before. His dark, wrinkly skin reminded me of a toad's and I couldn't stand him. Something about him gave me the creeps, especially his eyes. He even had toad like eyes.

"Now, that's enuff of that backtalk, Billie!" Big Ma said in a warning tone.

Sister didn't back down though, she kept going like a bull in one of those bull fights they have uptown during the carnival season chasing after a red flag. Sister rolled her neck and pointed a finger at our aunt before speaking again. "Yeah, I kno' all 'bout that baby ya' killed when ya' was in high school. Lou Mae heard 'bout it from her mama and told meh. You try ta' come 'round here actin' like you all high and mighty when ya' spread ya' legs just like meh and got knocked up, but oh nooooo... Miss Trisha Harris was too special, too fine, and too much of a holy roller to have a baby out of wedlock, so what did you do?" Sister glared at Aunt Trish with such disdain, I could've sworn that she had just taken a bite of something so vile, it had left a bad taste in her mouth.

"You went to the first clinic you could find down in Memphis that took Negro women and had that precious baby sucked right on outta ya'! All for what, Aunt Trish? Huh? So ya' could go ta' college and become a teacher? A lonely teacher wit' no husband and no kids ta' show? All ya' got is that stupid college degree ta' keep ya' warm at night! Well, I for one ain't havin' it! Neither you, Big Ma, Uncle Joe or tha' man in the damn moon gonna keep me from havin' mah baby!"

Sister spun on her heel and flew out of the kitchen. I stepped back quickly and hoped that she hadn't seen me peeping into the room just moments before. I tiptoed away from the kitchen door before any of the grownups could realize I had been listening to their little meeting with Sister. I mean, even if I hadn't of been eavesdropping it would've been hard not to overhear what was going on. Inching down the hall, I stopped outside of the doorway of our room. I was thankful that Isaiah was gone into town with Uncle Joe to pick up some things Big Ma needed for Thanksgiving supper. At least he wasn't here to hear and see all of the commotion which just took place moments ago. I hated to see him cry because of it.

From inside our room I could hear Sister crying, more like weeping. Slowly, I stepped into the room and saw her laid across the bed face down with her head lying on her forearms. Her shoulders were moving up and down as her crushed spirit poured out through her tears.

Coming closer to the bed, I touched her gently on the shoulder, allowing my small hand to rest there for a brief moment before massaging it gently.

"Sister..."

"Not now, Stripes..." Sister replied through her tears.

Ignoring my sister's response, I climbed onto the bed and lay down next to her, throwing my arm around her shoulder.

"I love you, Billie," I whispered into her hair which smelled of the strawberry shampoo she used to wash it with every other day. "I don't want you ta' give up tha' baby. I... I'll even help ya' raise it. Like I help out wit' Junebug." Patting her shoulder lovingly, I continued. "Don't be sad, Sister. They just wanna help ya'. They'll love tha' baby just as much as I will."

Sister rolled over and faced me. Wiping her eyes, she smiled. "You're an angel. Ya' know that?"

I shook my head and continued looking at her. I couldn't be an angel, 'cause I did bad things from time to time. Only angels I knew about were good ones like the angel that visited Jesus' mama before He was born. I had learned about that angel in Bible class at church.

Sister nodded her head and continued smiling. "Well, now ya' know." Sitting up in the bed she pulled me into her arms and hugged me tightly. Pushing some loose strands away off of my forehead she planted a kiss there.

"Thank you for being here, Stripes... And I love ya', too," she whispered into my hair as she leaned her chin down on the top of my head.

I don't know how long we stayed like that, Sister and I, just sitting on top of the bed with her holding me, but it felt great. Kinda like old times when we were really little. For a moment everything felt right, like how it was supposed to be. My big sister was my sister again and I was the little sister that looked up to her more than anybody in the entire universe. It was one of those moments I knew I would hold dearly to my heart and take with me into my adult life. One of those moments I would pray later on in life that my children held with one another. One of those moments that made a person believe that nothing in life was more important than family. For the first time in two months I felt at ease, like everything would be alright.

*

"Ohhhh, Zebra! Zebraaaaaa!!!"

"Somebody call the zookeeper and tell'em one of they's animals done got out!"

Some children on the playground taunted and jeered at me as I walked towards the heavy green door of the school building. It was the last day of school for the county children before Thanksgiving break and I couldn't wait to get it over with. Teresa walked by my side holding my hand tightly.

"Ya'll shut up!" she hollered back at a group of mischievous boys who were laughing at me while pointing their chubby fingers in our direction. Fourth grade boys could be so immature. Sticking her tongue out at them, she rolled her eyes and gave my hand a gentle squeeze.

"Don't pay 'em no mind, Stripes. None at all."

Smiling weakly, I nodded and continued on up the steps to the school. Coming to school was a chore some days. I got picked on just for being mixed like I could help my daddy was white. If I would've had a choice in the matter I would've told my mama to have me by someone like Mr. Leroy so I could've came out a real pretty brown baby like Teresa was.

Once we were inside the school, Teresa and I went our separate ways towards our respective classes. I hope with all my might that we are in the same class next year or school was really gonna be awful. The only time anyone said anything to me in class was when it was time to study together or when they were picking on me, other than that I was mostly ignored. Sometimes a sweet boy from up the road would turn and look my way and smile, but then his friends would pester him, and crack jokes and he would look away. Taking a seat at my desk which was the furthest in the back corner next to the window and radiator, I cracked open one of my readers and pretended to read, hoping that no one would disturb me. Sometimes sitting next to radiator was awful, but it was dreadfully cold outside today and threatening to snow, so I welcomed the warmth it gave out.

Soon, I drifted off into a daydream and didn't even notice when all of the normal hustle and bustle of the classroom quieted down suddenly. I had been thinking about how lovely it would be if my mama would show up for my 11th birthday which was in two weeks on the 8th of December. It would be both the best birthday and Christmas present a girl could ever ask for. I wonder what Mama looked like now. *Was she still as pretty as a black butterfly?*

I didn't look up from the reader that sat before me, where I hadn't even turned a single page since I cracked it open. Our teacher broke the silence with her boisterous voice.

"Class... Settle down now. We have a new student joining us today."

I really didn't care about any new student, so I focused my attention on the book before me with its faded color pictures telling the story of someone named Alice in some kind of wonderland. My eyes took in not only the pictures on the page, but the page's worn edges with its multitude of scribbles and marks made by former students before me. The entire book was aged and was no doubt older than I was since us colored students never received any new books. We only received the books from the white schools after they no longer needed them as a part of their required curriculum. I hated the way things were. What was so wrong with being a Negro? I couldn't understand for the life of me why we weren't treated the same. I honestly think the reason why so many of the kids I go to school don't like me is because they don't like the whites. They seem to hate the white part of me, but ignore the black part of me, too, like it doesn't even exist. Funny thing is that the whites never acknowledge my white part at all... Something about a "one drop" rule which I don't even understand.

It wasn't until I heard one of the boys who sat in front of and across the aisle from me whisper, "She looks just like the zebra" when I finally lifted my head upwards in curiosity. Scanning the room, I looked over my classmates' heads until they landed on her. The "she" the boy had been whispering about.

Standing in front of the room next to Mrs. Porter, our teacher, was a short, high yella girl with sandy, reddish-blonde colored hair, small nose, and green eyes. I couldn't see where the boy was thinking that she looked like me at, but I could tell one thing straight off the bat, she was mixed just like I am.

"Everyone, this is Zannie Mae Crenshaw," Mrs. Porter said with a smile. Placing a hand on the little girl's shoulder, she looked down at her and asked, "Is there anything you want to say?"

Zannie Mae blushed, face flushed crimson, as she shook her head. She fiddled with a notebook that she held in her hand and dropped her head low so no one could see her face which caused her hair to fall down all around her like spun gold.

"That's alright, young lady," Mrs. Porter said sweetly as she looked up and scanned the class through her bifocals until the fell down upon the empty seat next to mine.

"Why don't you take the vacant seat in the rear of the class next to Cora," Mrs. Porter said addressing Zannie Mae. "Cora... Cora, dear, could you raise your hand so Zannie Mae can know where to go?"

I lifted my arm in the air and watched as Zannie Mae quickly made it down the aisle to her new seat, right next to mine. She didn't even look my way as she sat down. She just kept her eyes downcast, staring at her hands which she now had folded together on top of the desk. I figured she must be shy something awful because she was still flushed in the face.

"Aw, man, now we's got two of them zebras in the class. Somebody needs to call the zookeeper and let'em kno' they's done got loose!" Arnie Hess, a pudgy, dark skinned boy with a missing front tooth said aloud with his ole' snagga-toothed grin and the class erupted in rolling fits of giggles. I couldn't stand

Arnie. He was like a rock that gets stuck in your shoe when you're walking along a dirt road and it keeps sticking you until you have to stop, lean up against a tree and take your shoe off, shaking it like crazy until the blasted thing falls out.

"Arnie Bartholomew Hess!" Mrs. Porter exclaimed with an annoyed expression her face. "Get up to the front of the class immediately!" Her jowls shook in anger as she pointed to the front of the class next to the chalkboard.

Arnie's grin was wiped off his face by being called out on by the teacher. Slumping his shoulders, he pushed away from his desk and walked slowly up the aisle to the front of the class.

"Was that Christ-like what you just said?"

Arnie hung his nappy head low in shame and shook it. "No, ma'am."

"Since you seem to think it's so funny to make fun of others, how about you stand here in front of the class and let them look at you while the rest of the class prepares for our reading time?"

Arnie frowned and stuffed his fat fingers into his khaki pants pockets. He looked like a tub of day old lard and I was glad he had gotten caught by the teacher for picking at me and the new girl. He thinks he's all that, but I can't stand the ground he walks on.

The class settled down and Mrs. Porter had us to open our readers up to page 49 to a story about some kings and queens in ancient times that lived over in England somewhere. Every now and again I would take a peek over at my new classmate who still hadn't said one word or even looked my way. She continued to look down at the reader Mrs. Porter gave her and ignored the rest of the class. *I wonder what she's like? Does she like to do the same things as me? Is her mama white or is her daddy?*

When reading time was over, we moved straight along into arithmetic, my most hated subject and the rest of the morning droned on. When lunch time came, I hurriedly took out my sacked lunch and tore into it retrieving the cold cut sandwich Big Ma made me, an apple, some teacakes and a thermos full of milk straight from the farm Uncle Joe works on as a farmhand.

Zannie Mae pulled out a tin lunchbox with the *Huckleberry Hound* etched outside of it. That cartoon was my most favorite one out of all of them, so I decided to spark up a little conversation with her about it.

"So... Um, you like *Huckleberry Hound*?" I asked, pointing at her lunchbox sitting on her desk.

Turning to face me in her seat, she smiled shyly. "Yup! It's my favorite cartoon."

The first thing I noticed about her was that she didn't sound like she was from around here. Her voice was kinda funny and airy, like she was from up north somewhere.

"Mine, too," I replied with a smile. "My name is Cora, but everyone else calls me Stripes." Taking a bite into my cold cut sandwich, I watched Zannie Mae curiously as if she were a new species of some sort. I was glad that another mixed kid had finally joined me at our small county school. It was lonely being so different all the time.

"Yeah, I heard earlier. I'm Zannie Mae, but my Aunt calls me, Pooh. You know, like *Winnie the Pooh Bear*." She took a sip of what appeared to be apple juice from a bottle sitting on her desk before speaking again. Arching her eyebrow, she asked, "Why do they call you that?"

"What?"

"Stripes."

"Ohhh... Well, it's tha' nickname mah Uncle gave me as a baby. 'Cause I'm, well, ya' kno', mixed. Like a zebra is." My face was burning in embarrassment. I think I'm gonna tell my folks to stop calling me by my nickname. I'm getting a little too old for it. After all, I will be eleven soon. That's more than halfway to being grown.

Zannie Mae nodded and picked up a peanut butter and jelly sandwich, bit into it, then chewed thoughtfully. The class was abuzz all around us, but it felt as if we were lost in our own little world. I felt as if

God had given me a special present by sending her to my class and I hoped that we would be good friends.

"I... I'm mixed, too..."

Smiling, I nodded my head. I had already figured that part out just by looking at her. She could easily "pass for white" as Big Ma says, just like me and Sister could. I watched as her bone straight hair cascaded down her back and wondered if it was naturally straight like that or if her mama had to press it out.

I could tell that she was very shy and hoped that she would warm up to me soon. I was always eager to make new friends seeing that the kids in my class could be kinda cruel at times. I missed having Teresa in class with me so I could have someone to talk to all the time.

Unwrapping some tin foil, I took out one of my teacakes and held it out to her. "You want one of mah teacakes?"

Zannie Mae looked at me funny, then frowned. "What's a teacake?"

What's a teacake? She really wasn't from here.

"It's like a cookie. My Big Ma makes them and they're really good." Thrusting the cookie out over the aisle, I motioned to her to take it. "Here, try it."

She shook her head, then blushed. "Sorry, but my aunt said I can't have too many sweets."

Pulling my arm back into my area, I shrugged my shoulders. "Oh, okay." Biting into the teacake, I eyed her suspiciously. I had never met any kid who could turn down a teacake before. She was very interesting, indeed.

We spent the rest of our lunchtime eating quietly. Not that I really wanted to, but because Zannie Mae wouldn't look my way again after I offered her the cookie. I couldn't understand why, but I kept throwing her glances throughout class hoping that she would at least smile at me and strike up a conversation, but she never did.

When the school day was over, I watched her gather up her belongings and head out the door. Picking up my book sack, I followed the rest of the kids out of the classroom. Teresa was waiting for me just outside the classroom door.

"Hi ya', Stripes!" she said excitedly, smiling brightly then pushing her glasses up on the bridge of her nose. For some reason the doggone things never seemed to be able to stay up.

"Hey, Teresa," I replied absentmindedly. All of my attention was focused on trying to see where Zannie Mae had run off to. Did she have a big brother or sister? Was her mama or daddy coming to pick her up afterschool? She was sure lucky if they were. Usually Sister and I walked home together with Isaiah, but today I was walking home alone because Sister didn't feel well, probably because her baby has been making her sick. She's been throwing up all night and morning. And Isaiah stayed home today because he had a bad cold. I hated walking home by myself.

"Ummm, so how was school today?" Teresa asked waving a hand in front of my face trying to get my attention.

"Oh... It was okay," I replied, still trying to see if I could catch a glimpse of Zannie Mae's blond hair. When it seemed as if I lost her among the crowd of students hurrying out of the building, I turned to look at Teresa. "We got a new kid today."

Teresa's eyes lit up in shock. "Really? This close to the holiday?"

"Uh, huh."

"I wonder why?"

Shrugging my shoulders, we began to walk down the hallway towards the school's exit. Before we stepped outside, I slipped on my hat and gloves. When we pushed open the door, our eyes fell upon little snow flurries swirling around in the air. The sky was gray and full of clouds and I couldn't wait to get home and sit in front of the wood burning stove. Stepping down the stairs, holding onto a railing so I wouldn't slip and lose my footing, I spotted Zannie Mae standing alone underneath one of the bare trees in the school yard.

Teresa followed my gaze questioningly. Arching an eyebrow, she asked, "Is that the new kid?"

Nodding, I pulled my coat up around my neck and shivered. I'd forgotten my wool scarf at home. If I got sick, Big Ma was gonna be mad and would more than likely fuss at me for forgetting it this morning.

"Wow... She kinda reminds me of you just by lookin' at her."

I shrugged and kicked at a rock in the schoolyard with my shoe. Why did people keep saying that? We looked nothing alike. She was just light skinned like me. That's all.

"So, what's her name?"

"Zannie Mae."

"Oh. Okay..." Teresa trailed off as she looked out beyond the schoolyard towards the road. Seeing her daddy's truck parked at the edge of the schoolyard, she smiled. "There's daddy's truck! Squirt and 'nem are already inside and everybody's waitin' fa' me!" Throwing her arms around my shoulders, she gave me a quick hug. "I gotta go! My gran'ma and gran'papa came into town today fa' tha' holidays and I can't wait ta' see them. Bye!" She took off down the yard heading towards her daddy's truck. I wished she would've offered me a ride home, but I doubt her daddy wanted to go all the way to the country if they were expecting company.

The schoolyard was nearly empty as all the children had drifted off headed in their various directions home and it was too cold out to be standing around talking or playing. I started to head out towards the road for my 20 minute trek home, but something made me stop and turn around. Out of the corner of my eyes I saw Zannie Mae sit down underneath the tree with her knees pulled up to her chest. Her dress rose slightly and showed her white stockinged legs. She covered her face in her hands and I watched curiously as hers shoulders shrugged up and down. *Is she crying?*

Walking slowly over to where she sat alone underneath the huge oak tree that in the spring offered us kids a huge amount of shade, I could hear her weeping getting louder as I approached her. Her first day of school didn't seem that bad to me except for when Arnie tried to crack a joke earlier, so that couldn't possibly be what was wrong with her.

Standing in front of her, I cleared my throat. She didn't look up, but kept right on crying. It was too cold for anyone to want to sit out here on the freezing ground like this. I hated to see people cry. I had a weakness for it.

"Zannie Mae?" I asked, quietly kneeling down. When my knee touched the cold ground, I shivered. It was so cold outside that it felt like tiny icicles were pricking me.

She sniffled as she looked up. Her green eyes were red rimmed and puffy and her nose was pink.

"Are you... You okay?"

Zannie Mae shook her head and wiped some tears away from her face with her gloved hands. I noticed that she didn't have a hat on and there wasn't a hood on her coat.

"What's wrong? Where's ya' mama and daddy? They ain't comin' down here ta' pick you up?" I asked looking around the school yard. Everyone else was already gone and we were the only lone souls left in sight.

"No..." she replied as fresh tears started to fall from her eyes.

Shivering, I moved closer to her side and set down next to her against the tree trunk. I was hoping that our body heat would jump off of one another and we would help each other stay warm for the time being. At least until I found out why she was crying and where her folks were.

"Why not?"

She sniffled again and it made me wish that I had some tissues in my back sack. I watched as she wiped the tears from underneath her eyes again. She reminded me of a newborn kitten searching for its mama blindly before its eyes opened up. She looked so small and lost.

"'Cause they are... Dead."

My heart lurched inside of my chest and I felt as if the living wind had been knocked smooth out of me.

"Dead? Then who you stayin' wit'? How'd ya' even get ta' school this mornin'?"

Zannie Mae lowered her eyes and twiddled her fingers. "My aunt brought me here this morning on her way to work at some white people house in town. We rode here with a nice man, but I guess she forgot about me. She was supposed to come get me from school, but I don't think she's used to having me around yet."

"Who's ya' aunt? I bet my Big Ma knows her. Big Ma knows everybody that live here. This town so small that darn near everybody some kin," I said with certainty. My grandma knew everybody's business it seemed and who was related to whom and who was creeping around with so and so's man or woman. I got a kick out of hearing the latest gossip when I eavesdropped while Big Ma was on the phone or talking to Uncle Joe about their so called "grown folks' business".

"Her name is Mildred Benton." Zannie Mae looked at me with a deep sadness in her eyes and my heart ached for her and I didn't know why. Maybe it was because she said her folks was dead. In a way I could understand how she feels because even though my mama is still living she might as well be dead to me because I don't ever see her.

"What's her nickname? Ion think I know a Mildred Benton."

Her face scrunched up like she was deep in thought. At least she had stopped crying for now. A northerly gust of wind shook us and I swear it felt as if Jack Frost himself had just cut me with a knife because that wind went straight through my coat to my soul.

"I think people call her Pinky because she's fair skinned," Zannie Mae replied softly. She shivered and I removed my hat from my head and pulled it down onto hers.

She looked over at me shocked. "Why you do that?"

I shrugged my shoulders. "'Cause ya' out here cold and cryin' and stuff." Standing to my feet, I tried to shake off the bone chilling cold that was invading my body. I already know that Big Ma is definitely going to fuss at me for coming home late from school and for not having a hat on my head in this cold weather, but I figured it was better for me to help out a friend who seem to need it more than I did.

"Thank you," she replied and the corners of her mouth turned upwards in a small smile. Pushing herself up off of the ground, she dusted off the backs of her legs and coat. "So, do you know my aunt?"

"I've heard of a Pinky befo', I think," I said, really unsure if I knew of her aunt or not, but I was sure that Big Ma did. Before I knew it I had decided to take her home with me so she wouldn't be left outside the school in the cold. I was really surprised that none of the teachers had saw us sitting out here in the schoolyard, but then again it was the last day of school before the holiday and I was quite sure that they had to get home and cook and entertain guests.

Taking her hand in mine, I said, "C'mon home wit' me. It's a bit of a walk, but you can call yo' auntie from my house. My Big Ma won't mind and I guarantee you she knows ya' kinfolks."

Zannie Mae looked a little nervous but bent down to gather up her belongings before walking out of the schoolyard hand in hand with me. She was really quiet, so I made an attempt at conversation to pass time.

"So, you got any brothers or sisters?" I asked as we walked along a dirt road towards home. Trees aligned both sides of the road, towering over us with their bare limbs. The snow was starting to fall faster now and I couldn't wait to step foot inside Big Ma's warm house. There wasn't a car or truck in sight and it made me wonder if there was about to be a big snow storm coming.

Zannie Mae shook her head and kept her eyes focused on the road ahead. "No. I was my mommy and daddy's only child."

The question that had been burning inside of me since she first walked into the classroom that morning slipped its way out of my mouth. "So... Who is ya' white parent? Ya' mama or daddy?"

She looked at me as if I had asked her if one of her parents were an alien. Frowning a little, she opened her heart shaped mouth and replied, "My mama was white and my daddy was black. Why?"

"Ion know? I's just curious. I mean, besides me and my big sister, I've never met another mixed kid before."

"Oh," she replied quietly. "Well, there were plenty of us at my old school."

My eyebrows shot up at that statement. Blacks and whites really didn't do too much of mingling in our small Tennessee town, so it was rare to see offspring of mixed races. What was even more unheard of was a white woman getting pregnant by a colored man. It was usually always the other way around like it was with Mama.

"Really?" Moistening my lips because the harsh wind was making the uncomfortably chapped, I looked at her in surprise.

Zannie Mae nodded and I watched as the ball on top of my gray winter hat she was wearing bounced about. My head felt awfully cold and I was regretting the decision of letting her wear it. Peeling my eyes away from the top of her head, I turned my attention back towards the road.

"Yeah, it wasn't a bad thing to be different where I'm from."

"Where ya' from anyways? Like, why did you start school so late?"

She didn't answer my question right away and for a moment all that could be heard were the sound of our footsteps as we trampled upon the dirt road, crunching fallen leaves as we went.

"I... I'm from New York." Her lower lip started quivering and it looked as if she may start crying again. I was hoping with all my might that she didn't.

"I had to move here because my mommy and daddy were killed in a car accident. I stay with Aunt Mildred now who was daddy's sister because my mommy's family wouldn't have nothing to do with her after I was born. My mommy's family is Italian and they don't really seem to care for black people. It hurts really bad because it always made me feel like parts of me are really ugly and dirty while the other parts are supposed to be good." Zannie Mae looked at me with sadness in her eyes and pain tugged at my heart for her.

"I kinda understand what you mean..." I replied softly. "I'm really sorry 'bout ya' folks, tho'. Really sorry."

I wanted to open up to her and tell her that my daddy had been killed when I was one years old, but I really didn't see how my story could compare to hers. I never even knew my daddy whereas she had grown up with hers and I was awfully embarrassed to tell her that my mama had run off with some rich man and abandoned all of her kids. Although I would never admit it aloud, I really couldn't understand why or how Mama was able to live with herself by leaving us behind while she did whatever she wanted to in life. It just wasn't right and it hurt me deeply to even think about it.

By the time we made it to Big Ma's house, the snow had fallen so heavily that it covered the earth like a soft, white blanket. As soon as we turned the corner and walked into the driveway, Big Ma came bursting out of the house wearing nothing but her pink housecoat and slippers, with a red kerchief wrapped around her head. At first her expression seemed like she was relieved then angry. She ran down off of the porch and took me into her arms in a hug, then released me.

"Cora Leanne!" Big Ma exclaimed with anger written across her dark face. Placing her hands upon her bony hips, she eyed me down. "Where have ya' been?! Ya' had meh worried sick! It's almost dark and ya' just now getting' home! I had been callin' all 'round town lookin' fa' ya'. I just called Joe at work and told him to gone on up there to that school of yours ta' look out fa' ya' ta' see if sumin' bad done happened ta' ya'!" Clutching her bosom, she released a frustrated breath. "I was just 'bout sick ta' death!"

"Sorry, Big Ma, I was just tryna help out mah new friend here," I replied weakly, gesturing towards Zannie Mae.

Big Ma stopped looking at me and looked over at Zannie Mae as if she were seeing her standing there beside me for the first time. A look of surprise flashed in her eyes and she smiled warmly at my friend.

"Oh, good, Lord, chile, I didn't see ya' standin' there," Big Ma said, adjusting her glasses upon her face. Squinting, she bent down and brought her face closer to Zannie Mae's. I held in a giggle as I watched Zannie Mae shrink back some and glance sideways at me. "Chile, who're ya'? Who's ya' belong to? I don't think I've eva' had tha' pleasure of meetin' ya' befo'." Standing back upright, Big Ma clucked her tongue.

"Um... Um..." Zannie Mae stammered then looked over at me for help.

"This is Zannie Mae Crenshaw. She's new in mah class, Big Ma and her auntie forgot to pick her up from school today." I said, folding my arms across my chest in attempts to block out some of the cold wind. Snow flurries were still swarming all around us and my grandma had us out here in the cold giving us the 3rd degree. I felt like an inmate on trial standing before the judge about to ask for the mercy of the court.

Big Ma looked down and saw that we both were freezing, shivering in our shoes damn near close to becoming Eskimos, so she ushered us up the yard and into the house. I melted as soon as I stepped foot inside of the warm house. Taking off my coat, I hung it up on the door hanger near the front door and took a seat next to Zannie Mae on the couch. She took off my hat and handed it to me but kept her coat on.

"So, Zannie Mae, who's ya' peoples?" Big Ma asked while walking across the room and picking up the receiver of the phone. Holding it up to her ear, she waited for Zannie Mae to reply.

"Mildred. Mildred Benton."

Big Ma nodded in recognition. "Ah, Pinky." Frowning, she looked down her nose at her. "I ain't kno' Pinky had no chil'ren."

Zannie Mae shook her head and I couldn't help but notice a few strands of hair that were standing up now upon her head since she had removed the hat. It looked like she was a cat that had just gotten spooked.

"No. She doesn't. I'm her niece." Zannie Mae bit her bottom lip. Her face was flushed, but this time I think it was because she was still cold since her nose was a bright red color, too. "I just moved here over the weekend and I don't think she's used to me being here, yet. I think she forgot about me."

"Mmm, hmm..." Big Ma said, then dialed a number on the rotary phone.

LeTresa Payne

We sat silent, listening intently at the rings over the phone. After three rings someone picked up.

"Yea', is this Pinky?" Big Ma asked with her hand on her hip, eyes darting back and forth between me and Zannie Mae.

"Hey, Pinky, I got ya' niece, Zannie Mae over here at mah house. Stripes brought her home wit' her after school."

I strained to hear the response, but I could've sworn it sounded like Zannie Mae's aunt said, "Thank Ya', Jesus," to Big Ma.

"Okay, well when Joe gits on back this way, I'll have him drop her off at ya' house."

Big Ma listened for a minute then said, "Mmm, hmm. Naw, it ain't no trouble, no trouble at all. Mmm, okay. You, too. Bye now."

Hanging up the phone, Big Ma called out to Zannie Mae. "My son Joe is gonna take ya' home as soon as he gits in." Heading towards the kitchen, she looked back and said, "Are ya' hungry, baby?" while looking our way.

I didn't know which one of us she was talking to, so I replied, "Yes'm."

Big Ma smiled, then chuckled. "I knows you are, Stripes. You're always hungry." Gesturing towards Zannie Mae, she continued, "I was talkin' 'bout that baby ova' there."

Zannie Mae looked over at me as if she was asking for permission to answer. I nodded my head telling her it was okay and she told Big Ma that she was hungry. Big Ma took off down the hall and went in the kitchen.

The rest of the house was quiet, so I was guessing that Sister was in the back room sleep and that Isaiah still didn't feel good. Any other time the TV would be blasting in the background, just on for Isaiah's amusement while he sat on the floor playing with his toys.

Rising from my seat on the couch, I walked over to the TV and turned the dial cutting it on. As I fiddled with the antenna, I asked Zannie Mae if she had a favorite show she particularly liked to watch at this time of day. She shook her head no, so I turned the dial to channel 3 and we sat and watched *Andy Griffith*. After a few moments of us sitting there, Sister came walking sluggishly into the room.

Yawning, sister stretched her arms high above her head then lowered them and rubbed her slightly protruding belly. Resting her arms down to her sides, she cocked her head and frowned. "Who's tha' kid, Stripes?" Walking over to Big Ma's favorite chair, she plopped down and crossed her legs. Her face was pale and dark circles had taken up residence underneath her eyes. She still looked sick. I hoped that she wouldn't scare off Zannie Mae because I really want us to become friends.

"She's a new girl in my class."

"Okay, so what's she doin' here? She ain't got no home ta' go to?"

Zannie Mae shifted uncomfortably in her seat next to me and I could feel myself getting heated. Who did Sister think she was questioning me like this? She ain't my mama and this ain't her house! If I wanted to up and bring a friend home with me, I very well could.

Feeling a braveness I had never felt before overcoming my body, I narrowed my eyes at her, rolled my neck and replied snottily, "Don't worry 'bout it. It's none of ya' business. She's mah company. Worry 'bout ya' own problems and stop being so damn rude all the time!" If I didn't know any better, I would have sworn that I was morphing into a clone of my sister.

Sister's mouth dropped open, her eyes bucked wide open at me. She started to say something, but Big Ma stepped in the room. Fear held me captive as my heart started racing and my palms started to sweat. I knew I was about to be in big trouble.

Big Ma twisted her mouth as she surveyed the room which was now as quiet as church during prayer time. Her dark brown eyes focused in on me and I swallowed hard. Closing my eyes, I took a deep breath, then exhaled and said a small prayer to God asking Him to please save my hind parts from the beating that was surely to come. When I opened my eyes, Big Ma was still standing in the doorway of the front room with an unhappy look upon her face.

"Cora, lemme see ya' fo' a minute." Without another word, she spun on her heel and went back down the hall, the floors creaking underneath her weight with every step that she took.

Pushing myself up off of the couch, my head hung low as I slowly followed after her. I couldn't bring myself to look at Zannie Mae because I was awfully embarrassed. As I walked past Sister, she smirked at me and I wanted to slug her in the jaw.

When I entered the kitchen, Big Ma was sitting down at the kitchen table. The warm, inviting smell of dinner hit my nostrils making my stomach growl and my mouth water. Big Ma gestured to the chair next to hers and said, "Sat down."

I noticed that she didn't have anything to hit me with in her hands. My eyes darted around the room searching for Big Ma's belt that she used to whip us with. Seeing it nowhere in sight, I relaxed a little. Pulling up a chair next to her, I sat down with my eyes cast downward. Nervously fidgeting with a loose thread on my shirt I felt like a prisoner waiting to be sentenced. For a moment all that could be heard in the kitchen was the sound of the clock ticking and the pots bubbling as they cooked the contents they held inside.

Big Ma reached over and I flinched thinking she may slap me like she did Sister that one time. Big

Ma had never laid a hand on me other than using a switch or belt to whip me, but I had said a cuss word and I knew I had been in the wrong. Instead of hitting me, she took one of my hands and placed it in hers before placing her other one on top of it.

"Cora, look at meh," Big Ma said and I raised my head and searched her eyes. I didn't see any anger behind them at all and I felt relieved.

Inhaling deeply, Big Ma looked me deeply in the eyes. "I'm not gone whip ya' if that's what you're thinkin'."

Visibly relaxing, I let out a sigh of relief.

"I called ya' in here so's that we could talk. I want ya' ta' listen ta' meh real good, okay?"

I nodded and waited on her to continue.

The light from the overhead bulb above us fell upon Big Ma's eyes and they glistened as if tiny diamonds were captured within them. I saw nothing but pure love within them that she held for me.

"I heard what ya' said and ya' knows that I ain't raisin' ya' up ta' be cussin' like no sailor." Big Ma eyed me from over the top of her glasses. I hated that I had disappointed her. I always wanted to make her proud just because she had stepped in and took care of me and my sister and brother when we had no one else, but the real reason I wanted to make her proud was because she loved me unconditionally. That was the type of love that no amount of money in the world could buy.

"Now, Cora, you are sumin' special. A real gem. You're different than most chil'ren ya' age. Ya' got wisdom far beyond ya' years and I want ya' ta' stay like that. Ya' hear?" Before I could reply she carried on. "I don't want ya' ta' grow up sassin' folks like ya' sister in there does. I loves Sister ta' death just like I loves you and Junebug like my own chil'ren, but ya' sister has a mean streak in her that's as venomous as a poisonous snake. She's full of anger at y'all mama which I can understand. She may not say how she feels 'bout mah daughter, but I knows she's hurtin' real deep inside 'cause y'all mama ain't here raisin' ya'."

Big Ma lifted a hand and raised my chin gently so that she could look me in the eyes. "The Lord is gone use ya', baby. You's real special. He's gone use ya' ta' do a mighty good work fa' His kingdom. Mark mah words. So, don't git ta' gittin' too big fa' ya' britches befo' yo' time. Stay in a child's place fo' as long as ya' can and remember that tha' words that come forth outta ya' mouth hits God's ears way befo' they hit tha' ears of whomeva ya' talkin' to in person. Make sure ta' always keep ya' mouth clean befo' tha' Lord. I want ya' ta' grow up and be a real respectable like lady. One that will turn heads whereva ya' go just because ya' is shinin' bright from tha' light of Jesus who lives within ya'. Understand?"

Nodding, I bit my bottom lip in shame. I realized then that sometimes getting a talking to was worse than getting a whipping. Big Ma's words were sure to follow me for a long time. Big Ma let go of my hand and pushed her chair back, stood, then leaned over and planted a kiss on my forehead.

"Now, go on in there and git' that friend of yours and brang ha' on in here fa' supper. Tell Sister it's ready, too." Turning towards the stove, she lifted the lid on a pot and steam swirled up in a misty pattern towards the ceiling. With her back to me, she said, "Don't worry 'bout feeding Junebug tonight. I got him. I want ya' ta' entertain ya' new friend. It looks ta' me like that chile gone need a good friend like you in ha' life."

The rest of the evening went on without any other issues. Sister even apologized to Zannie Mae for being rude and said she didn't mean anything by it. She said her hormones were raging like the Red Sea before God parted it so that Moses and the Israelites could escape that mean old Pharaoh. She even offered to braid her hair for her the next time came over if she wanted and that made Zannie Mae smile. She nodded her head eagerly and said she would love that.

Zannie Mae sat next to me at the kitchen table and ate everything clean off her plate. She said she had never tasted cooking so good before. When Uncle Joe came home, Zannie Mae and I piled into the truck next to him and we headed into town to take her home. She held my hand the whole way there and I couldn't help but smile. Gazing out the window at the rising moon, I silently whispered to God, "Thank you." I was glad that He had sent me a new friend and I could tell that we were destined to be good friends for a long time.

Chapter 6

Thanksgiving came and went and Aunt Trish left with it heading back home to Memphis. I hated to see her go, but she promised she would be back to visit for Christmas. Before she left, she came into Sister's and my bedroom while I was sleeping and left a small pink gift box tied with a light blue ribbon that was curled on the ends on the wooden back chair that sat near my side of the bed. When I woke up on the morning she departed, I rubbed the crust out of my eyes and smiled with glee when I looked down at the chair and saw the gift. Scooping up the box, I noticed a manila envelope laying underneath it. Picking the envelope up, I tore it open and pulled out the card that was inside. Opening the card, a crisp dollar bill fell out and onto the lap of my gown.

I decided to read the card before opening my gift and it read:

My dearest Stripes,

Happy 11th birthday, sweetheart. I know that this isn't much, but I wanted to let you know that you mean the world to me. I am so proud of the young lady that you are becoming. It seems just like yesterday when you were a tiny red baby who I couldn't get enough of holding and singing to you as if you were my own little girl. You are a bright, spunky, and special girl and I hope that all of your dreams come true for your birthday.

With Love,

Aunt Trisha

Laying down the card on the bed beside me, excitement bubbled up in my stomach as I grinned widely as I unraveled the bow on the gift box sitting in my lap. Carefully removing the top, my eyes grew big as they fell upon what was inside. Reaching down into the box, I retrieved the most beautiful necklace I had ever seen in my few years on earth. The gold chain of the necklace glittered in the light casted upon it from the bedroom ceiling's light bulb. Dangling at the end of the necklace was a gold letter "C" pendant. I fingered it gently and the chain swayed slightly back and forth.

"Oh, my Lord," I gasped in disbelief. How could my aunt claim in her card that her birthday gift to me wasn't much? This necklace alone must've set her back a pretty penny.

Shifting my weight on the bed, I tapped Sister, who was still fast asleep facing the wall, on the shoulder. I wanted her to see what a pretty gift I had received from our aunt. This was the first expensive gift I had ever gotten in my life. For the first time, I was the one receiving a lavish brand-new gift and not Sister. It gave me a warm and fuzzy feeling inside.

"Huh?" Sister mumbled without turning around so I pushed her on the shoulder harder this time.

"Dammit, Stripes, I said, 'huh?'" Sister cursed as she rolled over to face me.

Dangling my birthday gift in front of her face, I squealed excitedly, "Lookie at what Auntie Trish gave me!" Nobody could've wiped the grin off my face with an eraser if they wanted to. I was just that happy.

Sister's eyebrows shot up and she pushed herself up in the bed. Yanking the necklace out of my hand, she grimaced, "What in the hell?"

"It's pretty, ain't it?"

Sister rolled her eyes and turned the necklace over and over again in her hands. Squinting, she brought the clasp up to her eyes and peered at it, studying it hard. Frowning, I reached out to take it back from her, but she jerked her hands away.

Pouting, I said, frustrated, "Uh, uhhh. Give it back, Sister!"

Sister studied the necklace some more before thrusting it back at me. "Why she give ya' that for?"

Taking the necklace from her, I sighed. Sister's mood swings were really starting to get under my skin. "It's for my birthday."

"Uh, huh..." was all that she said.

Later on that morning, I showed the necklace to Big Ma who said it was really pretty, but since it was expensive I would only be allowed to wear it to church. She didn't want me wearing it to school and let some of the kids see it and make them want to steal it from me. I didn't like it, but I understood her reasoning. I couldn't wait to wear it to church the next day. I stuck the necklace, resting safely inside the box it came in, inside the top drawer of my side of the dresser that I shared with Sister, then I got ready for today. Uncle Joe said that he would take me and Isaiah into town today to buy one of those fake Christmas trees from the 5 and 10. I couldn't wait. It would be the first Christmas that we ever had an actual Christmas tree put up in the house like the white kids I saw on the old Christmas movies that they showed on TV every year.

When we were headed down the highway into town with Isaiah sitting in between Uncle Joe and me, an idea popped into my head.

"Uncle Joe," I called out to him.

Uncle Joe had one hand on the steering wheel driving the truck and looked so cool sitting there with his red fedora cocked to the side on his head with a cigarillo held firmly between his thick lips. He was about a decade older than me, but was the coolest guy I knew. I hoped to grow up and marry a man just as smooth as him someday.

Taking a drag on the cigarillo, he exhaled the smoke through his nostrils. "Yeah, Stripes?"

"Can we stop by Zannie Mae's house? Pleaseeee!" I begged and Isaiah looked at me and giggled. I must've looked or sounded funny to him, so I reached over and tickled him under the arms of his winter jacket. This made way for another volcanic eruption of giggles to break loose from him.

"Do ya' thank it'll be okay with her auntie?"

Nodding my head, I sat back in my seat and watched the road ahead. The sky was such a pretty clear blue outside today. Even though it was cold out there, it looked like a beautiful spring day minus the dead grass on the ground and the fact that there weren't any leaves on the trees except for the fir ones.

"Alright, then. I don't see no harm in that."

Uncle Joe turned off right on the highway and traveled down another road that led to the other side of town where Zannie Mae and her Aunt Pinky lived. Even though we had just seen each other at school the day before, I couldn't wait to tell her about the early birthday present I received from my aunt. Bare trees and endless fields whizzed past us in a blur of dark browns and yellows until we reached the street that she lived on. Her aunt didn't own a car, so it wasn't any surprise when we pulled up and there wasn't one in the driveway.

When Uncle Joe parked the truck, we all got out and I held Isaiah's hand as we strode up the walkway towards the front door. Unlike our house, Zannie Mae's didn't have a front porch, just three concrete steps painted white that were starting to chip away from the weather and sun. Bushes stood lined in a row underneath the windows of the red brick house with a gray shingled roof.

As we neared the front stoop, a black and white cat arched its back and glowered at us through its yellow diamond shaped eyes. Hissing at us, it shot off the front stoop in a blur and across the yard before climbing up a nearby tree. Looking up at it, I watched as it observed us from high above as we walked down below it. Isaiah started whimpering and I told him that everything was okay, the cat was gone and was more afraid of us than we were of it.

Uncle Joe raised his hand and rapped lightly on the screen door. A sultry voice replied, "Just a minute," from just beyond the wooden front door. Moments later, Zannie Mae's Aunt Mildred opened the door and peered out at us through the screen door. When she saw Uncle Joe, her eyes lit up and she smiled warmly.

Unlocking the screen door, she pushed it open and said, "Why hello, Joe, what a pleasant surprise in seeing you this morning." Looking beyond our uncle, she smiled at Isaiah and me. "Hello, children. Y'all sure looking nice today."

"Mornin', Missus Pinky," I said jubilantly.

Isaiah gurgled and played with his bottom lip. I was hoping that he would speak so that he would show others that he's learning how to communicate with the world using words. I guess we would still be taking things one day at a time. That's okay, though, I'm proud of my baby brother's progress. He's learning so much as each day goes by.

"Good mornin', Pinky," Uncle Joe said in a rumbling voice which was an octave deeper than it normally was. I caught myself looking up at him with an eyebrow raised, because his voice sounded a little funny just then. I wanted to ask him was he okay. Maybe he needed a cough drop 'cause a frog crawled in his throat or something. Cold weather could do that to you.

"Good morning, yourself, mister," she replied with a twinkle in her eye.

Mildred stepped back and held the door open with one hand so that we could enter the house. The house smelled wonderful as if she were baking cakes. As we stepped into the small living room, Isaiah and I took a seat together in a huge, poufy, plush blue chair sitting near one of the windows that had lace white drapes hung over it. Uncle Joe removed his hat and rubbed his goatee not taking his eyes off of Mildred for a minute. It looked to me like he was kinda sweet on her and she just might be kinda sweet on him, too.

"Pooh? C'mon in here. Your friend from school is here with her uncle and brother," Mildred hollered out.

The sound of Zannie Mae's feet could be heard as they excitedly pounded the floor as she ran through the house from the back of it towards the living room. Moments later she burst into the room, grinning. She looked radiant and sort of like an angel. Her blond hair, secured with a pink and black head band, was draping over the shoulders of her pretty pink dress that had a black sash around the middle which was tied in a bow on the back. On her feet were the prettiest black shoes that I had ever seen. They had a strap that went across the top of each foot and on the ends of each strap there was a heart shaped silver buckle covered with rhinestones which sparkled when the light hit them. The shoes even had a small heel! If only I could own a pair of shoes like that. It would surely be nice. My eyes were so in tune with her shoes that I didn't even notice that she was calling my name.

"Cora! Coraaaaa! Hellllloooooo!" Zannie Mae giggled and waved her hands wildly in front of my face.

I tore my attention away from her shoes, blinking rapidly. "Hey, Zannie Mae! Guess what?!"

Zannie Mae bent over and gave Isaiah a tight hug and he grinned. One of the things I was growing to love about my new friend was that she never treated my brother any differently than she treated me. She was unlike a lot of kids I knew who were so mean and made from of him because he wasn't like "normal" kids. To me, Isaiah was perfect, but to the outside world, they called him ugly things like, "slow" and "crazy" or "retard". My brother isn't any of those things. He's a precious soul who is unique in his own way. If people would just take the time out to get to know him first before judging him they would come to see that he is really smart. Smarter than what most people think and they would be really surprised at what he knows and can do.

"Hi, boyfriend!" she exclaimed to Isaiah when she pulled back away from him. Glancing my way, her green eyes sparkled. "So, what you want to tell me?"

I started gushing to her about the birthday card and gift I received from Aunt Trish while Uncle Joe and her aunt took off into the kitchen to talk. We were so caught up in our own little conversation that had jumped from my gift to school to the upcoming Christmas holiday, we didn't even notice when Uncle Joe stepped back into the living room. He cleared his throat to gather our attention. He had placed his fedora back on his head and his hand was on the door knob of the front door.

Mildred stepped into the living room then. "Pooh, go on in your room and get your coat so you can go around the square with Joe and your friends.

They're getting a Christmas tree today. Isn't that lovely?"

Zannie Mae's eyes lit up in glee and she clasped her hands together. "I can go with them?"

Mildred nodded, smiling warmly at her niece.

"Yes!" Zannie Mae took off back down the hall to retrieve her coat.

When we were heading out the door, Mildred called out to Uncle Joe. "It was really nice seeing you today, Joe. Really nice."

Uncle Joe tipped his hat and grinned, his smile reaching the corner of his eyes. "You, too, Pinky." Winking at her, he placed his hand on my back shooing me out the door.

When we got in the truck and were heading towards the square so we could go to the 5 and 10, I cupped my hands and placed them up to Zannie Mae's ear. She was sitting nearest to the door, leaning up against it watching the houses go by.

"I think mah uncle is sweet on ya' auntie," I whispered.

Zannie Mae eyes widened and she raised her hands up to her mouth giggling. Turning her head, she placed a hand up to my ear and whispered back, "I think so, too. But, guess what?"

She pulled back away from me and I replied, "What?"

With laughter within her eyes, she leaned back in and said quietly, "I think my aunt likes him, too."

It was my turn to giggle then. I really hoped that they did like each other. That would be amazing. Uncle Joe hasn't had a girlfriend in a really long time since his last one broke his heart. I didn't like his last girlfriend. She smelled like pig's feet and looked like one, too.

"If they get married, me and you would be cousins then!" Zannie Mae said excitedly in a hushed voice looking over at me, then looking beyond me to see if Uncle Joe was listening.

I nodded my head excitedly, then turned around to see if Uncle Joe had heard anything we had said. He had his eyes focused on the road, but I could see a small smile creep upon his face.

Pulling up to the 5 and 10, we all jumped out of the truck and walked inside the store. I was a bundle of excitement and could barely contain it. We were getting my first Christmas tree! Maybe Santa would bring my mama along with him this Christmas. I would have to have a little conversation with God and baby Jesus tonight to ensure that they could come through for me on this wish of mine.

The 5 and 10 smelled dusty, like it hadn't been aired out in years. Behind the counter stood a teenage boy around Sister's age with blonde hair and freckles that decorated the bridge of his nose and cheeks like specks of cinnamon. He watched us closely but didn't greet us.

Zannie Mae looked at him nervously and grabbed me by the hand.

"He surely looks mean," she whispered and I nodded.

Wrapping my fingers tightly around Isaiah's hand in my other one, we followed behind Uncle Joe towards the back of the store. The small bell above the door to the store chimed and I turned my head to see who entered it. It was an older, heavyset white lady and a little boy who had to be no more than four years old. The boy behind the counter smiled and greeted them.

"Mornin', Mrs. Buchannan." Bending down on the countertop, he smiled warmly at the little boy. "Hey ya', Jeff! You want a sucker?"

The little boy, who I presumed was called Jeff, nodded eagerly before sticking a forefinger up his nose and picking it. Lowering his finger, he popped a booger in his mouth. I cringed in disgust.

The shop boy bent down and reached behind the counter and I could see through the glass of the counter when he picked up a cherry lollipop. Pulling his hand back from behind the counter he unwrapped the lollipop and handed it over to Jeff.

"Here ya' go, pal."

Jeff grinned and stuck the lollipop into his filthy mouth. Turning my attention back to my uncle, I watched as he moved some small white boxes around that had Christmas trees in them so that he could get to the biggest box on the back of the shelf. Pulling out the box, he looked down at us kids and grinned satisfied with his efforts.

"This is the one, kids. What ya' thank?"

We all bent over and looked at the picture of the most beautiful Christmas tree I had ever seen on the outside of the box. I just couldn't wait to get it home and up so that we could decorate it.

"It's gonna be so pretty!" Zannie Mae gushed.

"Yup! I like it, Uncle Joe!" I said excitedly.

"Alright, then. This is it."

Uncle Joe took the big box in his hands and lifted it up onto his shoulder and headed back towards the front of the store with us in tow. When Mrs. Buchannan saw us approaching the counter, her face snarled up into an ugly scowl before rolling her eyes and turning her attention back to the shop boy. Uncle Joe sat the tree down on the store's floor and waited for his turn at the register with money in his hand.

The shop boy still didn't acknowledge our presence. He however began asking Mrs. Buchannan what she came into the store for.

"So, what can I do for ya' today, ma'am?"

"Well, Jimmy, I came in here today to purchase a Christmas tree here for little Jeffery. I want the biggest one your daddy has."

Jimmy's brown eyes lit up in a smile. "Oh, yes'm. I think we have one more big one in the back." Looking in the direction of where we were standing, his eyes fell upon the Christmas tree box that was now laying at Uncle Joe's feet.

"You can't buy that," Jimmy said with a cold stare.

I looked around to see who he was talking to and realized he was talking to my uncle.

"What ya' mean?" Uncle Joe challenged. "It was on the shelf fo' buyin' and that's exactly what I tend ta' do."

Jimmy glared, ears turning red in the process. "That's the last large tree we have and it's going to Mrs. Buchannan here." He gestured towards Mrs. Buchannan who had her nose turned up in the air. I studied her skin, intrigued by the yellowness of her old and leathery skin. I wondered how old she was because her face was so haggard looking and it appeared that she had a permanent frown etched onto it.

Mrs. Buchannan nodded, then said, "Yes, Jimmy. This one right here will do just fine."

An anger arose in my chest, churning hot embers and before I knew it I said, "This tree ain't yours, it's ours and ya' can't have it!"

Mrs. Buchannan gasped, a hand flying to her chest as if I had just cursed her out. Uncle Joe placed a firm hand on my shoulder and took a step in front of me.

Mrs. Buchannan cut her eyes at Uncle Joe. "Nigger, you better control that smart talkin' half breed of yours if you know what's best for you!" Her yellowed skin became tinged with red and her fat jowls shook in anger.

Letting go of both Isaiah's and Zannie Mae's hands, I balled my fists up at my sides. *Who did this old lady think she was talking to?!* The tree was rightfully ours because we had got to it first. She didn't even go to the back of the store to try to look for one.

The snotty nosed kid, Jeff, who was with her stood wide-eyed watching the ordeal taking place before him. He licked slowly on his lollipop as his eyes darted back and forth between Uncle Joe, Jimmy and Mrs. Buchannan. Slobber from the lollipop was slowly dripping down the sides of his mouth.

"Ma'am, no disrespect, but we got the tree first." Uncle Joe turned towards Jimmy and said, "Mr. Jimmy, I'd like to git' this here tree for the youngin's. They're really excited 'bout it."

Jimmy shook his head and placed his palms flat against the countertop. "Are you deaf, boy?" I peeked my head from around my uncle and glowered up at him. *How dare he call my uncle a boy!* Uncle Joe was way older than he was. This only fueled my anger more.

"I said that tree is goin' to Mrs. Buchannan."

Just then an older white man with wired framed glassed and a grayed mustache that looked like the fur of a squirrel's tail stepped out from an office in the back behind the counter. Glancing between us and Jimmy and Mrs. Buchannan, he said slowly, "Do we have a problem here, son?" Clasping a hand on Jimmy's shoulder, he eyed down Uncle Joe.

Jimmy tilted his head up and nodded. "Yes sir, these niggers trying to take that tree that I just promised to Mrs. Buchannan."

"I see..."

The older man turned towards Mrs. Buchannan and said, "I'm sorry, ma'am. I'll get Jimmy here to take that tree out to your car for you right now. You can pay for it here while he does that."

My mouth dropped open in disbelief. They were just going to give our tree away to this old lady like it wasn't nothing. Like we never even said it was ours.

"Sir..." Uncle Joe started but was cut off.

"Boy, if you know what's good for you, you will leave my store now."

Jimmy darted from around the counter and tried to pick up the box. He wasn't as nearly as strong as Uncle Joe, so he was experiencing some difficulties. Breaking into a sweat, he turned back and looked at the older white man before calling out, "Daddy, can you give me a hand here?"

Jimmy's father eyed Uncle Joe coldly, studying him. "No, son. Joe here will help you take that tree out to Mrs. Buchannan's car."

I looked up at Uncle Joe and shook my head, tugging on his hand. Uncle Joe didn't look down at me, but removed his hand from mine, his expression blank. Bending over, he swooped the box up with ease and followed Jimmy out of the store. Isaiah, Zannie Mae and I hurried behind him, passing by Jeff on our way out who stuck his red colored tongue out at us as we went.

The three of us stood on the sidewalk and watched as my uncle placed our Christmas tree in the trunk of Mrs. Buchannan's car. My heart sank as I watched my first Christmas tree be wrongfully given away to some racist, heartless souls. When Jimmy headed back into the store, Uncle Joe walked to the driver's side door of the truck and pulled on the handle, jerking it open. Without looking our way, called out to us. "Get in."

We hurriedly did as we were told and climbed into the cab of the truck. I was fuming on the inside. Zannie Mae appeared nervous and scared and was constantly biting the skin off of her lips. Isaiah was even quiet. He wasn't doing his usual happy humming.

As Uncle Joe steered the truck down the road heading back towards Zannie Mae's house, I watched him closely. His jaw was tightly clenched and I could see angry veins bursting through the skin of his neck. For the life of me I couldn't understand how he just up and let that white lady take our tree and I felt the need to let him know how I felt.

"Why'd ya' just let that mean and hateful ole' white hag take our Christmas tree, huh, Uncle Joe?" Popping my lips, I carried on in a tizzy. "Then you just let them call us niggers and me a half breed!" Slapping my knee in anger, I fought back the urge to cry. "I'm not a half breed and we ain't no niggers!"

Uncle Joe gripped the steering wheel tightly and I noticed the need for some lotion on his knuckles. Taking a deep breath, he released it slowly, not once taking his eyes off of the road.

"There wasn't nothin' I could do back there, Stripes, 'sides what I did."

"Why?" I asked in utter disbelief. Here he was a grown man getting told what to do by another grown man and even a child no older than Sister. How could he have allowed that to happen? Uncle Joe was the strongest man I knew and he demanded respect from everybody, but today he just acted like a coward and didn't even stand up for himself. He didn't even stand up for us!

"Drop it, Stripes..." He said in a warning tone.

But I couldn't drop it. What I had just witnessed and been a part of was wrong. That tree wasn't even theirs. It was ours and to just up and call us out of our names like that was awful. How could he just let them get away with that? As many times as we had been to the 5 and 10 before, that mean old white man just up and did us like that? Acted like our money wasn't any good for them and as if Mrs. Buchannan's was better or something. We had money to pay for the tree just like she did, but she should've gotten her own and not ours. It just wasn't fair.

"Uncle Joe, it wasn't right! That was our tree. You had the money out to pay for it wit'!" I was so angry that my skin felt heated, like it was on fire. I had never been so angry or hurt in my life. "Then that stupid shop boy, Jimmy, ignored all of us at first and when that nasty nosed lil' boy came in he gave him a lollipop, but ain't even offer any of us 'nam." I gestured in between me, Isaiah, and Zannie Mae. "Not like I would even want his stupid lil' candy or nothin' now anyways since he treated us like we were dogs."

"Cora, I said drop it!" Uncle Joe, who rarely lost his cool, spoke to me with such force, I clammed up immediately. He looked at me with eyes that held something behind them in which I couldn't decipher. It seemed to be a mix between anguish, sadness, or shame.

We spent the rest of the ride to Zannie Mae's house in silence.

*

Uncle Joe never spoke about the incident at the 5 and 10 when we made it back home. I don't even know if he explained the situation to Big Ma or not. As soon as we pulled up to the house, he went around back and later emerged with an axe and then disappeared into the woods. About an hour or so had passed when we heard a large thud upon the porch and he dragged a small fir tree inside the house. Big Ma looked up from her quilting but didn't say a word. We spent the rest of the afternoon decorating our new replacement Christmas tree while singing carols and drinking homemade hot chocolate. Sister was even in a good mood and sang right along with us as we trimmed the tree.

In the days leading up to my 11th birthday, I became increasingly anxious about Christmas and my Christmas wish. Each night I knelt beside my bed and said the same prayer to God and Baby Jesus, asking them to please send my Mama home for my birthday, if not then, at least for Christmas. I wanted desperately to know what it felt like to have a mother's love. I wanted to know what my Mama looked like now and if I resembled her in the slightest, but even more than that, I wanted to feel her arms wrapped around me in the sweetest, most loving hug.

After my 11th birthday came and went by quite uneventfully, I almost fell into a slump because God didn't answer my prayers and deliver my mama to me as my birthday gift. I didn't stay sad too long because I realized that maybe He was waiting to gift her to me on Christmas which would be even better. On Christmas Eve, I lay next to Sister who was snoring softly beside me on her side of the bed and looked up in the darkness towards the ceiling. I was hoping beyond hope that God would come through for me in the morning and answer my prayers or at least maybe Baby Jesus would have a little mercy on me since it was His birthday and all.

"Dear God and Baby Jesus," I whispered softly into the night, "Please let my mama come on home for Christmas just this once. I need her... Junebug needs her and Sister does, too... Even though she be actin' like she don't and stuff, I just knows she does. I just wanna kno' how it feels to be loved by my mama..." Feeling a lump rise up in my throat, I swallowed hard and fought to keep oncoming tears at bay. I despised crying because it made me feel weak and I didn't want to feel that way. I felt that I had to be strong for so many people in my life, especially for Isaiah. He looked up to me and I wouldn't ever let him down no matter what happened in life. Feeling my eyelids start to get heavy, they drooped until they fluttered closed and I fell fast asleep.

I awoke in the morning to the smells of bacon frying, hotcakes cooking on the griddle, and eggs sizzling in the skillet. My stomach started growling instantly. Rolling over on my pillow, I nearly screamed when I saw Isaiah standing by the side of the bed grinning.

"Co! Co!"

Willing my heart to calm its rapidly beating pace, I smiled back at him. "Mornin', Junebug and Merry Christmas!!"

Isaiah reached out to me as if he wanted to give me a hug, so I sat up on the bed and leaned over to wrap him in an embrace. When I let him go, I scooted out of the bed and looked behind me to see if Sister was still asleep. To my surprise, her side of the bed was empty, which was odd seeing that she was no early riser.

"Where's Sister?" I asked Isaiah, who stared back at me blankly with his huge eyes.

Taking his hand in mine, I said, "C'mon, let's go see what we got under tha' Christmas tree!"

When we entered the front room, we found Sister sitting by the wood burning stove smiling and looking radiant as she rubbed her hands over her growing belly. She was still wearing her gown and had rollers in her hair, so I don't suppose she had been up for very long. Big Ma was on the phone wishing someone a Merry Christmas and Uncle Joe was sitting on the couch watching *It's a Wonderful Life.*

"Ahhhh!!! The youngin's are here!" Uncle said excitedly when we neared the Christmas tree which was standing up proudly by the window. We had decorated it with pretty red, green, and gold ornaments and some pine cones that Sister, Isaiah, and I had found outside and painted. We didn't have any lights on the tree or an angel ('cause Uncle Joe said we wasn't gone put no white angel on top of our black folk's tree), but that's okay, because our first Christmas tree was perfect just the way it was.

Underneath the tree were a few presents wrapped in the funny pages from the newspapers Big Ma had Uncle Joe go into town and get every Sunday morning for her to read and our traditional Christmas shoeboxes. Every Christmas Eve each one of us kids would take a shoebox that we got from brand new shoes for the school year and place them out for Santa to come fill up with all types of goodies such as pecans, walnuts, apples, oranges, candy canes, orange slices and gumdrops. Getting my Christmas box filled every year was one of the highlights of the holiday and a family tradition that had been passed down since Big Ma was a little girl.

All of us gathered around the tree and we started unwrapping our gifts. Unbeknownst to anyone except God and Baby Jesus, I was still waiting on my biggest gift to arrive and my head kept turning back towards the front door every few minutes. I felt like I was sitting on pins and needles waiting for my Mama to walk through that door.

"Stripes, chile, what in tha' heavens is ya' lookin' back at the door fo'?" Her eyes were lit up in laughter behind her bifocals. "Ole' Saint Nick done already been here and gone now."

Uncle Joe winked at me, then said, "I bet she's 'spectin' one mo' gift."

Gasping, I sat as still as a fallen log. *Did he know? Had Uncle Joe overheard my prayers? Was my mama somewhere in the house? Was that why Sister had gotten up early and was in such a good mood? Had my dreams of our family being complete finally come true?*

"Hmmm... Is that right, Joe? Is that right?" Big Ma said with a hint of laughter in her tone.

A ball of nervous excitement was making its way around and around inside of my stomach. *Oh, my God, is my mama really here?*

"Yes ma'am, Mama... Thank we outta brang out one mo' gift fa' Missus Cora Leanne?"

My eyes grew wide at his question and I could barely contain my excitement. Nodding my head, I sat up on my knees and looked back and forth between Uncle Joe and Big Ma. "What is it?!" I asked, excitedly. *Please, dear Lord, let it be Mama!*

Uncle Joe left out of the room with a huge smile upon his face. The sound of the clock ticking on the wall just about drove me nuts as I sat on the floor beside Isaiah waiting for the Christmas present I had prayed for to appear before my very eyes. My smile was as wide as the Mississippi River, I was so happy. When I heard Uncle Joe's feet making their way back to the front room, I was shaking with excitement.

"Close ya' eyes, Stripes, and keep 'em closed 'til I say open 'em," Uncle Joe hollered from beyond the front room's entrance. I immediately shut my eyes tightly and waited for what seemed like an eternity for him to enter the room.

Moments later, I felt his presence standing in front of me and I heard him say, "Open 'ya eyes, baby gal."

When I opened my eyes, my heart dropped as did my smile as it slid from my face.

Uncle Joe, who was standing in front of me holding the cutest little yellow Labrador puppy, stopped smiling and confusion danced around in his eyes. The puppy wiggled and squirmed in his large hands before nipping at one of his thumbs. Uncle Joe scratched behind one of his ears, and then cocked an eyebrow as he studied me.

"Um, Stripes, what'sa matta? I thought you'd like ya' gift." Rubbing the puppy's head, he frowned. "I kno' ya' like dogs and all, so I thought I'd get ya' a lil' pup of ya' owns ta' raise."

I didn't want to hurt my uncle's feelings for bringing me home such a thoughtful Christmas gift, but my heart was aching something awful. I couldn't believe that God had forgotten me. He really didn't answer my prayers and bring my mama home. Blinking rapidly, I forced a smile upon my face and took the puppy out of Uncle Joe's hands. It was a cutie pie, but it wasn't my mama and no amount of puppies could take away that pain.

"Thank ya', Uncle Joe... I like him," I replied in the most uplifted voice I could manage.

Uncle Joe beamed down at me and dusted his hands off on his pants legs. "Good, babe. Ya' had meh scared. Thought I'd have ta' take tha' lil' rascal back ta' where I'd got him from."

"What ya' gone name 'em, Stripes?" Sister called out across the room from her spot on the couch where she was now laying down. She had removed her rollers and now her long curls cascaded over the arm of the tattered couch like flowing red lava.

Looking down at the puppy who gazed up at me with pretty blue eyes, I tried to think of a name real quick like. "Hmm... He looks like a Wally."

"Wally?" Sister scoffed. "As in Wally from *Leave it to Beaver*?" She started cracking up and I stuck my tongue out at her.

"I thank Wally fits him jus' fine," Big Ma said taking up for me, but Sister kept right on laughing.

Isaiah scooted over closer to me on the floor and reached out a shaking hand to touch the puppy.

"Doggy... Doggyyyyy!"

"Yup, this is a doggy my smart boy!" I said with a smile before I leaned over and gave him a peck on the cheek. Leave it to my little brother to lift my spirits.

After we ate breakfast, we piled into Uncle Joe's truck and headed to church for the Christmas service. Aunt Trish had phoned earlier and said that she would meet up with us at church because she had gotten held up in Memphis the night before with something unexpected at the last minute.

When we got to church I planned on giving God and Baby Jesus a piece of my mind. Although I was smiling, laughing and talking with my family, I was really hurt that my Mama hadn't showed up on Christmas morning like I had prayed for. Why hadn't God come through for me? Did He really care about me at all? Was He really in the answering prayers business like the fat old preacher in the pulpit claimed?

After we were seated on a pew near the front of the church, I glared up at grown Jesus on the cross hanging over the baptism pool behind the choir stand. I had a bone or two to pick with Him and God for how they broke my heart this morning. Sister caught me staring up at the wall and looked at me strangely. Nudging me, she asked, "You alright, Stripes? Ya's lookin' mighty funny. Why ya' lookin' at Jesus like that? What He done did to you?"

Before I could answer, I noticed that the preacher had stopped talking from behind the pulpit. His eyes grew as round as saucers upon his face and he broke out into a huge grin. Slapping the pulpit, he said, "Well, praise the Lord, praise the Lord! Who do we have here? It's a Christmas miracle!"

Everyone, including me, turned around in our seats to see what he was so happy about. An usher was escorting Aunt Trish down the aisle with someone walking closely behind her. I couldn't see who it was exactly, but whoever it was must be who the preacher was excited to see because he had just seen Aunt Trish last month at Thanksgiving.

When Aunt Trish made it closer to our row, she stepped out of the way and I got a good look at the person who was behind her and recognized them immediately. My breath caught in my throat and time stood still. I couldn't believe my eyes. The good Lord had up and done it. He had brought my mama back home.

Chapter 7

Sister and I both stared wide-eyed with our mouths gaped open at the woman we knew as "Mama" as she sat across from us at the kitchen table. I couldn't believe how much I looked like her. It was as if I was taking a look at an older, slightly darker version of myself in a looking glass. She was so beautiful and her thick hair stopped right above her shoulders as it was cut in a cute bob. We hadn't said much of anything as of yet, since church was packed and there wasn't much room left for talking while the preacher droned on and on during his all too familiar sermon about Baby Jesus' birth. As soon as church services let out, a slew of parishioners flocked at Mama's side hugging her and asking her a million questions, so Big Mama said to let them have their time to talk with Mama and we would catch up with her at home. I didn't think it was fair that so many people were taking up time with her when I was the one who had prayed she would come home. They were being just plain rude.

Aunt Trish, Big Ma, and Uncle Joe sat near to Mama around the table and they all watched her closely as if she was going to disappear at any given moment. It was so quiet in the kitchen that the only sounds going was the ticking of the clock and Isaiah's constant happy humming. I didn't know what to say to Mama. I was happy she was home, but I was scared, too. What if she didn't like me?

The silence was broken when Sister finally spoke up. "So, what the hell brings ya' here?"

"Billie!" Aunt Trish admonished while Big Ma and Uncle Joe scolded, "Sister!"

Sister rolled her eyes and crossed her arms over her large bosom. Narrowing her eyes at Mama, she demanded, "Well?"

Mama smiled faintly, then opened her ruby red lipstick painted mouth to finally address us. "I... I know that my coming back here has taken y'all for some kinda shock." Nervously placing some hair behind her earring-less ear, she looked around the table and continued. "But, I done realized that this is where I need to be. Home."

"Praise tha' good Lord above that He's done brought my gal home!" Big Ma said with a smile as she raised both hands upwards before clasping them together and whispering, "Jesus" several times.

"Glad ta' have ya' back home, big sis," Uncle Joe said with a toothy smile and nod in her direction.

Sister sized up Mama before speaking. "I'm jus' glad that this time 'round ya' ain't brought home nam' other mouth ta' feed like all them other times you jus' showed up and dropped one of ya' kids off on Big Ma like they's hers then up and hit tha' road with whicheva Tom, Jack, or *Billy* you done spread ya' legs wide fo' 'cause they done sold you all types of dreams and soon ta' be un-kept promises."

Uncle Joe sucked in a deep breath and struggled to hide the smile of laughter that was rising upon his face.

"Sister!" I cry in amazement. My ears were ringing from the rapidly beating pace of my heart after hearing the words that had just left my sister's mouth. How could she just up and say those things to our mama, even if they were true? Was she trying to run her back off or something?

"Lord, this child and her mouth..." Aunt Trish said shaking her head in disbelief.

"Sister, I ain't gon' stand fo' no sassin' and direspectin' ya' Mama up in here on the Lord's Holy day!" Big Ma warned eyeing Sister with a stern look. If looks could kill, Sister would have done died twice.

"But, Big Ma..."

Mama raised a hand and we fell silent again. "It's alright, Mama... My child has every right to say what she's done said. She's absolutely right." With tearful eyes, she allowed them to rest upon Sister, me next, then Isaiah before speaking again.

"I know that I haven't done right by y'all, but God be my witness that ends here. I'm home fa' good now so that we can be a family." Her fingers twitched as they lay upon the kitchen table and I couldn't tell if it was from emotion or if she just had some sort of nervous tick.

Mama addressed us, but kept her eyes focused directly on Sister. "I never meant to hurt none of y'all... 'Specially not my babies, but y'all gotta know somethin', I'm sorry, so sorry for how I did y'all. Ya' mama wasn't well... I left y'all here so that y'all could have a good life and I knew that Mama was gone be able to provide that for y'all. It's somethin' that I wasn't gone be able to do back then..."

Swallowing hard, she blinked back a few tears. Inhaling deeply, she smiled and looked at us with hopeful eyes. "I need to ask y'all for forgiveness. Can y'all forgive your mama and let me back in y'all lives?"

My heart swelled with emotion at Mama's request. All I wanted her to do was to come home and God had provided. There was no way in this world or the next that I was going to let her get away from me this time. Before I could open up my mouth to speak, Sister beat me to it.

"Hell naw! Forgive you?!" Sister pushed back from the table in anger as we all looked on in bewilderment. "You expect us to forgive you? After you abandoned us? After you just left ya' damn mommy duties to yo' mama and ran out on us chasing behind some funky men's pee worms?!" Sister's face was flushed in anger and her eyes bore holes into Mama. "I'll never forgive you! Ever! I fuckin' hate yo' triflin' ass more than anyone else in this God forsaken world! Where was you at when I needed you, huh? Where was you at when I lost my first tooth or when my titties started growin' and every night they hurt so bad 'cause they were sore and itchin' and I had no idea what was tha' matter wit' meh? Where was you when my women's flow started comin' on? Huh? Ya' kno' who had to teach me 'bout tha' rag? Ya' mama, that's who!!! Not you. And where was yo' funky ass when lil' boys started sniffin' up behind meh? Huh? Why wasn't you here to teach me 'bout keepin' my legs closed? Huh? I guess you couldn't teach me shit when yo' ass had yo' legs wide open fo' the highest bidder, huh?" Sister looked down and thrust her belly out, then looked back up with tears in her eyes and it scared me because she never cried. Ever. "Why I had ta' learn 'bout this shit tha' hard way?"

"Billie Christina Harris, that is enuff!" Big Ma declared as she rose from her seat, placing her hands firmly before her on the table. Her eyes were full of anger, yet her voice was steady and strong.

"Now, chile, I knows ya' is hurtin', but this here woman is still ya' mammy and you's gone respect her!"

Sister's eyes welled up with more tears and she angrily brushed them away as they fell one by one down the sides of her cheeks. Her button nose was as pink as the inside of a strawberry and she sniffled to rid it of snot. Noticing that she was shaking, I reached out to her and took her by the hand. To my surprise, she didn't snatch it away, but instead closed her fingers around my hand and held on tightly.

"Billie, baby, I am so sorry..." Mama began, choking back tears in her voice. "I knows I should've been here, but..." she trailed off as the floodgates opened and tears dampened her beautiful face.

"Save yo' gaddamn apologies... I don't want'em." Sister pried her hand out of mine and stalked out of the kitchen. I started to go after her, but Big Mama stopped me.

"Let ha' be, Stripes..."

Sitting back down at the table, I looked over at my mama. She looked as if her heart had been torn right out of her chest and trampled on. Picking up a snot rag, she started wiping her face before blowing her nose into it. My heart ached terribly for her, but surprisingly it hurt for Sister even more. I had never seen my big sister cry like that before in all of my eleven years on this earth. Big Ma had been right that time, Sister was hurting because of Mama and that was probably the main reason she acted out as she did.

Isaiah had stopped his humming and was observing everyone with watchful eyes. I was surprised that he hadn't burst out crying at our sister's rant but was also thankful because that showed he was growing up.

"Cora... Do you forgive your mama?" Mama asked in a small voice which made a lump form in my throat.

I paused for a minute to ponder her question and to separate my feelings from Sister's. Sister was right, Mama hadn't been there for none of those things, just like she hadn't been there to keep me from being picked on at school or to love on me and tell me that everything was going to be okay when I got called ugly names. She hadn't been there to take care of Isaiah and help him learn how to talk. That responsibility was left to fall solely upon me. On the other hand, here sat the mother I had been dreaming of for years, ever since I could remember. God and Baby Jesus Himself had answered my many prayers and delivered her to me in the flesh. I knew that despite of what my older sister was feeling, I had to forgive our mama because it was the right thing to do. It's what Jesus would have done, anyways.

Nodding my head, I looked back at this older reflection of myself and wondered if we would ever truly have one of those mother daughter relationships like I saw on TV or like the one Teresa had with Missus Carol Ann Taylor. Mama, scooted her chair back from underneath the table, stood and walked over to me.

"Give your mama a hug, sweet girl."

Standing from my seat, I did as I was told. Mama opened her arms wide and I leaned into her.

Wrapping her arms around me, she enveloped me in the sweetest hug I have ever experienced. I rested my cheek on her small bosom and inhaled her sweet fragrance. She smelled like honeysuckles and buttercups. *Is this a dream? No, it feels too real... Way too real.* Closing my eyes, I willed myself to keep this memory close to my heart. I never wanted to forget this moment for as long as I lived. I had finally received all that I had ever dreamed of and all was well... For now.

*

Days have passed by at a swift pace since Mama has been back home. She's walked with me and Isaiah to school every day and has been standing outside waiting on us when the bell sounds at dismissal. I finally feel like how the other kids my age must feel when their parents pick them up. I finally feel as if I have a complete family except for the fact that my daddy's dead. Life seems to be picking up in every way, shape and form. It's a new year, I'm a year older, my mama has come home, Isaiah's talking more and more each day, Sister's belly is getting rounder and I even felt her baby kicking, and Zannie Mae's aunt has been letting her stay the night over the weekends while she works. Life couldn't possibly get any better!

Sister still wasn't on good terms with Mama and had barely said two words to her or acknowledged her presence in the home. It really hurt my feelings to see how angry Sister was at our mama and that she just couldn't seem to shake the past. One night as we sat up in bed shooting the breeze, I expressed to her how I felt about the matter.

"Sister, why you jus' can't up and forgive Mama? She's home now and she's tryin' really hard to be here for us."

Sister groaned, then exhaled in irritation. "Look, I'm not fallin' fo' her lil' show she's puttin' on... You don't kno' that woman. She gone leave agin'. Mark my words."

Fear thumped in my chest. God wouldn't be so cruel as to take my mama away from me again after I had prayed so hard for her to come back home. I couldn't see living my life without her, especially now that she's become a part of my everyday routine over the past three weeks. I've had such a good time talking with her and laughing with her while we've gotten to know each other. And Isaiah... Isaiah latched onto her really quick like a newborn babe to its mama's teet. The look of adoration in his eyes when he looks at the woman who has those exact same huge mocha eyes as his melts my heart. I know he can't say it yet, but I know he loves her... Just like I do.

"Naw, she ain't, Sister... You got it all wrong." I took some strands of my hair and twirled it around my finger before letting it go. My curls bounced back and hit me in the face. "Mama said she's truly sorry and that she's not gonna go anywhere this time. She promised."

Sister guffawed at my expense and I didn't take to kindly to that. "You have gots to be kiddin' meh." Eyebrows raised in disbelief, her blue eyes bore into mine. "That woman is nothin' but a lyin', conniving, slutty lil' skank and I can't believe that you're fallin' for whateva dreams she's tryna sell you!"

She placed her hands firmly on my shoulders, but I shrugged them off and glared at her. *How dare she talk about our Mama in this way?!* Mama may have done some wrong things in the past, but she was truly trying to make up for what she did and correct her wrongs. I couldn't believe that Sister was trying to judge her when she had her own indiscretions to worry with.

"Mama ain't lying to me." Folding my arms over my flat chest, I narrowed my eyes at my sister. "She loves us, Sister... Just talk wit' her and you will see that."

Sister tousled her hair gently, then ran a hand through it. Rolling her eyes, she shook her head. "Babe, you have a lot ta' learn 'bout life, a lot. I can't stand tha' way you's always lookin' fa' tha' bright side in folks. Even those snotty nosed brats at yo' school who picks on ya' fa' being two races. If they was ta' come up ta' ya' tomorrow and say 'let's be friends' you would forgive them and carry on wit' them as if they ain't never said a harmful word ta' ya' in tha' past. I don't kno' who ya' picked that mess up from. Maybe ya' git' it from daddy's side of tha' family..."

Frowning, I cocked my head to the side and looked at her funny. *Daddy's side of the family?* Clearly, I ain't hear her right. She must've made a mistake in saying that and ain't know it.

"What ya' mean by daddy's side of tha' family?" I eyed her curiously to see her reaction. "We ain't got tha' same daddy..."

Sister's eyes widen at my statement, and then her face fell. Looking upwards she took a deep breath before bringing her head down to look at me again. "Look, I ain't supposed ta' be tha' one ta' tells ya' this, but ya' daddy ain't die in no damn tractor accident in the next county. That was some bullshit ass lie that Big Mama told ya' 'cause she hate our daddy, Billy Baxter."

Pursing her lips, Sister rubbed her hands over her belly and for a slight moment my attention span was thrown off track because I wondered what she was carrying inside of her. *Is it a boy? A girl? Will they look just like her or that God awful Johnny Ray?* Heavens forbid that baby come out looking like that peckerwood. When my mind drew back to our conversation, sweat began forming on my brow and I suddenly started feeling ill.

"Big Ma hates our daddy 'cause he knocked up Mama when she was just 15 years old and he was already 25. She says that he was way too old ta' have been messin' 'round wit' Mama like tha' way that he was and then got her in tha' family way wit' meh... So, when Mama came back 'round here pregnant wit' you and dropped me off on Big Ma for the third time, she said that she would rather tell ya' that our daddy was dead than fa' ya' ta' grow up knowin' how corrupted of a man he is. I don't blame Big Ma fa' that 'cause Billy Baxter ain't shit and he knows it. He gots white kids that he doesn't even take care of either. He lives in a trailer down on Cherry St. right next ta' tha' cemetery and every time he sees meh, he acts as if I'm invisible when he knows that I look exactly like him... Red hair, blue eyes and all. Even got his freckles..."

My world was reeling. My palms started to itch and become sweaty and my breathing was labored. *My daddy isn't dead?* He was alive and well and was still one of those deadbeats who ain't want nothing to do with me?

"So... My daddy ain't dead? And we got tha' same daddy who don't want us?" I asked as small bursts of bright lights darted in front of my eyes making it hard to see Sister fully. She was busy chipping away some old nail polish from a fingernail and wasn't paying me any mind.

"Yeah... I heard he don't like our kind either... He supposedly hates Negroes, so I don't even kno' how him and Mama even hooked up not once, but twice to make us."

My heart was thumping madly in my ears at this point and my head was starting to pound. I didn't know what was going on with me and why finding out that my daddy wasn't dead was bothering me so. I guess it's because I hated being lied to. I started hyperventilating and that sure enough caught Sister's attention. Her head shot up quick like a rocket and she leaned forward and grabbed me in her arms before I fell backwards off the bed and onto the hard linoleum floor. "Big Maaaaaaa!!!!" was all I remember hearing her holler as my eyelids fluttered closed and everything went dark.

*

"She's going to be alright now," I heard a strange male's voice sound muffled in my ears. My body felt extremely weak and my head was pounding harder than when Uncle Joe nails thick plastic up to the windows in the winter time to keep the cold air from seeping into the house. I don't know why he even bothers doing that because somehow the cold air still manages to get inside.

"Thank you, Dr. Jones," a voice that sounded like Mama's replied. "We was real scared for my lil' girl for a while."

"Yeah, it was touch and go fa' a min'. Glad her fever's breaking," Big Ma said gratefully.

I struggled to open my eyes so that I could look around the room, but they were as heavy as the tin buckets full of cow's milk that I helped Big Ma tote to the house during the spring and summers when she lets me help her milk her lone cow Bessie. *Why can't I open my eyes? What's wrong with me? And why is*

Dr. Jones here? I hated that man. He gave me the heebie jeebies... *Did he touch me?* I hated frogs and I didn't want his frog hands touching me.

"Just remember to keep her hydrated and cool. Give her this medicine about every four hours or so until she starts feeling better." Dr. Jones cleared his throat, then continued, "About five other children from her school are out sick with this Scarlet fever..." In a lower voice, he said, "And two children in the next county over recently died from it, so you all did the right thing by calling me or this could've been worse than what it is."

"Oh, no... I couldn't take it if something had of happened to my baby... God knows I just came back into her life," Mama choked out, her voice full of emotion.

"She should be alright now, ma'am," Dr. Jones said. "I'll take my leave now."

After hearing the doctor's heavy feet retreat out of the room with what sounded like Big Ma's shuffling, I tried to moan to get my mama's or whomever was left in the room attention, but no sound came out. My throat was awfully sore and felt as if it was closed up. *What did the doctor say I have? Scarlett fever? What is that? Do I look red or somethin' right now?*

I tried shifting my body on the bed, but I felt extremely weak and drowsy. I felt someone's presence near the bed and then a cool hand touched my forehead.

"Be still, Cora," Mama said in a quiet voice. "Your body may feel a lil' weak right now, but you'll feel better in the mornin'. Don't fight that sleep that's tryna come over you right now. It's the medicine that Dr. Jones gave you just doin' it's job. Rest up, baby. Mama's right here. I'm not going nowhere."

Mama began to sing softly and I couldn't help but to succumb to the medicine induced sleep and slip away into dreamland. This is what I had wanted all of my life... Mama right by my side when I needed her most. When I awoke the next day my body felt achy, but signs of the fever were gone. I looked around my room and saw that I was alone. Sunlight streamed through the dingy glass of the window and landed on everything in sight, illuminating the room with a warm glow. Pushing myself up on the bed, I scooted back against the headboard and pulled up the quilt that Big Ma had made for me and Sister around my shoulders and tucked it underneath my chin. The house seemed oddly quiet and I tried to remember what day it was. *Ahhh, it's Tuesday, that's right.* Sister and Isaiah are no doubt at school and Uncle Joe done probably already left for work, but where are Mama and Big Ma?

As if she could read my thoughts, Big Ma came shuffling into the room carrying an old wooden serving tray she had gotten from the old white lady she used to work for way back when she was younger.

On the tray held a glass of orange juice and a bowl of homemade chicken noodle soup. When she saw me sitting up, she flashed a loving smile my way.

"'Bout time my precious Stripes wakes up. Thought ya' was gone sleep halfway 'til suppertime, I did." Big Ma pulled out the chair that set next to my bed, sat down, and then set the serving tray down on the lap of her duster. Picking a spoon up off of the tray, she stirred the soup which had steam rising up from the bowl into the air. Dipping the spoon deep down into the bowl, she scooped up some soup, took it out and blew lightly upon it to cool it. Holding out the spoon with her other hand underneath it to catch any spills, she said, "Open up, youngin'."

I quietly obliged. Big Ma loved to baby us for some reason when we are sick. I don't ask any questions or fight it anymore since the last time I asked her why she does it and she simply stated, "Y'all's my babies, that's why. If ya's sick, I's gotta be tha' one ta' make ya' all betta. Ya' sick, ya' gotta save ya' strength."

I swallowed the soup and winced. My throat was still a little tender. Big Ma noticed and reached down into her duster pocket and pulled out a bottle of medicine and a throat lozenge. Shaking the bottle's contents, she twisted off the cap and poured a little in another spoon she had laying on the tray. "Here gal, take this. I knows ya' throat still likely on fire."

I took the awful medicine and swallowed it with a frown. I had to shut my eyes at the pure taste of the nasty stuff. Big Ma continued to feed me until I had eaten my fill of the soup and she let me rest. Sucking on the cherry throat lozenge, I mulled over my current life and wondered what Teresa and Zannie Mae were doing today at school. I wished that I was there because today was story day and Mrs. Porter told some amazing stories and today we were going to hear one about slaves who made it to freedom. Big Ma's mama had been born a slave but was set free when she was just two years old. It's amazing to think about stuff like that. Sister said if we would've been born back then we would've been called "House Niggas" all on a count of our "High Yella" skin complexion. Teresa told me that her teacher, Mrs. Gray, doesn't tell good stories and most of the kids just end up falling asleep when she starts talking about the past, but not Mrs. Porter... She tells stories with such enthusiasm and in different voices it makes you feel like you was there.

There's something that's been bugging me really badly lately. You see, Teresa and Zannie Mae don't like each other much. They don't get along at all. Teresa doesn't like her because she feels that Zannie Mae is taking her place as my best friend and Zannie Mae doesn't like Teresa because she feels that she's stuck up and acts all prissy. It has me feeling kinda strange because I don't know who to spend my time with in the school yard when we have free time during the day. See, Teresa gets all in a huff and has her panties in a wad because I want to play with Zannie Mae during free time and complains because me and Zannie Mae gets to spend time together during class since we got the same teacher. Zannie Mae on the other hand complains about Teresa hanging out with us and playing because she says Teresa doesn't like her since I like her so much. It's really starting to get on my nerves. I don't like either girl over the other, but they sure enough act like I do. I treat them both the same, but one or both of them always got their lips poked out at me like I'm doing them wrong or something. I just hope and pray that they start getting along so we can all be friends because I need them both and don't wanna lose either of their friendship.

Eventually I dozed off to sleep since the medicine makes you extra drowsy and woke up to Wally licking on my face. Giggling, I sat up in the bed and grabbed him, giving him a big squeeze. He's gotten bigger in the past month and I know that after a while I won't even be able to pick him up at all.

"Heyyyy, mah big boy," I say smothering him in tiny kisses. "Who's mah big boy? Who's mah big boy?"

Wally starts barking his cute little bark that he has, then licks my face which tickles something awful. I start having a fit of giggles when Big Ma comes into the room and swoops Wally up out of my lap.

"That's enuff you lil' rascal," she says fondly to the puppy. Placing him gently down on the floor she watches as he cocks his head to the side and peers up at her with his big brown eyes as if he's trying to figure her out. "Off ya' go!" Big Ma waves her hands at him in a shooing motion and Wally takes off out of the room in a flash.

"Aw, why'd ya' go and do that, Big Ma? We was just playin'."

Big Ma turns to face me with a smile. Reaching behind me, she fluffs my pillow and kisses me gently on the cheek. "'Cause ya' still needs ya' rest lil' gal and ya' don't need ta' be up in here gigglin' and loosin' ya' breath and thangs. Ya' voicebox needs ta' rest so it stops being all tender. Understand?"

My throat was actually feeling a little better, but I knew better than to try and argue with her, so I just nodded. Big Ma checked my temperature, then gave me another throat lozenge. She clucked her tongue which made me think that something was wrong. I didn't feel hot anymore, so had my fever come back and I didn't even know it?

"What's wrong, Big Ma?"

Big Ma didn't readily respond. She had a far way look in her eyes as if she was no longer there in the room with me. The ends of her short, plaited salt and pepper colored hair were peeking out from underneath her yellow kerchief and a lone tear began making its way down her face from her left eye. I had never seen Big Ma cry outside of catching the Holy Ghost at church, so to see any tears at all was unusual coming from her. Big Ma stood frozen in place without uttering a word and it was beginning to unnerve me.

Reaching out a hand, I gently took one of hers in mine and softly rubbed the back of it with my thumb. "Big Ma... You alright?"

"Bertha..."

The mention of my deceased Aunt's name, one I had never had the pleasure of meeting since she died as a child, caused my eyebrows to shoot up on my forehead. Why was Big Ma calling out Aunt Bertha's name?

Big Ma continued to stand in a daze, eyes locked straight ahead staring at nothingness. For a while the only sounds audible in the room was our breathing, then she spoke again. "No, Bertha, baby... Gone and sat down. Sat down right 'chere under that there Walnut tree. Mama got it. No, baby, I said, Mama got it. Go on and sat down there and mind ya' brother fa' meh..."

Frowning, I looked up at Big Ma in confusion. *What's happening here? Is Big Ma reliving a scene from the past?*

"Don't sass meh, Bertha... I want ya' ta' mind Joe for meh while ya' daddy and I work these fields..."

Big Ma's hands began to tremble and I held on tightly to the one that I was holding. "Willie B., have ya' seen Bertha? I's been lookin' fa' that gal some of everywhere... She was 'pose ta' be mindin' Joe fa' meh while we was off in tha' fields, but when I went back ta' tha Walnut tree round the bend alls I found was Joe laid out on his blanket fast asleep." Big Ma's voice suddenly got louder. "Y'all, has anyone of y'all seen Bertha?"

Big Ma's voice shook in fear and her eyes darted back and forth. "My Lord, where's that chile of mine done run off to? She knows betta than ta' run off and leave her brother behind like that... Willie B., here, take a hold of Joe's hand while I goes off through the woods ta' look fa' her. No, I'm just goin' right beyond the brush, no further. She can't be done slipped off that far nowhere... I promise I'll be right back."

Big Ma's hands clenched at her sides and the one I was holding squeezed mine so tightly I thought it may break, but I didn't say a peep. I had never seen Big Ma like this before and it scared me. *Is Big Ma gonna be okay?*

"Where's that chile at?" Big Ma started breathing heavy as if she was running. "Bertha?! Berthaaaa!!!"

Big Ma's voice got softer then as if she stumbled upon something she ain't want to see. "Bert..." The dam broke then and tears rushed Big Ma's face. "Oh, my Lord... Bertha! BERTHA!" Big Ma's entire body started trembling and I feared she would fall. Slipping out of bed, I still held her hand as

I wrapped my other arm around her waist to steady her. In her memory she must've come across Aunt Bertha dead, but I thought she had been found in the field passed out from working in the sun, not in the woods.

"Dear, Lord, not mah baby. Not mah precious lil' gal." Big Ma sniffled and choked back more tears as her eyes remained focused in the past. "Who done did this ta' mah lil' gal?"

Scrunching up my face, I cocked my head to the side just how Wally did not too long ago and I looked up at my grandma curiously. *What is she talking about?* For all my life I was told that Aunt Bertha had died in the fields from a heat stroke, not that somebody did something to her. *What does all of this mean?*

"Dear, God, my God! Look at mah baby gal... Oh, no suh, no suh, dear Lord, how could ya' jus' let somebody come and do this here evil deed ta' mah flush and blood?" Big Ma's body shook in apparent sadness and anger. "Who done raped and kilt mah baby? Who done did this?!"

My eyes grew wide at the words coming out of my grandma's mouth. *Aunt Bertha was raped and killed? By who? Why?*

While I was busy contemplating this heavy piece of information I'd just learned, Big Ma stumbled and fell back against me causing us both to come crashing down on the hard, dusty floor. It took me all but a second to scramble up to my knees to check on her.

"Big Ma!" I cried, shaking her shoulders. Big Ma lay on the floor, unmoving, her eyes were shut tightly and I couldn't tell if she was breathing or not.

Frantically I sprung to my feet and ran through the house calling for Mama, Uncle Joe, Sister, or anybody who could help me. No one was there. I was all alone in the house to tend to Big Ma, except for Wally who ran underneath my feet nipping at my ankles as I ran through the house because he thought we were playing a game.

"Not now, Wally!" I hollered at him which made him yelp and run and hide underneath one of the old couches. He peered out at me from behind one of the wooden claw feet of the couch with his huge eyes and it pricked my heart with a twinge of sadness. I hated to holler at him and hurt his feelings, but right now wasn't a time to play any games. I needed to get Big Ma some help and fast. Running into the front room, I stopped in front of the end table that held the rotary phone. Picking up the receiver I tried with all of my might to remember Dr. Jones' number but couldn't. Placing the receiver up to my ear, I started to dial Ms. Pinky, but there wasn't a dial tone. Dropping the receiver in frustration, I ran back to my room and slipped on some tennis shoes without any socks and grabbed my coat and scarf and threw them on. Big Ma was still lying on the floor, not moving and I prayed she wasn't dead. I don't think I could live my life without her. Running back over to where she lay, I bent down and kissed her softly on the forehead. "Be right back, Big Ma. Hold tight, please, just hold tight fa' meh." Coughing, I flipped the collar up on my coat and left the room.

Flying out of the house, down the porch steps and across the yard, I headed for Mr. Leroy and Miss Bessie Mae's house. The cold wind nipped at my cheeks like ice picks and my chest started to hurt from inhaling it. My throat ached and felt as if it were about to close up on me and my skin felt warm. Combing my way through dead leaves, fallen limbs, and leafless bushes, I tumbled into their yard. Mr. Leroy's sleek black 1959 *Chevy* four door car that he was sure enough proud of was sitting clean as a whistle in their driveway. I said a silent "thank you" to God that he was home which more than likely meant Miss Bessie Mae was there, too.

I stomped up the porched steps in record time and banged on the front door. I heard some movement within the house and moments later a hand pushed back the window curtain and Miss Bessie Mae's light brown face appeared. She unlocked the door and opened it.

"Stripes! My Lord, girl, what are you doin' over here in this cold weather?" she asked with concern. Her pretty face was twisted in worry and her eyes focused in on me with seriousness. "Your grandmama told me you fell down ill last yesterday some time, so why are you out here? You gonna get that walking pneumonia if you keep this up!"

I didn't have time to explain about my sickness or catching another illness. All of that was irrelevant at this point. "Big Ma..." I replied, panting. My chest ached something awful and my throat felt as if it were getting even tighter. Leaning up against the doorframe, a cold sweat dampened my face. "Big Ma... Somethin' bad done happened ta' mah Big Ma!"

Miss Bessie Mae's hand flew up to her chest and she pulled me inside the house. The warmth of the heat felt so good to my nearly chilled limbs. "Leroy! Leroy, come quick! Somethin' done happened to Missus Virginia!"

I flopped down on their sofa without asking first like I normally would. I was feeling sick from the mixture of adrenaline, cold weather, Scarlett Fever and Big Ma's current condition. I felt like I was sitting on the spin cycle of Big Ma's washing machine, I was so dizzy with fever. Mr. Leroy came running into the front room from their back bedroom. His eyes darted back and forth between me and Miss Bessie Mae. "What happened?" Rushing over to my side, he took a handkerchief out of his back pocket and gently wiped the sweat from my face. I knew right then and there I would forever remember his gentle, caring touch and hoped that I would be as lucky as Miss Bessie Mae is to find a good man like him when I'm older.

"Bessie Mae, this child is drenched in sweat! What happened? Did I hear ya' say sumin' 'bout Missus Virginia?"

Miss Bessie Mae nodded eyes full of fear. "Let me get our coats. Take us over to their house right away."

Since I was too weak to move on my own now after exhausting the slight energy I had running over to their house, Mr. Leroy scooped me up in his huge, strong arms and carried me out to his car. Miss Bessie Mae opened the back door and Mr. Leroy sat me down easy on the backseat. His car smelled sweet and smoky like the huge cigars he smokes. Miss Bessie Mae felt my forehead and clucked her tongue.

"That child's burning up, Leroy. That ain't good. Have mercy. C'mon, we gotta get to their house to check on Missus Virginia and get this baby some medicine. She ain't lookin' too good."

Mr. Leroy turned around in his seat and looked back at me and nodded in agreement. Cranking the car, we peeled out of the driveway and headed down the road to Big Ma's house. Uncle Joe still wasn't home from work and I couldn't tell if anyone else had made it in, yet. Mr. Leroy picked me up and carried me up the stairs while Miss Bessie Mae knocked on the door before pushing it all the way open.

"Missus Virginia?" she called out into the empty house, but the only reply she received was a whimper from Wally who was still camped out underneath the couch.

"Where is she at, Stripes?" Mr. Leroy asked me, still cradling me like a baby.

My throat felt as if I had swallowed a million hot chili peppers and I strained to speak. "In... there..." I said weakly, pointing to my bedroom in the back of the house.

Miss Bessie Mae rushed to the back while Mr. Leroy took his time carrying me to my room. The world around me was starting to spin viciously. When we entered the bedroom, Miss Bessie Mae was cradling Big Ma's upper body in her arms.

"She's still alive... She's breathing, but its real shallow-like. We need to get her to the Negro hospital."

Mr. Leroy laid me down on my bed and went over to Miss Bessie Mae's side. "What are we gonna do 'bout Stripes? We jus' can't leave this sick child here by herself, we gotta..." Before he could finish his sentence, Sister came rushing into the room with Uncle Joe and Isaiah on her trail.

Sister's eyes grew wide in fear. "Big Ma!!! Oh, God, what done happened ta' mah grandmama?!!!!!" She ran over to Big Ma and Miss Bessie Mae, blue eyes glistening in unshed tears. "Is she gonna be okay?" She looked up at Miss Bessie Mae with fear washing away the beauty of her face.

"I don't know, Sister. Get back some so Leroy and Joe can help me get her to the car."

Uncle Joe looked as if he had just saw a ghost. "What happened to mah mama, 'Roy? What happened?"

Mr. Leroy filled in Uncle Joe on the tidbit of information I had provided them at their house, then Uncle Joe lifted his mama up off of the floor. Miss Bessie Mae and Mr. Leroy tried to help, but he pushed them away. "Naw, she's mah mama. Imma carry mah mama out ta' tha' car. Let's go." Looking back over his shoulder at Sister, he said, "Sister, watch afta Junebug and make sure Stripes gets some medicine in her. She ain't lookin' too hot. Have ya' mama call tha' hospital as soon as Miss Rochelle Green drops her back off at home. She went down ta' tha' beauty shop today in search fa' work and seein' that she ain't here, Miss Rochelle must've done hired her."

Sister swallowed hard and nodded. "What's gone happen ta' Big Ma?" she asked in a small almost child-like voice.

Uncle Joe didn't say a word, but left out of the room carrying our grandma with Miss Bessie Mae and Mr. Leroy closely behind him. When I heard the front door shut and the screen door slam shut behind it seconds later, I tried my hardest to sit up in the bed, but couldn't. My entire body ached and I was sore from head to toe.

"Sister..." I croaked out.

Sister rushed over to my side and felt my forehead with the back of her hand. "My Lord, Stripes, ya's burnin' up jus' as bad as last night!" She ran out of the room and returned moments later with a wash pan full of water and a wash rag.

Isaiah took a step closer to the bed from the other side of the room where he had been standing watching me wide eyed. "Co sick... Co sick... Bad."

Sister turned and looked at him and replied softly, "Yes, baby boy. Cora is sick and don't feel good." Pointing to an empty chair near the dresser, she said, "Can you do Sister a favor and sat down in that chair ova' there?"

Isaiah nodded and limped over to the chair slowly, then sat down to watch us some more. I hated that he still had to drag one foot when he walked and I hoped that one day he would be able to walk normally without any problems. I remember Big Ma saying that when she got enough money saved up we was gonna take him up to Nashville to see a specialist of some sorts that deal with walking and feet problems.

"That's a good big boy," Sister said to him with a tenderness in her voice that I had never heard from her towards him before. I didn't know whether it was Big Ma falling ill or my being sick or her being pregnant which was making her be extra nice tonight, but whatever it was felt good. I wished she paid more attention to our little brother like this all the time.

Sister swished the washrag around in the pan, then removed it and squeezed the water out. Removing my winter hat, she began dabbing my forehead with the cool rag. Looking at me with love in her eyes, she said, "Everythang's gonna be alright, Stripes... You gon' git' betta and so is Big Ma." She dipped the washrag back into the pan again and brought it back out. Squeezing it, she folded in into a rectangular shape and laid it across my forehead. Then she began removing the coat, I was still wearing and my shoes.

"Lil' gal, no you didn't leave out this damn house wit'out no socks on in the dead of winter while you're sick..." Shaking her head, she sat down on the edge of the bed and placed my feet upon her lap. Rubbing my feet softly, she warmed them up for me. After a few minutes she placed my legs on the bed behind her, then rose from her seat and crossed the room. Stopping at the dresser, she opened a drawer and pulled out some socks. Coming back towards me, she placed the socks on my feet. Picking up the medicine bottle Big Ma had laid on the seat earlier, she shook it up and poured a generous amount in a spoon.

"Here, Stripes, take this so you can get that fever of yours ta' break agin'. We can't afford ta' have both you and Big Ma off in the hospital."

I weakly parted my lips and Sister placed the spoonful of medicine up to them and tilted the spoon. I didn't even wince this time in disgust when I felt the medicine travelling down my throat. I was just too weak. Sister picked up a blanket that was neatly folded on the end of the bed, unfolded it and covered me with it.

Gently brushing my damp hair back with her hand, she leaned over and kissed me on the cheek. "I'm 'bout ta' take Junebug into the kitchen and warm him up some supper real quick. I'll be back ta' check on ya' soon. Get some rest, Stripes."

My eyelids fluttered closed and I heard Sister call out to Isaiah to follow her. It sounded like he said, "Co... feel betta," before they left the room but I couldn't tell if that was real or if I was imagining things since the world around me was still spinning, although now at a slower pace than it had been earlier.

When I woke up the room was pitch black except for a soft glow streaming into it from the front room down the hall. I could hear whispered voices carrying on and I wondered what they were talking about and what was going on. Sitting up slowly on the bed the events from earlier on during the day came flooding back to me all at once.

"Big Ma!" I choked out in a hushed whisper. I reached an arm over to Sister's side of the bed and patted gently only to discover she wasn't there. *Where is she?* Weakly, I forced my aching limbs to move and I slipped quietly out of bed. Easing my way down the hall, the whispered voices began to get louder. I carefully watched my step so that I didn't step on any of the weakened floor boards in the floor that tended to groan underneath my feet from the weight of my body when I walked. Pausing just right outside of the front room, I peeked inside, but kept my face hidden from view. Sitting up solemnly in the room with saddened faces were Mama, Uncle Joe and Sister. My heartrate quicken and my mouth went dry. Fearing the worst, I tried to push the thought that immediately flooded my mind away... *Is Big Ma dead?* No, she couldn't be dead. I wasn't ready. I was her little baby, she even told me I was. I'm only eleven years old. *What am I gonna do without her?*

Uncle Joe opened his mouth to speak and I strained to hear him. "They's sayin' it ain't lookin' too good, Glory Jean... I's... I's don't kno' what we gone do if Mama leaves us."

Mama, pain stricken in the face, nodded and gave Sister's hand a squeeze which I was surprised to see her holding. I learned that night that tragedy had a funny way of bringing people closer together. "She gone be alright, Joe. That's our Mama. She's strong and she's gonna pull through. I jus' came back home, so I kno' God gone give me the chance I need to make things up to my mama. Don't fret. Mama gone make it."

Sister looked up at Mama and swallowed hard. Her eyes were red rimmed as if she had been crying all night long. "I've been so mean ta' her... God knows I have... What if my Big Ma don't make it? I ain't git tha' chance ta' say ta' her that I'm sorry. I ain't git tha' chance ta' tell her that I love her and I ain't really mean ta' be so disobedient." Sister pulled her hand out of Mama's and covered her face as she cried. Her shoulders heaved up and down with each sob and Mama leaned over and pulled her into her arms to console her.

"Billie... You'll get to tell her all of those things. I promise you will. Your Big Ma ain't going anywhere anytime soon. God's not ready for her just yet."

"Can I go see 'bout her on tomorrow?" Sister asked as she dabbed at her tears with a snot rag Uncle Joe had given her out of his shirt breast pocket.

"Not just yet... Uncle Joe is gone go back down there to the hospital first thang in the mornin' to see 'bout her while I go to work at my new job. I just started, so I can't afford to take off. I gotta come up wit' some money to take care of y'all and things around the house." Mama lifted Sister's chin and looked lovingly in her eyes. "We need you to stay here to tend after Cora and Isaiah. Since Cora is sick and there's no one else to take Isaiah to school, he will have to stay home with y'all until Cora feeling better. Okay?"

Sister sniffled and nodded in response. For the first time ever, she appeared to be nothing more than a mere little girl in my eyes as she sat next to our mama. Big Ma falling ill had definitely taken its toll on her. She didn't look like the strong-willed teenager that I knew her to be nor did she look like a soon to be mama herself. No, she looked like the lost little girl who had been needing and waiting for her mama to show up and find her. She looked just like me.

I turned away from the front room and tiptoed slowly back down the hall. For the first time in my short life I thanked God that Isaiah didn't really know what was going on. I knew that he really couldn't comprehend why Big Ma wasn't at home and I hoped that she would be back home soon and feeling like her old self before he started to miss her being here.

Chapter 8

Big Ma stayed in the hospital for a whole two weeks. The doctors said she had suffered a stroke and would have to start taking things a little bit more slowly at home. When she finally was released from the hospital I noticed a change in her immediately. She had always been a fairly small framed woman, but she now appeared ghastly thin and it saddened me. Big Ma was the rock of our family and without her strength I didn't know how we were going to make it. I was glad that God had sent Mama home because she had now stepped into her mother's shoes, with the help of Sister, and was cooking our breakfast and supper daily. Sister helped out more around the house by doing the laundry and tending to Big Ma's cow, the handful of chickens we had, the rooster and our two pigs in the slop house out back. I did my part by minding Isaiah, making sure he was washed up, dressed, and ate all of his food. I walked him to and from school each day while Mama was at work and while Sister did some afterschool work at the corner bakery cleaning up in the kitchen to earn some money for her baby that would be due around April. I was secretly hoping that the baby would be born on April 16th which was also Sister's birthday.

Our winter went by fairly quickly with all of the recent changes we had at home adjusting to our new lives where Big Ma wasn't no longer the main person in charge over everything we said or did. We, as a family, focused more on making her as comfortable as we could so that she could heal and recuperate from her stroke. I really missed having special times to just sit down and talk with Big Ma like I used to when she was well. We used to sit and talk just about anything and now all she wanted to do was lay in bed and sleep. She had nightmares often now and in the dead of night she would sometimes wake up screaming and moaning about Aunt Bertha. I still hadn't told anyone about what I heard her say when she had the stroke that day because I was really scared to repeat it. *Who had raped and killed Aunt Bertha and why hadn't Big Ma ever told any of us about it?* It made me wonder how many other secrets my grandma was holding down deeply inside of her that haunted her day and night. I also couldn't wait until she got better so I could ask her why she lied to me all these years about my daddy being dead when he clearly wasn't.

On this seasonably warm Mid-March afternoon, Sister decided to pick Isaiah and me up from school and walk us home since she didn't have to work today. I was extremely happy to see her because on most nights I didn't get to see her until it was really late and after supper since she would be working long hours to save up money. I had noticed over the last few weeks that she had been peculiarly quiet about Johnny Ray and I was happy about it. I couldn't stand the ground that cracker walked on. Something was really evil about the boy and I couldn't lay a finger on it. Every time I saw him I got the heebie jeebies.

Birds sang merrily in the treetops above our heads, no doubt excited that spring had finally arrived. Sister pulled her jacket off as we walked down the dirt road that led us home and draped it across her arm. Her belly was bulging underneath her flowery printed mauve colored dress and she looked like she would be due any day now. Droplets of sweat decorated her forehead and she brushed them away with the back of her hand as she let out a "whew". I couldn't imagine how hard it must feel to be pregnant and I didn't think that I ever wanted to have a baby after watching how Sister struggled with her weight and getting around, not to mention how sick and moody she had gotten early on in the pregnancy.

"Y'all hold up for a min'," Sister said struggling to catch her breath. She looked completely worn out and we hadn't even walked a full half a mile yet.

I stopped abruptly and pulled on Isaiah's hand to get his attention because he was still marching on ahead. He turned around and looked at us blankly, no doubt wondering why we were stopping so suddenly.

"You alright, Sister?" I asked, swatting away a few gnats that decided to have a dance off in front of my face. One thing I despised about the weather getting warmer was the presence of bugs. I hated bugs... All of them except butterflies. Butterflies were God's special gift to world with their carefree flittering and fascinating patterns and colors. They reminded me oddly enough of my mama, who was as mysterious and beautiful as they were.

"Uh huh. Just needed ta' catch my breath fa' a spell. This baby is kickin' mah ass. I can't wait 'til they git' here." She fanned her face and blew out some air. When she had collected herself, she looked at us and said, "Alright, lets git' goin'."

As we headed down the road, we came upon a clearing off to the side and heard music playing and loud voices trying to out talk the radio along with the sounds of laughter. I nervously looked over at Sister to see if she could possibly know what was going on and I was thankful that she was here with us because I would be scared to death to have to walk past a field full of people on the way home, especially if it was some rowdy white teenage boys up to no good. As we got closer to the clearing, Sister's eyes began to narrow and her face became redder when we saw who was in it.

Leaning up against his 1959 cobalt blue *Ford* car with a lit cigarette held tightly in between the fingers of one hand and a bottle of booze in the other one, was none other than the little devil himself, Johnny Ray. Laying snuggled up against him with her head tucked gently underneath his neck was some super thin, yet top heavy blonde headed girl with dimples, small turned up nose and cornflower blue colored eyes. Her skin was as pale as porcelain itself and she looked as fragile as one of those china dolls I saw in the window of the antique store around the square one time. Sitting on the hood of another car was two lanky redneck boys who were also drinking.

The door to the back of the car was open and sitting in the backseat were three white teenage girls, a blonde, brunette and a girl who had hair as black as coal. They seemed to be engrossed in a deep conversation as they laughed and whispered care freely.

Hearing a loud crunching sound, I looked up and saw Sister gritting her teeth in anger. I reached out and touched her on the forearm lightly, but I don't think she felt my touch. Eyes blazing, she marched over the where Johnny Ray and the girl were standing. My grasp on Isaiah's hand became tighter as I apprehensively steered us behind her. All five of my senses kicked into overdrive and the hairs on the back of my neck began to stand up warning me that something really bad was about to happen. Nothing good at all could come out of three Negro children being alone around all of these white kids. Nothing good at all.

"Sister!" I whispered with an urgency that screamed to get her attention. I wanted desperately to beg her to walk away and leave whatever issues she had with Johnny Ray and whoever this new girl was alone. I knew that no matter what I said or did, Sister wasn't going to listen to me. She was too headstrong.

Sister marched right up to Johnny Ray and the girl and stood directly in front of them with her hands placed firmly on her hips. Her baby belly was poking out at Johnny Ray as if the baby inside was accusing him of doing wrong, too. Anxiety mounted as I watched the two lanky fellows jump off the car and slowly walk over to where Sister was standing. They stopped just a few feet outside of her.

"What in tha' hell is this, Johnny Ray?" Sister asked, glaring at him. The sunlight streaming upon her head made her hair appear to be a blaze of fire. It reflected how heated she was at the scene sat before her.

Johnny Ray stared coldly at Sister with a look that chilled me to my very soul. Raising the beer bottle in his hand to his lips, he took a swig and lowered his arm back down and rested it on the girl's shoulder. She looked up at him with pouty lips and said, "Baby, who is this Nigra?"

Johnny Ray bent his head down and kissed her lightly on the lips and I wanted to puke at the sight of it. Pulling his head back, he said, "She ain't nobody, Sarah."

Anger flashed wildly within Sister's eyes. "Nobody?" she scoffed. "You wasn't sayin' I was nobody when ya' had ya' pecker all up in meh now was ya'?"

Sarah pushed away from Johnny Ray and stood upright. Tucking some hair behind her ears, she eyed him. "You slept wit' this Nigra, Johnny Ray?!" Looking at him in disgust, she twisted her mouth and snarled. "I know you ain't done slept 'round wit' a dirty Nigra and then messed 'round with me!" She wiped her lips hastily with the back of her hand and stomped her feet as if she was a toddler throwing a tantrum. "I can't believe that I saved myself for you and you had already given yourself to a fuckin' monkey! Unbelievable!"

Sister reared back and slapped Sarah hard across the jaw leaving a bright red mark upon her face. "Bitch! Who ya' thank ya' is callin' dirty you ole' trailer trash whore?!"

Sarah stood holding her jaw, whimpering as she looked at Sister in disbelief that she had touched her, let alone slapped her. By this time the music that had been playing loudly before we walked up had been turned all the way down and the girls in the car were watching the scene closely. All of my instincts at the moment were telling me that we needed to hightail it out of here now.

"Johnny Ray, you got a problem, brother?" One of the lanky boys who was dressed in overalls with no shirt underneath asked. "You need us to help you git' rid of these Niggers?"

Johnny Ray's dark eyes were full of pure evil as he took a slow drag on his cigarette. He studied Sister with those eyes that looked as if they belonged to Satan himself, watching her intensely. Flicking the cigarette off to the side, he stood upright and positioned himself right in front of Sister, towering over her by at least half a foot. "Nigger, I think you betta be gittin' yo' ass on home now if you kno' what's best for ya'."

Isaiah squeezed my hand and started to hum loudly as tears streamed down his cheeks. He waved the fingers on his free hand wildly in front of him.

Johnny Ray's eyes darted towards our direction and he shouted, "Shut that fuckin' retard up now!"

Before I knew it, a strange sense of bravery overcame me and I hollered back, "He ain't no retard, you ole' redneck!"

Sister reared back again to take a swing at Johnny Ray, but the two lanky boys grabbed her from behind by the arms. I let go of Isaiah's hand and ran towards her, but Johnny Ray shoved me down on the ground.

"Don't you touch mah sister!" Sister screamed at him.

Johnny Ray chuckled with an evil glint in his eyes. "Bitch, I'll do as I please to you ole' porch monkeys. Fuckin' half breeds think you're somethin' special 'cause you got a lil' white blood runnin' through yo' veins." He lifted Sister's chin and squeezed it hard. She tried to snatch her face out of his hand, but he held it steady. Bringing his face down closely to hers, he said, "Let me remind you of somethin', Billie... Yo' ass will never be white no matter how much you wanna be white. I ain't never fuckin' love you and only fucked you because you gave up the pussy so freely. You ain't nothin' but a piece of cunt to me. Understand?"

Sister cut her eyes at him as she struggled to free herself from the grip that the boys had on her. Isaiah's humming increased and he flopped down on the ground, rocking back and forth while twiddling his fingers in the air.

"Fuck you, Johnny Ray!" Sister spat in his face and he punched her solidly in the jaw.

"Stupid Nigger, what yo' ass just say?" Wiping the spit out of his eyes, Johnny Ray's eyes gleamed red and he kicked Sister in the stomach and she cried out in pain.

"Stop it, Johnny Ray!" The black-haired girl, who I hadn't even noticed had exited the car and was standing nearby, screamed.

Springing to my feet I ran over to where they were and jumped on his back. Wrapping an arm around his neck, I squeezed hard in attempts to choke him as I clawed at his eyes with my free hand. Johnny Ray pulled at my arm and I squeezed tighter.

"Git' off me, lil' Nigger!"

I didn't take too kindly to being called that, so I found one of his ears and bit into it as if it was the most delicious sandwich on earth. Johnny Ray squealed like one of Big Ma's pigs when they get caught in the barb wired fence and threw me off of him with such force that I hit the ground with a loud thud that nearly rattled my brains. I looked up and saw Johnny Ray approaching me, when the black-haired girl walked up and grabbed him by the arm.

"I said, stop it, Johnny Ray!" The girl tugged at his arm and he looked at her as if she was crazy, but he didn't take another step closer to me.

The girl turned around and faced the guys who were still holding on to Sister who looked as if she were about to pass out. "Frankie, Bobby, let her go!" The guys just looked at her without saying anything, then looked pass her at Johnny Ray. The girl then turned around to face Johnny Ray again. "Call them off of her, Johnny Ray. This ain't right and you know it ain't! You the one got that poor girl pregnant and neither she nor her family deserves this!"

Johnny Ray's rage could be seen clearly written across his face, but he nodded to the guys holding Sister. "Let her go."

Sister collapsed on the ground in a heap and I rushed over to her side. Pulling her upper body into my lap, I gently caressed the side of her face and brushed back strands of hair off of her forehead. "You alright, Sister?" I choked out.

"Annie, I can't believe you're taking that Nigra's side, you fuckin' Nigger lover!" Sarah shot at the black-haired girl.

Annie looked back at Sarah coldly, dark eyes killing her softly with her gaze. "Sarah, I think you better hush your mouth right on up before I lay a hurtin' on you worse than what Billie ova' there just did."

Walking back to the car she had originally been in when we walked up, she called out to the guys, "Frankie, Bobby, let's book it. Now!"

Frankie and Bobby got inside the car and let Sarah get in the front seat in between them. I was guessing that she didn't want to ride anywhere else with Johnny Ray now seeing that he had messed around with Sister. Annie stood outside of the car and called out to Johnny Ray. "Johnny Ray, leave, before I tell Mother about this incident."

Johnny Ray looked down at Sister and me, then shook his head. Darkness clouded his features and it was like I was staring into the eyes of death standing before me. Before walking off he said, "Bitch, I better not ever see you 'round here agin' or you're gonna be sorry. Next time my sister won't be around to save you. I hope that fuckin' coon you're carryin' doesn't make it. It ain't no child of mine." He headed over to his car, got it, cranked the engine and peeled out of the clearing lickity split with Frankie's car trailing right behind him, leaving us alone.

Isaiah was still humming loudly, but I noticed his tears had stopped. He was still rocking back and forth at a rapid pace and fidgeting with his fingers. Looking down at Sister, I choked back tears. I knew I had to be strong for her right now even though I was scared beyond the meaning of the word.

"Sister," I said softly, "Do ya' think you can stand up?"

Sister groaned and struggled to push herself up off of the ground as I grabbed her underneath the shoulders. She looked positively green in the face as if she were about to puke all over the place. Tears streamed down her face and plopped onto the soft earth beneath our feet. I stood and held her up by the waist as she leaned on my small frame for support.

"I's gon' kill him, I swear I am," she muttered, then groaned in pain. "If he hurt mah baby, I swear he's a dead man walkin'."

We walked slowly over to where Isaiah was sitting and I called out to him. "C'mon, Junebug, let's go." Isaiah stood and flapped his arms while humming. I knew right then that it was going to be a long walk home because Isaiah was more than likely going to flail his arms the entire way and I had no way to calm him down and tend to Sister at the same time. My only hope would be that God would send an angel our way so we could hitch a ride home, but on this country road, that wouldn't be very likely.

By the time we made it home twenty minutes later, Sister had grown extremely weak. When we stepped upon the gravel driveway, I looked down at her feet and nearly screamed. Not wanting to create a panic, I said as calmly as I could to her, "Sister, you's got blood runnin' down your legs."

"Mmmm..." was her response and I knew something was wrong. Very wrong. Walking her up the porch steps slowly, I called out for Mama and Uncle Joe. Mama came to the door first and her hands flew up to her mouth as worry darkened her face.

"Cora! What in the high heavens done happened?"

I didn't know whether to tell the truth or skid around it. I was scared to death of what would happen if it got out about what happened with Johnny Ray. Coloreds and Whites just didn't get along in this town. Some whites were nice to us, but others acted as we were less than human. It made me hate the white part of me. I felt like I would never be a whole person. Before I could open my mouth to say anything, Sister beat me to it.

"It was Johnny Ray, Glory Jean," Sister said to Mama as she gasped for air. "He kicked meh in mah stomach. I hurt so bad."

"My Lord!"

"And she's bleedin', Mama!" I said, pointing down at Sister's legs.

Mama looked down and then caught Sister in her arms just before she collapsed as a bolt of pain pierced her body. "You're gonna be alright. You hear me, Billie?" Mama said as we helped Sister get inside of the house and Isaiah followed closely behind us. Once we were inside Isaiah ran off into Big Ma's room and climbed into bed with her leaving us to tend to Sister alone.

"Joe!" Mama called out. "Joe! Git' on out here, we need you! Sister's in trouble!"

Uncle Joe came running out of Big Ma's bedroom and saw us hovering over Sister who we had laid down on the couch.

"What happened to Sister? Why her face bruised and where's tha' blood coming from?"

I looked down at the floor and saw that droplets of blood had made a trail from the door all the way over to the couch, staining the linoleum. Looking back at Sister, her face scrunched up in pain and she became red in the face. "Ahhhhhhh!" she screamed and a gush of blood streamed out from in between her legs, dampening the couch.

"She said that no good white boy she messed with done did her like this, Joe." Gesturing towards the phone, Mama looked up at him with pleading eyes. "Call the midwife. We gotta git' her over here right now if there's any chance to save this baby."

Sister looked up at Mama with a pain stricken face. Grabbing ahold of one of Mama's hands, she coughed out, "No... Save mah baby. Please, save mah baby."

Mama wiped the sweat that had formed on Sister's forehead away with her hand and let it rest there while she lovingly looked into her eyes. "We gon' try everything that we can to save it, Billie. Just stay calm."

"I can't lose... I can't..." Sister gasped for air as tears steadily made their way down the sides of her face. "Mama... I can't lose this baby."

Mama's face became full of emotion as she choked back tears. This was the first time that Sister had ever referred to her as "Mama". Patting Sister's hand, she replied, "God gone save your baby... It's gone be alright."

"Sister Gwen ain't answerin' tha' phone, Glory Jean," Uncle Joe said soberly. Rubbing the back of his neck, he looked at the scene before him tightlipped.

"Joe, my daughter needs help, right now. Is there anyone you know who can help us deliver this baby tonight?"

Uncle Joe's face brightened as an apparent revelation crossed his mind. Snapping his fingers, he said, "Bessie Mae!" Without another word, he was out the door and in his car.

Standing nearby watching Mama tend to Sister, I asked quietly, "Mama is there anything I can do?"

Mama turned her head and looked at me as if she forgot I was in the room. Smiling weakly, she nodded. "Yes, baby... Go into the kitchen and boil some water in the teapot. Then bring me out a washbasin full of cold water and a towel. By the time the hot water is ready, Bessie Mae will be here and she'll know what to do."

Following her orders, I went into the kitchen and did as I was told. My hands shook as I filled the metal teapot up with water at the kitchen faucet. "Please God, don't let Sister lose her baby," I whispered and my voice cracked with unshed tears. Turning the burner of the gas stove on, I watched the blue flame jump and dance for a moment before placing the teapot on top of it. What if my sister did lose the baby? What would happen to her? What would happen to all of us? We were already still hurting over Big Ma's stroke and weren't anywhere near close to being over it.

Shaking off my thoughts, I grabbed a washbasin and filled it with cold water and grabbed a rag, then rushed back into the front room. The sight of blood and the pain on Sister's face was heart wrenching. Handing Mama they washbasin and rag, she sat it down on the floor at her feet and begin wiping Sister's face with it. Seconds later, Uncle Joe and Miss Bessie Mae burst through the front door.

"Glory Jean!" Miss Bessie Mae said excitedly, "Joe here told me that awful boy Johnny Ray hurt Sister and that the baby is in trouble." Making her way over to Mama and Sister, she reached down and gave Sister's shoulder a loving squeeze. "Don't worry 'bout a thang, Sister. I'm gonna help you bring this baby into the world. Sister Gwen taught me well and it ain't nothin' new under the sun that I ain't seen wit' a pregnancy."

Mama stood from her seat in an old wooden chair and beckoned for Miss Bessie Mae to take it next to Sister. Miss Bessie Mae sat down and began prepping herself for the delivery of Sister's baby. Mama stood looking at her daughter for a minute with tears welling up in her eyes, then hurriedly went outside on the front porch. I followed after her to make sure that she was going to be okay.

Mama stood halfway bent over at the far end of the porch with her hands placed firmly on the wooden railing. She seemed to be silently sobbing and it tugged at my heartstrings to see her that way. I quietly made my way over to her, stood behind her and gently rested my hand on her arm. She stood upright, wiped away her tears before turning around to face me. Giving me a small smile, she chuckled, "I didn't want you to see me like this, baby..."

Giving her a knowing look, I replied, "I know, Mama, but everythang is gonna be alright. Sister's baby gonna make it."

Mama leaned up against the porch railing and let out a long sigh before speaking again. Sniffling, without looking at me, she said, "You know, all of this is my fault. All of it."

My brow crinkled as I tried to comprehend how Johnny Ray hurting Sister had anything to do with Mama. For the life of me it didn't make any sense.

Johnny Ray was just a mean-spirited boy and Mama by far didn't have anything to do with what happened to us in the clearing today. I know Jesus is all about forgiving people, but I don't see how I'll ever be able to forgive such a nasty boy as him, especially if Sister's baby dies.

"Mama, you ain't got nothin' to do wit' what happened out there wit' Johnny Ray... You don't know him. He's jus' a mean boy..."

I tried continuing my attempts of reassuring her that she had nothing to do with the current situation, when she raised a hand, cutting me off. Looking me dead in the eyes with her tearful ones, she said, "Baby... There's so much you don't know, yet. You're too young, far too young to understand. I have everything to do wit' what done happened. All of it."

I stood watching Mama's face become even more twisted with emotion as I waited on her to fill me in by what she meant. How could she have had anything to do with Johnny Ray? It just made no sense. No sense at all.

Taking a deep breath, she exhaled and continued. "See, ya'll are payin' for my past sins. Especially Sister in there." Mama nodded her head towards the front door. "See, I ain't been a good mama to y'all and everything I've done since I've left y'all here wit' Mama has finally caught up wit' me. My daughter is knocked up at 15 just like I was. She's in there right now about to give birth to a baby that ain't gone know nobody but one parent. That baby will never be accepted by Johnny Ray or his folks. If I had of had my head on straight and raised y'all up, Sister would probably be getting ready to go off to college somewhere and getting herself a fine education, so she could end up marrying a respectable young man. Now, she's gone have to deal wit' raising a baby when she ain't nothin' but a baby herself." Mama stared off into the distance and a lone tear escaped the comfort of her eye and travelled down the side of her face at rapid speed. I longed to wipe it away from her face but knew that reaching out to her right now wasn't the time.

"Then, my precious baby boy, Isaiah, can barely speak and walks all funny. That's another punishment for my sins. God punishing my babies because I forgot about serving Him and went out there in the world like I was all big and bad and made some really bad decisions. Isaiah is like that because of me and my stupid ways. If I hadn't of been so messed up, he would've came out normal just like you and Sister did."

My heart nearly skipped a beat at what Mama was saying. Had she done something wrong when she was pregnant with my brother? All six years of his life on earth being delayed was due to something she had done? It wasn't right.

"Wh... What did you do for Junebug to be like he is, Mama?" I asked quietly in a voice I didn't recognize.

Mama looked at me with sadness in her eyes. I noticed her fingers wiggling and when she caught me looking at them, she clasped her hands together and rested them on her flat stomach. "I don't know if you're old enough to understand it, yet, Cora."

This just about burned me up inside. I was so tired of everyone claiming I was too young to understand things. *I'm eleven years old for God's sake and if I don't learn about life now, how will I ever learn about it?* Frowning, I looked at Mama with seriousness within my eyes and plastered across my face. "I'm not too young. I'm the one that's been takin' care of Junebug since he was a baby! What did you do to him?" I could feel pent up anger rising in me that I had been keeping inside towards my Mama. When it came to Isaiah and his well-being, all bets were off. That little boy meant more to me than my very life did.

Swallowing hard, Mama looked away. For a moment she was quiet and this just fueled my anger more. Placing my hands on my narrow hips as a gentle breeze made its way upon the porch, I demanded, "Mama!"

Mama's lower lip was quivering and fresh tears sprung up in her eyes. "I... I was on drugs, baby. I met up with a man that was really bad for me and he introduced me to some bad stuff... He had me doing some things that I... " Mama buried her head in her hands and mumbled, "That I'm not proud I did."

My heartrate escalated as this newfound information hit my ears. My little brother was different from everyone else due to Mama's careless mistake? He had to suffer going through life being teased and not being able to walk straight and was unable to communicate to the rest of the world all because Mama had wanted to get high when she was pregnant with him? I couldn't believe it. Not my Mama. Not the woman I had been yearning for all of my life. Not the woman who I thought would be a Heaven sent angel to me. At that moment all the dreams and fantasies of the woman I had spent a lifetime wishing for evaporated. How could I ever trust her if she was able to put her own child's very life at risk the way she did? My heart sank as Sister's words from months ago came to mind, "That woman is nothin' but a lyin', conniving, slutty lil' skank and I can't believe that you're fallin' for whateva dreams she's tryna sell you!"

Narrowing my eyes, I backed away from where I was standing. My very blood felt as if it were boiling and I couldn't recall ever being so angry in my life. "It's yo' fault Junebug is the way he is! How could you do that to him?!"

Mama looked up and focused her attention on me. Wiping some snot away from her nose with a handkerchief she retrieved from her dress pocket, she nodded in sorrow. "Babe... I was sick... Mama was sick back then, but I'm better now, I swear. I got my life together to come on back home and be with my babies. I promise on God's Bible that I love y'all and I never meant to hurt Isaiah. I didn't even realize I was pregnant with him until I was a good five months along and by then it was too late to do away with the pregnancy. I was so messed up in the head because of the drugs and dealing with my own issues that I hadn't even noticed that I hadn't had my menstrual cycle in months."

Swallowing hard, I fought to blink back tears. My mama had been a junkie. She was one of those druggies that Big Ma told me to stay far away from when we visited Aunt Trish in Memphis. I swear the last time we visited Aunt Trish there was a drugged-out person on every street corner. It was either that or a wino.

"How could you be so selfish?" I asked, blinking fast. "Junebug ain't deserve that. Don't you know how bad that stuff is for you? I'm only eleven and I know it'll mess you up bad."

Mama raised her head and took a step closer to me. "Cora, baby, I was sick. I ain't know what I was doing let alone what I was thinking about. I never meant for Isaiah to be hurt. If I could take it all back I would. Please believe me."

Before I could even think if I was going to take a page from the Bible and be like Jesus and forgive my mama for her many sins and wrongdoings towards Isaiah, a piercing howl from inside the house broke my thoughts. Mama rushed past me and into the house. When I neared the front door and placed my hand on the knob, another ear-piercing scream met my ears. I was fearful of what I may see on the other side of the door when I entered it. Was Sister losing the baby? My heartbeat was thunderous in my ears as I pushed the front door open. It creaked loudly, but no one in the front room paid my entrance any mind. All eyes were focused on Sister.

"I need you to push one more time, Sister," Miss Bessie Mae urged as she felt between my sister's legs.

Mama now sat on the couch beside Sister and was holding her up behind her back so that she was in a sitting position. "It's okay, Billie. Take another deep breath and push with all your strength so you can bring that beautiful baby into the world."

Sister moaned, scrunched up her face and pushed with all of her might. Sweat poured off of her face and dripped onto the top of the dress she was still wearing. Her hair was matted upon her forehead and her eyes showed that she was beyond drained.

"Ahhhhh!" Sister yelled before falling back against the couch. Her chest heaved up and down rapidly as she struggled to catch her breath.

Miss Bessie Mae removed her hands from in between Sister's legs and held up a red and purple colored baby. Cleaning the baby's nose and mouth, she then smacked it firmly on the buttocks causing it to scream out. Hearing that baby's cry was like music to my ears. *It's alive! Sister's baby didn't die!* Miss Bessie Mae wiped off the baby and cleaned them up as good as she could before wrapping it in a towel.

"What is it, Bessie Mae?" Mama asked expectantly. Her eyes grew wide in excitement at the sight of the newborn baby.

Sister struggled to sit up against Mama, then held her hands out to Miss Bessie Mae. "Bring meh mah baby."

Miss Bessie Mae smiled warmly before rising from her seat and handing the baby over to Sister. Sister took the baby in her arms and shed tears of joy as she cuddled them to her bosom.

"It's a lil' girl, Sister and she's just as pretty as her mama," Miss Bessie Mae cooed.

Sister beamed. Bending her head down she kissed her little girl softly on the forehead. "Hi, baby gal. It's so nice to meet tha' lil' person who done kicked my insides for the past few months." Picking up the baby's hand, she kissed her little fingers one by one. "My sweet baby gal."

"Well, Billie, what are you gonna call her?" Mama asked as she smiled down on Sister and the baby.

Sister's eyes lit up as she looked at her daughter with eyes full of love. "Nora. Imma name her Nora."

Turning her head towards where I was still standing by the door, Sister beckoned towards me. "C'mon and meet ya' niece, Stripes. C'mon and meet Nora Leanne."

Tears stung at my eyes as the corners of my mouth turned up. "You... You're giving her mah middle name?" I walked over towards them on shaky legs. I was a ball full of emotions. I was nervous, excited, happy, you name it. When I stood over Sister and little Miss Nora Leanne, my heart swelled. The baby had a healthy pink tone under her light skin, full rosy cheeks and wispy blonde hair. Her eyes were already wide open and she was looking out at the world in curiosity.

"Hi, Nora, I'm yo' Auntie Cora." Reaching out, I touched her hand and marveled at how small it was. Baby Nora wrapped her hand around my finger and the world stood in place at that very moment. I couldn't remember being so in love ever except for the day when I first met Isaiah.

Bending down, I kissed my niece lovingly on the forehead and whispered. "I promise I'll always be here for you no matter what. I'll never let anyone hurt you. I promise."

It was a promise that I meant with my very soul and would keep at all costs, no matter what dangers may come our way.

*

Six Months Later

"Stripes, I really think you should stop being friends wit' that girl," Teresa said as we sat on a two swing swinger in the far end of the school yard. It was a cool, crisp Wednesday afternoon and Teresa was waiting on her daddy to come pick her and her siblings up from school. Since I would be walking home alone today, I decided to keep her company. Isaiah had a doctor's appointment in Nashville and Mama and Uncle Joe had taken him up there really early this morning to get fitted for leg braces that would help him walk better. Sister stayed at home today to tend to Big Ma and watch after little Nora, whom I affectionately called Norie. Our folks seemed to like that nickname that I picked out for her, so it has kinda stuck.

Leaves rustled ever so slightly in a breeze as I turned my attention towards my best friend. After all of this time, I still couldn't figure out why she and Zannie Mae just couldn't seem to get along. I mean, it's been a year already. Both girls held a special place in my heart.

"Teresa, why don't you just drop it?" I asked in annoyance. I was tired of having this same old conversation with her week after week. As far as I knew, Zannie Mae had never done anything to Teresa to make her not like her or make her not want to be friends with her.

Teresa rolled her eyes, then placed some newly permed hair behind her ear. Missus Carol Ann Taylor had recently allowed Teresa to get a perm just like her older sister, Lou Mae. Ever since she had straightened her hair out you couldn't tell her nothing. She was constantly shaking it or throwing it over her shoulder. She was starting to get on my very last nerves. She always had her nose up in the air about something and it was really irritating.

"I ain't gon' drop it because she's bad news for you," Teresa replied snottily. "I mean, who does she think she is? Just because she's from New York, she thinks it's alright to come to school wearing all those ruffled dresses and Mary Janes. And for some reason, she thinks she can eat up all of your time so that you don't have any time to spend with me! I don't like her one bit!"

Frowning in utter confusion, I looked at her as if she were crazy. As many pretty dresses as she owned and nice shoes, how could she get mad at the fact that Zannie Mae liked to come to school looking nicely? I was about to tell her just how I felt when Zannie Mae ran up and stood in front of the swing set.

Smiling, she looked directly at me and ignored Teresa's presence. "Hey, Cora!" she said breathlessly. "My auntie wanna kno' if you want to catch a ride home with us? Her friend from work decided to give her a ride over here to the school to get me and since I knew that Uncle Joe wasn't coming to get you today I asked if we could take you home and she said yeah."

Nodding appreciatively, I smiled and said, "Yup... Thank yo..."

Teresa caught me off guard when she stood from her swing and waltzed over towards Zannie Mae and stood in front of her. She was a tad bit shorter than her, but that didn't seem to faze her at all. Placing her hands on her fall jacket covered hips, she eyed Zannie Mae evilly. "Heffa, I kno' you seen me sittin' over there!" She pointed behind her towards the now vacant swing which was swinging wildly back and forth from the force of when she had jumped up out of the seat.

Zannie Mae's eyes narrowed. "So?"

"So?" Teresa mocked. "So, you betta speak. I ain't invisible."

Rolling her eyes, Zannie Mae took a couple of steps back away from Teresa, but Teresa wasn't having it. She inched her way right back in front of Zannie Mae.

"You need to get out of my face," Zannie Mae warned, green eyes flashing with anger. Her face was reddening and it wasn't from the chill in the air.

"And if I don't?"

"We gonna have a mighty big problem on our hands."

My body tensed up watching them. I couldn't believe my two best friends were acting a plum fool and arguing over nothing. "Y'all stop it!" I yelled from my seat on the swing, but neither one of them paid me any mind.

Teresa shoved Zannie Mae and she hit the dirt ground with a loud oomph. I jumped off the swing and tried to help her up off of the ground, but she pushed my hands away, stood and reared back and slugged Teresa dead in the nose. Tears sprouted up in the corners of Teresa's eyes as both hands flew to her face.

"You broke my nose! You brooooke... Broke... My nose!" Teresa sobbed in pain.

Walking over to her, I gently lowered her hands to inspect the damage that Zannie Mae had inflicted upon her face. Blood was everywhere, on her hands and streaming down her face in little red rivers from her nose. Mixing in with her tears, the blood plopped onto her green jacket, staining it. Fishing in my coat pockets, I found a faded light pink handkerchief and held it up to her nose.

Looking behind me, I yelled out to Zannie Mae, "Why'd ya' have to hit her so hard, Zannie Mae?"

Face expressionless, Zannie Mae stood watching me tend to Teresa as if she could care less about a possible broken nose. Dusting off the backs of her legs to remove dirt and leaves from when Teresa pushed her, she remained silent.

"'Cause she's an evil bitch, that's why!" Teresa yelled furiously as she wiped some tears from under one eye.

I looked at Teresa shocked by the words that just came out of her mouth. She rarely ever said a curse word and I hadn't uttered one since Big Ma got onto me that day I got into it really badly with Sister when she was pregnant last year.

"Teresa!"

Teresa glared at Zannie Mae and ignored me. Lifting one of her hands, I held it up to the handkerchief I had on her nose and placed it there. "Here, hold your own nose."

Teresa smacked her lips and rolled her eyes at me. "Why you doin' that? You're gonna take her side of this?"

"I'm not taking anybody's side, but I will say this, you shouldn't have been pickin' wit' her in the first place."

Hearing footsteps approaching us from behind, we turned around to face whoever it was. Miss Pinky walked up to us with a look of concern plastered across her beautiful peach colored face. Her hair was in curly tendrils just like *Shirley Temple*'s only prettier. Seeing Teresa's bloody face, she asked, "Girls, what in the world is going on here?" Turning to Zannie Mae then looking back and forth between where I was standing with Teresa and then back at her niece, she said, "I came out here ta' see what in tha' world was takin' y'all girls so long. Gertrude got her car running with the heat on and we are wasting her gas. I don't have a lot of gas money to be giving her for giving us a ride as it is." Eyeing Teresa closely, she asked, "Teresa, chile, what happened to your face?"

Before Teresa could say anything and get Zannie Mae in a heap of trouble, I spoke up. "We were playin' and she fell out of the swing when we were racin' too fast tryna see who could touch the sky the highest, ma'am." Sensing that Teresa was about to say something, I nudged her in the side to keep her quiet.

"Oh, my Lord! Y'all kno' betta than ta' play like that on those ole' rink-a-dink, rusted out swings!" Coming over to where we were standing Miss Pinky, placed a hand on Teresa's shoulder and asked, "Is your Mama or Daddy on their way?"

"Yes'm," Teresa mumbled.

"Well, let's walk out to the side of the road and wait for them. I think I saw your little brothers and sisters standing near the fence watchin' out for your parents."

Looking over at Zannie Mae, Miss Pinky said, "Let's go, young lady." By the tone of her voice I didn't think that she really bought my little story that I just told her, but I didn't want my friends to get in trouble for fighting. It was my sincere hope and desire that one day they would end up friends, but at the rate they're going hell would freeze over before that happened.

*

"Cora, are you almost finished getting ready for church?" Mama hollered down the hallway to my bedroom.

"Yes ma'am!"

"Good! I need you to come help watch Norie while I help your brother get ready."

"'Kay!"

Sister was in town this morning working at her second job as an early shift candy stripper at the nursing home. She said she hated the job because most of the elderly white patients treated her like cow manure on the bottoms of their shoes, but the money was good, so she kept going. She did whatever she could to raise Norie without asking for help from anybody else and I was extremely proud of her. She worked the early shift on the weekends at the nursing home from 5 a.m. 'til 10 a.m. and she still worked at the corner bakery around the square after school.

Sister never asked anybody for money to help raise her daughter. I had asked her one time what she would do if Johnny Ray decided to pitch in and help out with Norie and she darn near cut my head off with her words. She told me to never bring up Johnny Ray around her or Norie again and I really couldn't blame her. I hated him but was really curious as to what she would do if he decided to pop up one day and claim Norie. When you looked at her, Norie could easily pass for being a fully blooded white baby. She had almost no Negro features in her at all. Her eyes were the bluest blue I had ever seen and one could almost get lost in them if you looked at them for too long. Her hair was curly and blonde and it looked as if God had spun it from a spool of sunshine rays. She was the most beautiful baby my eyes had ever laid upon and I'm not just saying this because she's my niece. I'm saying it because it's the absolute truth.

When I entered Big Ma's bedroom, I was delighted to see that she was sitting upright in the wheelchair Sister had brought her home from the nursing home she worked at. She said they were throwing away a bunch of old ones and her boss lady said she could bring this one home to our grandma. The left side of Big Ma's face still drooped from when she had her stroke and some of the light had disappeared from her eyes, but she was still beautiful. Mama had dressed her in a gorgeous red dress with black buttons down the front and placed a big black church hat on top of her pressed-out salt and pepper hair.

"Mornin' Big Ma!" I said ecstatically as I bounded over in her direction. Wrapping my arms around her small frame, I gave her a squeeze before planting a kiss on her sunken in cheek.

Big Ma didn't respond which was normal for her nowadays. Long gone were the times when she would bestow her infinite wisdom upon me or make me laugh with her stories from the past. All that was left of her was really nothing more than a shell of the strong woman we once knew but having her still here with us was better than not having her here at all.

Mama turned and looked at me and gave me a small smile. Behind her eyes held a deep sadness that only she knew the reasoning of. "Here, Cora, come get Norie so I can help Isaiah finish getting dressed." Picking Norie up off of Uncle Joe's bed, she handed her to me.

"Eeeeeeeee!" Norie squealed in excitement as I took her in my arms.

"Hey, my sweet little niece!" I said, smothering her with love and kisses which caused her to giggle. Words couldn't begin to describe how much I loved this little girl.

"You know, Cora, I am so proud of Isaiah. With your help he's learned how to put his clothes on darn near perfectly!" Mama exclaimed before turning to Isaiah who was standing in front of her grinning a gap toothed smile, wearing a crisp yellow button-down shirt, navy blue tie and gray slacks.

"Ohhh, my sweet little handsome boy! Look at you! Look at this good job you've done!" Mama praised my brother as she bent over to tighten the leg braces that he wore over his pants legs.

"Good jobbb!" Isaiah replied, then twiddled his fingers in the air excitedly before clapping.

Mama looked up at him with love in her eyes and said, "Yes, Mama's baby, you did a good job!"

Uncle Joe drove us to the church and carried Big Ma into the church while Mama carried her wheelchair inside. I held Norie on my hip and held Isaiah tightly by the hand as we walked up the six green carpeted concrete steps that led to the church's porch. I was a little nervous because today I would be singing a solo to Big Ma. I wanted to do something really special for her to show her that I loved her and Mama and Uncle Joe both had suggested that I sing her favorite song, *Precious Lord*.

Sister walked into the church with Lou Mae, who now as the Taylor's oldest child had her own car, just as I took my spot in front of the congregation behind the announcer's podium. My palms were sweaty and my heart was beating a drum solo all of its own as my eyes scanned the crowd. It was the Sunday before Thanksgiving so nearly everyone in our small town had shown up for morning service.

"Mornin' y'all," I said to the church members.

A resounding collective response of "Good Morning" greeted me.

"I wanna sing this special song ta' mah grandma if ya' don't mind."

I heard a couple of "That's alright" and "Amen" and "Sang baby" from out in the crowd.

"Sing, Sister Cora!" Pastor Solomon boasted proudly from his seat in the pulpit.

Swallowing, I took a deep breath and glanced over in my family's direction. Big Ma's eyes were downcast and I fought hard to keep the lump forming in my throat away. Looking upwards, I said a quick prayer to God and Baby Jesus to help my song come out right, then I opened my mouth and began to sing.

"Precious Lord, take my hand, lead me on, help me stand..."

I looked back over at Big Ma as I was singing and to my delight she slowly raised her head and it looked as if she was focusing in on me. This gave me courage to continue singing and I belted out the rest of the tune. By the time I was finished, there was hardly a dry eye in the church house. As I handed the microphone to the church secretary before taking my seat, I noticed that Big Ma had a half smile on her face and her once dull eyes had lit up. Giving her a hug, I whispered, "I love you, Big Ma."

"Love you, Stripessss," came her reply loud enough for most of the congregation to hear and happy tears dampened my face.

"Praise the Lord!" Uncle Joe shouted as he threw his hands up in the arm.

"Thank you, God!" Mama cried out to the heavens before breaking out into a Holy Ghost dance in the aisle of the pews.

Big Ma had just spoken her first words in over 10 months and she had spoken them to me. I would never forget this day as long as I should live.

"God surely does work in mysterious ways... Mysterious ways," Pastor Solomon said from the pulpit.

That night while everyone else was in the front room watching TV and talking amongst themselves, I sat alone in Big Ma's bedroom with her and watched her sleep. I was still amazed at how God allowed her to speak today after being silent for so long. The soft rising and fall of her chest as she took each breath comforted me in a sense. It gave me a sort of peace that God was able to perform miracles even when you weren't expecting them. Big Ma stirred in her sleep and opened her eyes. Turning her head towards me she opened her crooked mouth slowly.

"Stripes..."

Hearing Big Ma's voice startled me, but I took her frail hand in mine and held it on top of the bed covers. This very hand had loved me, bathed me, fed me and comforted me for so many years. Now, I felt as if it were my turn to do the same for her.

"Yes ma'am?"

"Do you 'member what... What I tolds ya' awhile back?"

I frowned slightly because she had told me a lot of things before, so I shook my head. "No ma'am. What you tell me?"

"God's gonna use you, baby..."

Ahhh, I do remember that. She had told me that after she heard me cussing Sister out that time. "Oh, yes'm. I remember now."

"Cora..."

"Ma'am?"

"I want ya' ta' always trust God. I want ya' ta' serve tha' Lord no matta what happens in ya' life. He is a good God and He will see ya' through. Don't let nobody make you's feel less than 'nem 'cause of ya' skin color or 'cause of who ya' came from. Be proud of who ya' is. Don't fa'get ta' give Him tha' glory in everythang ya' do. I want ya' ta' keep sangin' fa' Him. Let Him..." Big Ma started coughing, then cleared her throat. "Let Him... Let Him use ya' chile," she finished as another coughing spell erupted inside her body. Her eyes teared up and she looked as if she was getting choked. She hadn't spoken in so long, I think that her throat probably forgot how to work properly and was causing her pain.

"Big Ma!" I cried out as I jumped up from my seat and lifted her back off of the bed.

"Sister! Mama!" I hollered out panicky and I heard their footsteps dashing madly as they entered the room.

"Oh, God! Mama!" Mama cried as she stepped in front of me and gently pushed me out the way.

"What's tha' matta wit' Mama?" Uncle Joe asked as he stepped foot into the room. His chocolate eyes were wide with fear.

Mama looked at Uncle Joe sternly and said, "Joe, git' this baby out of here," referring to me.

"No!" I cried out. "I wanna stay right here wit' Big Ma!"

Big Ma's coughing increased and she sounded strangled causing a thunderous fear to erupt within me. Sister placed a hand on my shoulder and tried to steer me away, but I jerked away from her and turned back towards where Big Ma lay in the bed. What I saw next was a sight I wished I hadn't seen. A sight Sister was trying to divert me from. As Mama struggled to pull her mother into an upright position on the bed, Big Ma's eyes rolled in the back of her head and in an instant, she was gone.

Chapter 9

5 Years Later- September 1967

"Cora, what are your plans for after graduation?" Zannie Mae asked me as we walked down the path from the newly integrated high school towards her home. Since Zannie Mae lived within city limits, I spent most of my afternoons at her home studying and just hanging out until Sister got off work and picked me up.

This was the first year that I was attending school with the white kids in the community. Schools all over the South were finally being integrated just like the schools up North already were. After *Martin Luther King Jr.* fought so hard for freedom and equal rights for Coloreds and the *Brown Vs. the Board of Education* trial in 1954 stating that separate schooling for Coloreds and Whites was unconstitutional, our schools in our small country town of Tennessee had finally provided us with the option to attend classes at the what used to be "Whites Only" high school. The *Civil Rights Movement* was making strides, but some white people in our community were still hell-bent against equality for all and claimed that they liked things better when they were "equal, but separate". Some of the teachers and students at our high school were really accepting of the changes, while others gave us cold stares and icy shoulders every time we entered the room. I was really glad that this was my last year of school in this town because I don't know if I could really handle being ostracized for my race more than I have already been in my life.

"Well... I don't know," I replied quietly. And it was the truth. Part of me really wanted to go up North to attend college at the University of Chicago where my Uncle Sammie worked, but another part of me wanted to get a job around here and stay home until Isaiah turned 18. He was 11 going on 12 now, so I had another six years to go. Honestly, I really don't know if I can stick around this town or the South for that much longer. There were just too many hurtful memories here.

"Well, I know what I want to do," Zannie Mae said dreamily as she turned her head up towards the sky. "I want to get married to Jimmy and have his babies." She smiled warmly and blushed. I cringed inwardly at her plans for the future. I mean, seriously, why would she want to stay down here and get knocked up by the first guy who told her that he "loved" her? The thought of being tied down to one guy, especially an ole' country run of the mill Joe was not appealing to me in the least.

"Um, so you're not thinkin' of goin' off to college somewhere and continuing your education?"

Tilting her head towards me, she smiled, then giggled. "No, not at all. I am so tired of school. I'm ready to get this senior year over with so me and Jimmy can run off and get hitched." She looked at me curiously with her large green eyes as if she were trying to probe my thoughts. "You're thinking of going off to school somewhere? You're really going to leave home? What about Isaiah?"

I ran my hands over my gray cardigan and didn't answer immediately. Was it really so wrong of me to want to leave this God-forsaken town? Was I wrong for wanting to have a life of my own now? I felt a twinge of guilt for actually wanting to leave home and go off to school somewhere far, far away from Tennessee. I don't want to leave my little brother behind, but in order to take the best care of him I would have to get a really good education and a good paying job. *He would understand that, right?*

"Mama is taking really good care of him, Mae," I replied. She really was. Ever since Big Ma passed, Mama has been the rock of our small family. It took a minute to forgive her for doing drugs and drinking heavily while she was pregnant with Isaiah, but if Jesus could forgive us sinners, surely I could forgive my mama for her mistakes. "Besides, it would only be until I graduate college. I would come back and get him. Wherever I go, Isaiah will never be too far behind."

Zannie Mae nodded and blew out a small pink bubble from the gum she was chewing. Popping the bubble, she sucked the gum back into her mouth. "I love how you take care of your brother, Cora. You're so strong and such a sweet person. I don't know of any other kid our age who would be able to do the things you do for him. He is God awful lucky to have you as a big sister."

"Thanks... I do it because I love him and I made a promise to him that I would always look after him. My brother is my heart."

"I wish I had a sister who loved me just as much as you love him."

Linking my arm in hers, I nudged her shoulder and smiled. "You do. You have her in me!"

Giggling, Zannie Mae nodded in agreement. "You're surely right about that! Ever since we were eleven years old!"

After we had walked arm in arm in silence for a moment, she paused in her stride which caused me to stop walking. "So, if you're planning on going off to school somewhere, where is that gonna leave you and Ashner?"

Ashner... I really hadn't given him too much thought as I gave my future first priority in my mind. Ashner had been sweet on me since ninth grade and made no secrets about it. He was a kind-hearted fellow, but I wasn't sure that I wanted to forfeit my college education to remain living here in this backwoods town that doesn't seem to want to progress as quickly as the rest of the world was. Ashner Jones would probably be a dreamboat for any other sixteen-year-old Negro girl, but for me, he was just a good friend of mine. He was seventeen years old, tall, slim, with skin the color of pecans and had pretty, straight white teeth. He always wore his hair in a short afro which was seemingly the style lately. His dark, serious eyes drew you into him and would make any girl go weak at their knees if they looked into them for too long. He also made good grades and worked hard on his daddy's farm. As far as rank goes in the Negro community, Ashner Jones' family was up there in elite status. Most girls would jump at the chance to be with him just due to social status and the family's' financial status, but not me, things like that just didn't seem to interest me much.

I softly slipped my arm out of hers and started back up walking. I listened to the sound of my black and white saddle shoes hit the pavement along the sidewalk and inhaled deeply before responding.

"Mae, I'm just not as into him as you are into Jimmy…"

Truth of the matter, settling down scared me. I didn't want to become someone's wife and ultimately their "property". I wanted to be free to do what I wanted to do, when I wanted.

Zannie Mae skipped a few steps to catch up with me. Clutching her books and notebook to her chest, she looked at me in horror.

"But why not, Cora? That boy adores you! He would bend over backwards to do anything for you." Smiling coyly, she batted her eyelids, her long brown lashes fluttering over her eyes like butterflies. "If I wasn't already spoken for, I wouldn't mind claiming him for myself. Just about every girl at school wants to be with him!"

This was a subject where Zannie Mae and I differed on. Out of all of our years of being friends, she has always been the one that has obsessed over boys while they barely touched my radar. My life consisted of taking care of my brother and watching after my five-year-old darling of a niece while my sister worked. Other than that, I was engrossed in my studies because I had decided to become an advocate for Civil Rights. Being someone's baby maker just didn't appeal to me. I couldn't stand the thought of being "barefoot and pregnant". Somehow, I believe when Sister got knocked up at 15 it killed any future desire of mine to become a mother. Besides, I had been taking care of Isaiah all my life and I knew that adding any other responsibilities to me outside of him would prove to be more than tasking.

"Zannie Mae, I think I want to go off to school and focusing on boys right now instead of my studies would keep me from attaining my goals."

Shrugging, Zannie Mae kept in stride with me as we walked down the street that led to her house. Her cute little facial features were twisted up as if she were deeply in thought. "You know, Cora... I really admire you. You're not like me in that way. You know exactly what you want and you're so independent." Placing some of her wavy hair behind her ear that had a pearl earring in it, she continued. "You see, my mama raised me to always depend on a man like she depended on daddy. She always told me that I was to make sure I did everything right that I needed to do to attract a successful husband that was going to take care of me. I guess even after all these years since her death those words of hers have stuck with me. I never thought about what life would be like without trying to get married. I just want to be a good housewife like she was and raise me a bunch of kids and have dinner ready and waiting on my hardworking husband when he comes home from work."

I nodded but didn't say anything. I could understand that her upbringing differed from mine, but I didn't want to put her down in anyway. There just wasn't any way I could agree with graduating from high school and just sitting at home cooking and cleaning, besides, I had been doing it pretty much all my life anyways when I helped out Big Ma.

When Sister picked me up a little after 5 p.m. that afternoon, I told her what Zannie Mae had told me about wanting to be a housewife and waiting attentively for her opinion on the matter. At 21, Sister was poised with elegance and grace and had so much wisdom under her belt now.

Taking a slow drag on her cigarette as she steered what used to be Uncle Joe's truck down the old windy country road leading us home, she blinked her eyes thoughtfully. Her fire red hair was cut into pixie cut style which seemed to make her freckles a more prominent attraction on her beautiful face. Her blue eyes were focused on the road as she lowered her cigarette and tapped its ashes outside the open driver's side window.

"I can see her viewpoint on this, Cora, I mean, that's what most gals want straight outta high school, ya' kno'." Turning her head towards me, she looked at me for a second before placing her eyes back on the road. "You on tha' otha' hand are different and that's not a bad thang, so don't git' meh wrong. You want more outta this life and I don't blame you. If I was as half as smart as you are when I was yo' age, I would be wantin' ta' do tha' same thang ya' wantin' ta' do. I would've went off ta' college somewhere and made somethin' real proper outta my life, but I made my choices and I have ta' live wit' 'em now."

Reaching over the seat, I touched her lightly on the arm. "It's not too late, Sister. You can still go off to school."

Sister shook her head and chuckled. "Naw, babe girl. My main focus in life now is to make sure that my daughter is taken care of. Norie comes first. Every extra penny I git' ta' mah name goin' towards her future and her education. I want her ta' make sumin outta herself just like you are. She looks up to you, ya' kno' that? I want her to be somebody, that's why I named her after you."

I blinked back tears. This was the first time I ever heard of the reasoning why my sister decided to name her firstborn child after me. "She looks up to you, too, Sister."

Sister pulled the car up in our driveway and killed the engine. Turning towards me, she looked at me intently and said, "Yeah, she does, but jus' not in tha' same way. There's somethin' so special about you. Even Big Ma knew it. I feel it in mah bones that you're gonna change how this old world operates one day." With that being said she opened the car door and stepped out and greeted Norie who was bounding down the front porch steps towards her.

Smiling widely and giggling, Norie opened her arms wide and flew into her mother's arms.

"Mommmmmmyyyyyy!"

Sister picked up Norie and swung her around a couple of times before kissing her softly on the forehead and lowering her back down to the ground. Pulling gently on one of Norie's pigtails, she said, "Hey, Tuggah. Mama's missed you. You have a good day at school ta'day?"

Norie nodded excitedly and begin to spew out all she did at school at a rapid pace. I sat in the truck and watched them interact together. *Am I wrong for not wanting what Sister has? What Zannie Mae wants as soon as we graduate?*

Exiting the truck, I smiled brightly as my niece skipped over to me with her pigtails bouncing as she went. Her purple plaid dress was wrinkled and her frilly white socks were dusty and I was sure that just by the sheer looks of it, she had an amazing day of Kindergarten. Norie hugged me by the waist and I gave her a squeeze back.

"Auntie Corie, guess what?"

"What?"

Norie motioned for me to bend down, so I did and she cupped her small hands and put them up to my ear. "I made Mommy a popsicle stick dolly today at school."

Leaning back, I smiled and looked her in the eyes. "Really?"

"Yup," she nodded proudly. Putting a pointer finger up to her lips with her blue eyes shining she said, "Shhh! Don't tell her though."

Sister, who had been watching us closely, laughed and placed her hands on her hips. "Are y'all two gals over there talkin' 'bout meh? What ya' tryna keep your auntie from tellin' meh, Norie?"

Norie beamed up at me and put a pointer finger up to her lips as if she were trying to shush me, then turned her head and put on an innocent look as she faced her mother. "Nothin', Mommy!" Running away from me, she bounded up the stairs and onto the porch with her long pigtails swinging madly as she went. In another second she had disappeared behind the screen door and into the house.

Sister laughed and her blue-green eyes sparkled as she looked after her child. "Now, jus' what are we gonna do 'bout that lil' girl, Cora?"

I laughed along with her. "I have no idea."

When we entered the house, Norie ran up to her mother with her hands behind her back, grinning.

"What 'cha grinnin' fo', lil' lady?" Sister asked, placing her hands on her hips in amusement.

"I gotta surprise for youuuuu!" Norie proclaimed in a sing-song voice.

"Is that right?"

Norie nodded her head eagerly. "Uh, huh."

"What is it?"

"Close your eyes then you will get a sweet surprise!"

My sister did as she was told and held out her hands in front of her awaiting the surprise her daughter had for her. Norie's hands came from behind her back and she placed the popsicle doll she had told me about a few minutes earlier in her mother's hands. The popsicle doll wore a pink felt dress cut in the shape of a triangle and had two buttons for eyes, a bead for a nose and red yarn for hair.

"Open them!" Norie asked of Sister.

Sister opened her eyes and grinned down at the doll in her hands. Fingering the felt dress, she bent over and embraced her daughter. "Awww, thank you, Tuggah." Pecking Norie on the cheek she stood upright.

"You like her?"

"Yes, love, she's beautiful."

"Guess what her name is?"

"What?"

"Billie!"

Sister laughed heartedly at the fact that her daughter had named the doll after her. Sister was rarely called by her given name and had once told me when we were younger that she despised it because she was named after her daddy. This was before I found out that Billy Baxter was my father, too.

Sister and Norie started chatting about her day at school and I set my books down on the end table near Big Ma's favorite chair and exhaled. My mind drifted back off to the conversation that I had earlier with Zannie Mae about Ashner and just as if he knew that he was on my mind, I noticed through the front window that his sleek black pickup truck was pulling into our front yard kicking up swirls of dust from the gravel driveway along with it.

Pushing open the screen door, I stepped lightly onto the porch and watched him as he got out the truck and strolled over towards the porch. The setting sun cast a warm glow upon his golden skin which highlighted his handsome features even more. Leaning against the doorframe, I eyed him warily wondering why he had shown up at my home. It wasn't as if we were dating or anything... To me, he was just a boy from school and nothing more, even though he wanted there to be more.

Ashner joined me on the porch and leaned up against the wood railing, flashing me a toothy grin. "So, how come you've been avoiding me, Cora?"

Nibbling on my bottom lip, I cast my eyes downward and studied my shoes. I had been avoiding him ever since he had asked me to accompany him to the Octoberfest Formal on last week. He just wanted something from me that I couldn't give him. I wasn't ready to court anyone and accepting his offer to the dance would give him the idea that I liked him as much as he liked me. That just wasn't the case.

"Um... Ashner..."

Coming closer to me, my breath quickened as his steps hit the porch. Okay, so maybe I liked him just a little. I just didn't know what to do with my feelings or lack thereof for him. I didn't want to end up like Sister. I wanted to get my education and make a difference in this country. I had no time for the likes of boys.

Ashner reached out and gently caressed the side of my face. His hand felt slightly rough from all of the years he had been working on the farm, but it also felt warm and strong against my flesh. A shiver shot through me making me press back up against the doorframe and wall behind me even harder.

Lifting my chin, he gazed into my eyes forcing mine to meet his. "Cora... Why are you fighting this? Us?"

Tearing my eyes away from his, I pushed his hand down and moved around him. "I'm not fighting anything, Ashner... There's nothing going on between us."

Ashner turned around to face me once more, a smirk tugging at the corner of his lips. Placing a hand in his jeans pocket, he leaned up against the wall of the house. I was suddenly embarrassed by the chipping yellow paint on the walls of the outside of my house. No one had tried to paint it in years, not since Uncle Joe had painted it last. "I beg to differ."

Memories of seeing Sister mess around with Johnny Ray flooded my mind and I shook my head slightly as if that would get rid of them. I couldn't end up like her. No. No puppy love was going to keep me from achieving my dreams. I would get out of this country town and make something of myself. I refuse to end up pregnant as a teenager like Mama and Sister did. That wouldn't happen to me. I wasn't like them and I wouldn't and couldn't let my Big Ma down.

"There isn't." Flicking some imaginary lint off my cardigan, I tried to control the ever-growing thumping of my heart. For the life of me I couldn't understand how he could bring forth feelings from me that I had never experienced before. I felt warm all over whenever he was near me as if he was the sun and I was a flower he shined brightly upon, encouraging it to spread out its petals and grow.

"Cora... At some point in time you're going to have to stop resistin' me." Crossing the porch, he took my hands in his and leaned over planting a kiss softly on my forehead. I nearly melted into the porch railings at this sweet gesture.

"Ashner, I think you should leave," I breathed quietly, silently begging my heart not to deceive me and inform him that he had this effect on me.

Leaning back, he took one of my hands and held it up against his cheek. I felt myself caving, melting, just from his touch and it scared me.

"I just had to see you. You don't even come around to see the horses anymore. You've been avoiding me since I asked you out to the dance." Smiling warmly, he pressed a kiss on my palm. "You still haven't given me your answer."

Snatching my hand away from him, I frowned. "I don't want to go to the formal, Ashner. Take another girl. You have so many to choose from at school who all swoon over you. Why ask me?"

"Because I don't want any other girl but you, Cora Harris. I'm sweet on you and I love you."

Swallowing hard, I sidestepped away from him and walked quickly towards the front door. I could not handle what he was saying. I just couldn't. Mama had loved a man and ended up with Sister and Sister had loved Johnny Ray and ended up with Norie. And where are the men that they loved? Nowhere to be found. I wasn't going to end up like them.

"Go home, Ashner," I replied as tears clawed at my throat. I just couldn't bear to look at him any longer.

Opening the door, I walked inside the house leaving Ashner and a piece of my heart on the porch alone. I had to focus on my future and he just wasn't a part of it.

*

"Are you sure you don't wanna date, Ashner?" Zannie Mae asked, face flushed as she folded a piece of loose leaf paper in half and fanned herself with it. It was the middle of October, but the Indian Summer was kicking our butts heating up the South with temperatures hitting the mid-90s every day this week. We were sitting in the sweltering hot cafeteria of the high school eating lunch. The air conditioning unit had long since conked out on us back in August at the start of the school year and we all were miserable. It was so hot inside that even the walls appeared to be sweating.

Groaning, I rolled my eyes at her and tapped my fork on the plastic tray sitting before me. "We've been over this countless times. No, I don't."

Zannie Mae stopped fanning herself for a moment and pushed her tray out of the way as she leaned over so that her chest wouldn't fall in her food. She had a large chest like my older sister, something that I was lacking tremendously. My breasts were small and it often made me feel self-conscious around the other girls my age who were fully developed.

"Well, I bet you'll think differently after this..." she replied, green eyes flashing, "Rumor has it, he's dating Teresa now."

My pulse quickened at her statement. *Teresa? As in my ex-best friend? How could he? Did he do this to hurt me because I wouldn't go out with him?* I could feel my cheeks and ears getting warm, so I took a hand and tousled my curls so that they fell forward hiding my face. Reaching out in front of me, I brought a cup of lemonade up to my lips and took a deep gulp before placing it back down on the table.

"So, what do you think about that?"

Stalling so I could gain my composure, I cleared my throat and shrugged while looking her directly in the eyes. "That's their business. I couldn't care less," I lied. But inside my heart was being torn into a million jagged pieces. *Teresa and Ashner? This just couldn't be...*

Zannie Mae sat back on the lunch table bench and narrowed her eyes. "Mmm hmm... Say what you want, Cora, but I know you. You are my closest friend and I can see that this bit of news is clearly bothering you."

"It's not..."

"Lies... Stripes... C'mon, I have seen with my very own eyes how you look at Ashner whenever he's around. You're smitten! I just for the life of me can't understand why you won't just give in and go out with the boy already!"

"I don't like him, Mae!" I hissed under my voice and then looked from side to side to make sure no one else was paying attention to our conversation. My cheeks were flaming red in an embarrassment that I didn't totally understand. *Why did I even feel this way and why couldn't I be completely honest with my best friend about how I was feeling?*

Eying me closely, Zannie Mae crossed her arms over her bosom and tsked. "Girl, you're in such denial. Ashner makes you hot under the collar and don't lie. It's okay to like a boy, Cora. There's nothing wrong with it. In fact, it's natural. We are teenagers for Heaven's sake."

"You just don't understand, Mae..." I said as I toyed with the mashed potatoes on my tray with the fork in my hand. No one would ever understand how much liking a boy scared the beejesus out of me. To me, boys equaled trouble and I wasn't about to get into trouble with any one of them. No matter how much I liked one of them.

"What's there not to understand, Cora?" Zannie Mae said as she bit into her turkey sandwich. Chewing thoughtfully, she swallowed and sat the sandwich back down on her tray. "You like him, but you're scared of ending up like your mama and sister. I get that. I'm neither blind nor dumb. You must forget sometimes that I know you?"

"I don't like the boy. Case closed and..." My words trailed off as Ashner entered the cafeteria with a pretty and poised Teresa hanging onto his arm. He was wearing his purple and white football team jersey. It was the very jersey that made his muscles pop and had me growing weak in the knees at the sight of them.

Zannie Mae turned around in her seat to see what had just intently caught my attention. Seeing Ashner and Teresa, she turned back to me and shook her head. "I thought you didn't like the boy, huh?"

I opened my mouth to utter a rebuttal, but my voice got caught in my throat as I watched Ashner steer Teresa, who happened to look like some kind of model out of the teen magazines that brightened every magazine rack in the 5 and 10 store, towards the popular kids' corner of the cafeteria. Her hair was long and straight down towards the middle of her back and parted in the center. She wore a pretty baby doll pink mini skirt with pleats and a white fitting polo

T-shirt which accentuated her breasts. On each wrist she wore silver bangles which clinked with every movement she made and on her feet, she wore 3 inch white heels. I couldn't even walk in heels, let along stand up in them. Teresa personified everything that I wasn't. She was the perfect Negro teenaged girl and she came from money. It's no wonder Ashner didn't give me a second thought after I turned him down and headed straight towards Teresa.

Zannie Mae reached across the table and gently touched my hand which caused me to jump, taking me away from my thoughts.

"Cora, you're staring at them," she whispered.

"Huh?" I replied distractedly as I watched Ashner sit down next to Teresa at the popular kids' cafeteria table. My heart felt as if it were about to shut down on me and die. How could he have decided to go out with her? She's nothing like me. How could he have claimed to love me, then turn right around and go out with her? It didn't make any sense at all.

"Cora!" Zannie Mae said loudly as she jerked my hand.

Tearing my eyes away from Ashner and Teresa I looked at her. Zannie Mae's green eyes were focused on me and her pretty face showed her concern. Softly patting the back of my hand, she continued speaking, "You have to let go of that fear that you're gonna end up pregnant like your mama and big sister, Stripes... You're in love with Ashner and you're gonna let him just up and get snatched away by that snake all because of something that ain't even gonna happen. Ain't nobody ever said that just because you like a boy that you have to sleep with him. Don't miss out on love just because of a mistake that people in your family made."

Swallowing the ever-forming lump in my throat, I pulled my hand away from hers. Standing from the bench, I picked up my tray and replied softly, "It's just not that simple, Mae. If I get involved with him I'm giving up on everything that my future stands for. I'm not living just for me, remember? I'm living for Junebug, too." Walking away from the lunch table, I left her sitting there alone with her mouth gaped open in disbelief.

*

Later on that evening, I sat alone on the front porch in Big Ma's old rocking chair looking up at the ever darkening sky as the sun set. Brilliant reds, oranges, and pinks painted the blue sky above me and I was in awe at God's creation. My mind was a million miles away, but my heart was stuck right here in this little old country Tennessee town and pinning for Ashner Jones. *Am I doing the right thing by pushing him away and into the arms of another girl?*

A cool breeze blew across the porch causing me to shiver. Wrapping my arms around myself, I exhaled deeply. My heart felt as if it were being torn from my chest at the very thought of Ashner being with Teresa.

Would their relationship progress so much that he proposes to her? Would they get married? Would she have his babies one day? I couldn't stomach the thought of it all. I was so consumed in my thoughts that I didn't hear Mama step onto the porch.

"Cora, baby?"

Turning my head towards the sound of her voice, I forced a small smile and replied. "Aw, hey, Mama."

Mama walked over to me and stood by my side. Running her hair through my still vicious red curls, she peered down at me with love in her eyes. How I loved this woman so. Next to Big Ma, she held one of the biggest places in my heart. "What's the matter, baby? You've been sitting out here on this here porch by yourself for about an hour now."

I didn't want to tell her the truth. I was embarrassed to admit that I didn't want to end up like her and Sister. I also didn't want to hurt her feelings by letting her know that I was ashamed of how she just up and got knocked up with three kids and forced them on her mother to raise for years.

"Nothing's wrong, Mama. I'm just getting some fresh air."

Mama raised an eyebrow and looked at me all knowingly, an expression on her face that mothers have when they know that something is bothering their children and that their child is lying to them about it.

"Cora Leanne..."

Sighing, I clasped my hands together in my lap and fiddled with my thumbs. I didn't feel like talking about Ashner. I wasn't even sure of how to process how I even felt about him.

"Cora... I'm waiting."

"Ah... Okay, Mama... There's something on my mind, but I don't wanna talk about it."

"But, it may make you feel better. Does it have anything to do with that handsome young fella that came around here for you the other day?"

Whipping my head upwards, I cringed. "You saw him?"

Placing her hand upon her hip, Mama chuckled. "Of course I did. It's not too much that gets past me, even when I got my hands full with your brother. Now tell me about him. What's got you so bothered?"

Shrugging, I diverted my gaze and looked out at the dying grass in the yard. This was hard enough to think about, let alone express out loud.

"Do you like this boy?"

Nodding, I looked back up at her and watched as a smile spread across her face.

"Oh, that's lovely, baby. He seems like a nice young man. So, when are you gonna introduce him to the family?"

"Never."

Mama frowned. "What do you mean by that?"

"He's going out with another girl."

"Oh, baby... I'm sorry."

"I'm not... I can't focus on boys anyways. I gotta focus on my future and that doesn't include any time for boys. They're nothing but trouble. Look at what happened to you and..." I stopped myself before any harmful words could spill out from my mouth.

Mama gently cupped my chin in her hand and forced me to look up at her. "Are you afraid to end up like me and Billie? Is this why you're saying that boys aren't apart of your future?"

I couldn't bring myself to utter the words, so I just nodded.

"Ah, baby. What Billie and I did was irresponsible, but you aren't anything like us. Don't miss out on being in love and experiencing life as a teenager just because of mistakes from my past. I want you to live your life. You have plenty of time to be serious when you become an adult. And quit using your brother as an excuse to push people away and not have fun. I am Isaiah's mother, not you. Now, I admit, I made a lot of mistakes with you children, but I am here now and I'm never leavin' y'all again until the good Lord calls me on home to glory. Understand?"

"Yes ma'am," I replied quietly. Could I believe Mama's words? Could I truly love Ashner and not have to worry about my future being ruined? I wanted nothing more than to get as far away from this "go nowhere" small town of Tennessee and make it big for myself. I saw myself being an advocate for Negro Women's rights and becoming big with child by some guy in high school wouldn't get me closer to that dream.

"Call that boy up, Cora... You don't wanna let your future get beside you just 'cause you're afraid." Mama kissed me lightly on the forehead, tied what used to be Big Ma's apron tightly around her small frame and stepped lightly towards the front door. Once she was back inside of the house, I was left alone with my many thoughts again.

I had never admitted to myself how much I enjoyed Ashner's presence in my life until Teresa stole it away from me. He was just a figure that I thought would always be a part of my life until graduation. Without him around, everything in my world felt a little bit duller.

I spent the rest of the afternoon in a daze, watching my niece play with Isaiah, halfway listening to Sister and Mama talk about what all had happened at Sister's job that day, and thinking about how badly I had messed up things with the only boy that had ever shown me any real interest. My heart had never experienced such an ache and longing as it was right now. How could I have been so foolish? Zannie Mae was right... I was in love with that boy. I had to tell him. I had to get him away from Teresa's clutches. She was all wrong for him and would deliberately try to trap him. She had changed so much from when we were little girls and all she cared about now was "status" and money. Since she knew that Ashner came from money and from one of the wealthiest Negro families in town, she would make it her business to marry into his family. I was for certain that she could care less about winning his heart or getting to know his mind and boy did Ashner have a wonderful mind. He was as smart as they came and wasn't just another dumb jock who was only known for his actions on the field.

As I got ready for bed that night, I stood in front of the mirror inside of our recently installed bathroom. We had only had it for less than a year, but I was truly thankful that I no longer had to run out to the outhouse or use a chamber pot (or piss bucket, as Big Ma used to call it) every time I needed to do my business and relieve myself. I barely noticed when Sister entered the bathroom and stood behind me as I brushed my long, curly locks upwards on top of my head and secured it into a high ponytail.

With her blue eyes focused intently on my reflection in the mirror, she spoke in a calm, nurturing voice, one that she usually reserved for speaking to her daughter in. "Stripes..."

My eyes reached hers in the mirror and I saw a world full of concern swimming around in hers. "Yeah?"

"Mama and I had a talk 'bout ya ta'night... And I want ya ta kno' that you ain't gotta be scared 'bout turnin' out like meh... You won't, okay?" I noticed that tears were beginning to well up in the corners of her eyes, but she quickly blinked them away. "You ain't nothin' like me, Stripes... You're smarter than meh... Always have been and always will be. If you like some boy... 'Specially if it's that cutie pie that done came by here befo', I say go for it. Let him kno' how you are feelin'... Don't let what I did when I was yo' age keep you from happiness. You deserve all of the happiness in the world. You didn't have much of a childhood 'cause you was always lookin' out for our little brother. You barely played 'cause you was so concerned at motherin' him in the absence of our mama, so this is yo' time to spread yo' wings and enjoy life befo' life gets away from you. Date. Go ta' all the dances that ya can, hang out... This is your senior year, Have fun, Cora..."

"I... I'm scared... I... I just don't know what to make of all of this." Exhaling deeply, I lowered my head. "He told me that he loved me and all I had to say in response was for him to go home. Now... Now, he's dating Teresa and I feel like a fool."

Sister placed her hands on my shoulders and gently spun me around so that I was facing her. Lifting my chin, she looked at me with eyes full of sisterly love. "If you love that boy back, tell 'em... Don't let a lil' thang like him being wit' her stop you. That boy has a good heart from what I see and Teresa ain't the right gal for him. She's too shallow and will drag that boy through the mud later on in life if they make it far." Reaching upwards, she gently brushed down some wild curls that had sprouted out on the side of my head. "I want you to go into town ta'morrow and tell that boy just how you feel. If you need me ta' take ya' to his house I will."

Shaking my head, I looked upwards at the cracked plaster in the ceiling before looking back at my sister. "I'll think about it, but I know I won't need a ride. This will be somethin' that I'll have to do on my own terms."

"Okay, babe girl..." Sister nodded and left the bathroom heading towards our still shared bedroom. Nothing much had changed over the years with our living arrangements except the fact that I now had my own bed and that Sister and Norie now shared our old bed. I had inherited Uncle Joe's bed when he moved in with Zannie Mae's aunt years ago. Isaiah now slept in Uncle Joe's old room. As the only boy, he got his own room.

My heart grew heavier with the thought of Uncle Joe. He had been dead now for six months. He was another tragic case of the unjust ways of the South for the Negro population. He had a run in with some evil, racist white men at a diner one evening and they had trailed him on his way home. According to some eyewitnesses, three white men had made him stop his car on the side of the road and had pulled him out of the driver's seat and forced him to get into their car. Uncle Joe never made it home that night. When his wife, Mildred had called around looking for him without any luck, she called on a search party and Mama and some of Uncle Joe's friends went out searching for him. His body turned up hanging from a tree in an apple orchard not too far from town. It was the last time that Uncle Joe's strong will and mouth had caught up to him.

Many of the racist whites in town had been after him for years and wanted to kill him, so it was no surprise to the Negro community when Sheriff Bradford did absolutely nothing to prosecute the men who killed Uncle Joe. Word had it, much to my dismay, my dad was one of the men who had played a part in our uncle's death. As much as I hoped it wasn't true, there wasn't anything that I would put past a Baxter. They were well known for their hatred of Negroes and wasn't shame of it. One day I would ask Mama just how in the world and why she even laid down with the likes of Billy Baxter in the first place. *Just how could she have fallen in love with a racist white man?*

As I lay alone in my bed that night, thoughts of Uncle Joe drifted to the back of my mind while thoughts of Ashner came back to the forefront. Sister was right and so was Mama. I needed to tell him how I felt and fast, before things with him and Teresa got any more serious.

Chapter 10

I awoke the next morning with determination in my heart and a huge smile upon my face. Today I would tell Ashner that I loved him, too and explain to him why I had pushed him away. I just hoped he would understand. Throwing on a light blue t-shirt and a pair of worn jeans, I nibbled lightly at the breakfast that Sister had prepared for us before bolting out of the door. I was far too nervous to eat anything at all because my mind was only on what I was going to say to the only boy that I had ever loved.

Dashing down the freshly paved road headed north towards Ashner's family farm, my heart felt as if it were about to burst. *Can I actually do this? Can I tell him how I really feel? Yes, I can... I have to.* Rounding the curve in the road, I took a shortcut through the thicket and fought my way through the dying brush until I came into the clearing that was just on the outskirts of Ashner's home. I could hear cows mooing and chickens cackling loudly which meant that someone was up early feeding them. Walking alongside of the white posted, barbwire fence that held the cows, I rehearsed in my mind the lines I would say to him when I saw him face to face. I just prayed to God that I would have the nerve to finally express my feelings to him.

As I came upon the driveway, I saw Ashner's dad, Raymond Jones, stood outside of a huge chicken coop wearing blue jean overalls, a white muscle shirt, and a straw hat, dropping out chicken feed from a metal pan onto the dirt floor of the fenced in henhouse. When he heard my footsteps approaching, he turned around at the sound and gave me the same toothy smile that Ashner has.

"Well, hi there, Ms. Cora. Long time no see."

"Hi, Mr. Jones. How are you fairing today?"

"I'm guessin' I'm doin' alright. You come down to see 'bout that knucklehead boy of mine? Been missin' you comin' 'round here lately and so has Roberta. She was just askin' Ashner 'bout you the other day and why we haven't been seeing much of you."

Nodding, I replied with a smile, "Yessir..." Digging the tip of my sneaker into the earth, I blushed. "Is your son home? I kinda need to talk to him 'bout somethin' important."

Mr. Jones nodded his head in the direction of the backyard where the horse stable stood tall and firm. "That boy is back yonder messin' off wit' those horses. You know that boy loves his horses. I'm thankin' that his sister is out there, too, so whatever it is that you need to discuss wit' him, you might want to have him tell Connie to come on back up to the house so that y'all can talk in peace. I love that little gal of mine, but she is as nosey as they come," he answered, chuckling heartily as he wiped a trail of dripping sweat off the side of his face.

"Thanks, Mr. Jones."

Mr. Jones nodded and resumed feeding the chickens as I headed towards to back of the house. From the distance I could see two figures out near the horse stable and figured that their father had been right, and that Connie was out there helping out her big brother. As I neared the stable, my assumption couldn't have been any more wrong. There were indeed two people out there, but it wasn't Connie with Ashner. Sitting on a wooden stool near one of the doors of the stable that held Ashner's favorite horse, a black stallion with a silky, long mane, was none other than Teresa. Connie was nowhere in sight.

"What is she doin' out here so early in the morning?" I whispered under my breath as I inched nearer to the stables careful not to crunch on any of the fallen leaves on the ground which may alert them of my presence.

My heart sank as I watched Ashner gesture wildly into the air and Teresa tilt her head back in laughter. As her laughs met my ears, I knew that he had to be telling her one of his famous jokes that would rip anyone's stomach to shreds from laughing so hard at them. I had fell victim to many sore sides and cheekbones from laughing at his jokes in the past. My heart ached slightly at the realization that it had been weeks since he last told me a joke and it was nobody's fault but mine for pushing him away.

Teresa touched his forearm lightly in a flirtatious way and it made me nauseous. Ashner bent downwards and his face was inches away from hers when I forgot all about being quiet and stepped on a twig which crunched loudly beneath my shoe. Ashner jumped back away from her before their lips could meet and his eyes widened in surprise when he saw me. Teresa turned her head towards the sound and her face initially bore confusion before it turned to irritation at the sight of me.

"Cora?" Ashner called out.

My breath caught in my throat as I stared back at them, unable to utter a word. Ashner started to head towards me, but Teresa reached out and grabbed his arm stopping him. Ashner looked down at her and said something that I couldn't hear before removing her hand from his arm. Jogging over to where I still stood frozen in my tracks, he stopped a few feet in front of me.

He stood for a moment with his hands on his hips trying to catch his breath in the shade from a maple tree above him. Sweat had begun beading upon his hairline and I wanted to wipe it off of his brow. He had never looked as attractive as he did in that moment to me. His dreamy eyes that every girl at school had fallen in love with were now focused in on me and I never again wanted him to take his eyes off of me.

"Cora..." My name breathlessly escaped his beautiful, full lips. *Oh, God, what has become of me? Since when did I think of guys like Zannie Mae did?* I silently chastised myself at my unusual thoughts, but right then I couldn't help but to wonder how his lips would feel pressed against mine. I had never been kissed before.

"What are you doin' here?"

"I... I..." Stammering, for a lack of words, I looked at him in embarrassment. I could feel my cheeks growing warm and I wished that I had worn my hair long today so that I could cover my face with it. I had never been so ashamed in my life. I felt like a fool for showing up at his home unannounced just like things had never changed between us and our friendship recently.

Ashner took a few more steps closer to me while stuffing his hands in his jeans' pockets. Not taking his gaze off of me, he asked again, "What are you doin' here, Cora?"

My pulse was racing wildly, and it felt as if the temperature outside had risen 20 more degrees since I first walked up on the two lovebirds.

"I... I needed... Um," I just couldn't seem to find the words to say to him as to why I was at his house so early in the morning on a Saturday even though I had been to his house so many times before in the past. Now, it just felt wrong. Terribly wrong.

Spinning around on my heel, I mumbled, "I gotta go," before bolting back up the yard and past Mr. Jones who was now feeding their goats with Connie standing beside him talking a mile a minute. Seeing me running, Mr. Jones called out to me, "Ms. Cora, won't you stay fo' breakfast?"

I didn't respond but kept running until I was out of their yard and down the clearing. Dry, knee high grass whipped at my jeans covered legs as I went. I didn't stop to catch my breath until I reached the thicket. Tears blurring my vision, I wiped madly at them as I leaned up against a tree. Birds chirped sweetly while bullfrogs croaked contently in the cool shade of the trees. How I wished my life was as simple as those animals. Right now, it was anything but. Once I caught my second wind, I trudged home in disappointment. This will most likely be the first and last time that I ever go out of my way to tell a boy how I felt about him.

When I made it home, Norie was waiting for me on the front porch playing with her dolls. She looked up from them and smiled brightly at me as I climbed the stairs to the porch. I wish I still held the innocence of a 5-year-old child. Life seemed so much simpler then.

"Heyyyy, Auntie Corie!"

Rustling her hair with my hand, I smiled back at her. It was so hard to be upset around this kid, she just made everything seem better instantly. "Hey, Norie... What are you up to?"

Norie held up one of her rag dolls and handed it to me. "Playing dollies. Wanna play?"

Sitting down next to her on the wooden porch, I said, "Of course."

Playing dollies with my niece lightened my mood, which I was extremely grateful for. During the 30 minutes that we were playing I didn't think about the incident that just happened with Ashner not once. We were so engrossed in our fairytale child's play, that you could imagine my surprise to hear the sound of a pickup truck entering our yard and parking in our driveway.

Norie lay the doll she was holding down in her lap and pointed out to the yard. "Auntie Corie, there's that cute boy again."

My heartrate quickened as I looked out into the yard and saw Ashner climbing down out of his black truck. Glancing over at my niece, I said, "Norie, do auntie a favor and go in the house for a minute. We'll finish playing dollies in a bit."

Norie looked out into the yard at Ashner who had just shut his truck door and was now leaning against it watching us. Giving him a small wave and a smile, she stood up, kissed me lightly on the cheek before running to the front door and entering the house.

Placing the doll that I was still holding down on the porch, I stood up slowly, brushing off my pants with my hands before descending the steps and heading out into the yard. I could feel the anxiety I had been trying to fight earlier rise back up with every step that I made towards him. When I was finally standing in front of him, his face bore an expression of curiosity.

"Cora, why did you show up at my house this morning?"

"It doesn't matter now, Ashner... It was a mistake."

Ashner raised his eyebrows. "A mistake?" Rubbing his chin, that upon further examination I noticed had sprouted the beginning hairs of a beard, he chuckled. "A mistake. It was a mistake for you to come running alllll the way over to my house at nine this morning?" Pushing himself off of the truck, he stepped closer to me. "Do you really expect me to believe that?"

He was so close to me that I could smell his cologne. Swallowing, I nervously bit the bottom of my lip and nodded. My heart was beating wildly against my ribcage. Could he hear it, too?

"My daddy told me that you came over there to 'cause you had somethin' very important to tell me. So how was your coming over to the house this morning a mistake?"

He had me there. I should've known Mr. Jones was going to tell him what I had said. I started looking at the world around me, at any and everything I could so I wouldn't have to look at him.

"Cora..." Ashner said as he cupped the sides of my face with both of his hands and stared me directly in the eyes. "What did you want to say to me?"

I tried to turn my head away from him, but he wouldn't let me. How could I tell him how I really felt about him now after seeing him this morning with Teresa? He had almost kissed her, and God knows how many other times he has kissed her before today.

"Cora... Tell me what you wanted to tell me earlier... Please."

"I... I can't now. It doesn't matter anymore. I saw you there with Teresa at the stables. It doesn't matter." I moved my hands upward and placed them firmly on top of his and attempted to push his down off of my face, but he wouldn't budge.

"It does, matter, Cora. Anything that you could ever have to say to me matters. Cora, I meant it when I told you weeks ago that I love you and even though you basically told me to get lost, that hasn't changed. I've loved you since we were kids. When you wore your wild red hair in pigtails and I used to chase you around the playground with dead bugs and lizards. You ran away from me and squealed like you were scared even though we both knew you weren't scared of those types of things. So, please... Cora... Tell me what was so important that it couldn't wait until you saw me at school on Monday."

He still loves me? How can he if he's with Teresa now?

"Ashner... It's hard for me to say this to you after how badly I treated you. After how, like you said, I pushed you away."

"Baby, none of that matters now... The only thing that matters is that you have somethin' you want to tell me now. The rest is history. In the past. So, what is it? Or are you gonna make me grow old out here waitin' on you to spill the beans?"

Inhaling deeply, I exhaled my response in one quick sentence. "Ashner Jones, I love you and have just realized that I have always loved you and I am so sorry that I had pushed you away because I was scared of fallin' in love and what it all meant."

I tried to look away from him, but he wouldn't let me. My nerves were just about all shook by now. Ashner smiled brightly and before I knew what was even happening, he bent his head down and kissed me hard on the lips. Lowering his hands from my face, he held me in an embrace and my body felt like jelly in his arms. *My first kiss... Oh, my God, this is my first kiss!*

Pulling away from me, Ashner grinned. "I've been waiting half my life for this moment."

Blushing, I couldn't contain my giddiness. I felt dazed and intoxicated, as if I were flying high in the sky right now. Who knew that a kiss could make a girl feel so good? I sheepishly looked up at him through my eyelashes and saw that he was still grinning as if he had just won one of the football grand championships or something.

"Why are you grinnin' so much?" I couldn't help but ask.

"'Cause I feel like I just won a million bucks."

"But, you didn't."

Ashner reached down and grabbed one of my hands and held it tightly in his. "No, I won somethin' even better."

"What's that?"

"Your heart."

Frowning slightly, an unpleasant thought of Teresa entered my mind. What would become of their relationship now? Did this kiss and my confession mean that they were over or was I foolish for even telling him how I felt?

"What about Teresa?"

Shaking his head, he lifted my hand that he was holding and placed it to his lips. Kissing it softly, he looked me in the eyes and said, "I ended that as soon as you ran off this morning, Cora. She wasn't the right girl for me. I only went out wit' her because she asked me to and all the boys on the team said I should be wit' her since she's a cheerleader and all. You know how that goes. Star quarterback of the team and the head cheerleader sort of deal. But my heart wasn't in it because she isn't you. No one else could ever compare to you. I was eventually going to break up wit' her anyways."

"But I'm just a nobody. A goody two shoed, bookworm. People at school call me a nerd."

"You are somebody to me. You're that same overly smart, beautiful, and talented girl that I fell in love with way back in grade school. The girl I used to seek and peek at in class. If you're a nerd, you're my nerd, now." Ashner leaned in and gave me another kiss on the lips, quicker this time. "I could get used to this. I don't think I'll ever stop wanting to kiss those beautiful lips of yours."

"Me, too," I said giggling and I meant it. I never wanted him to stop kissing me.

"Now, since we got the big part out of the way... Tell me why you were so scared of me? Of us? I hope that you know that I would never intentionally hurt you."

Ashner and I got into his truck and we talked for a long while about my fears of being involved in a relationship and how I had been fearful of ending up like Mama and Sister. He was really understanding, as I should've known he would have been. We had been close friends for years ever since his father had started bringing Big Ma corn, tomatoes and other vegetables that the family grew on their farm. Mr. Jones' dad and my granddaddy had been best friends coming up, so our families went way back.

After Ashner had left, I went inside the house and found Mama, Sister, Norie and Isaiah all sitting down in the front room watching our black and white television. No one looked my direction, as I was headed towards my room, Norie burst out singing, "Corie and Ashes sittin' in the tree, K-I-S-S-I-N-G!"

Mama and Sister burst out laughing as I spun around, embarrassment written all over my face. "Norie!" I exclaimed as she exploded in a fit of giggles.

Looking at my sister and mama, I asked, "So, I guess you all saw what happened in the yard, huh?"

"Yup... Gone head wit' yo' bad self, babe," Sister said, her smile reaching her eyes in glee.

"I'm so proud of you, baby," Mama replied.

"Kiss... Kiss!" Isaiah said while looking up at me from his position on the linoleum tiled floor in front of the television.

"Oh, dear, Lord, not you, too, Junebug! Please tell me that they didn't have you in on this, too," I said, laughing.

"Is Ashes your boyyyyyfriend now?" Norie asked as she jumped up from her seat on the couch and ran over to me.

"His name is Ashner, kiddo, and yes, I think he is."

Norie frowned at the correction, then said, "I like Ashes better," with a shrug before walking over to where her mother was sitting and climbing up in her lap.

"I'm happy for you, babe," Sister said as she ran a hand through her daughter's hair.

I smiled. I was happy for me, too. I just hoped that it lasted.

*

The next few weeks of life were pure bliss for me. Ashner and walked around school as a couple to the envy of all the Negro girls in our class. Teresa really hated me now, more than she had before Ashner broke up with her, but it really didn't bother me much. We had stopped being friends in grade school shortly after she and Zannie Mae got into that fight. When she had asked me to choose between the two of them and I refused, she'd called me a "two-faced bitch" and had never spoken to me again.

We had accompanied Zannie Mae and Jimmy to the Octoberfest dance and I had a ball with my boyfriend. I found myself wondering if it would've been worth it not telling Ashner how I felt about him and missing out on being with him. He was the best thing next to sliced light bread in my opinion and I couldn't picture life without him now. The only thing that worried me was my future. I still planned on leaving Tennessee after graduation and going off to school somewhere up North. Maybe I could stay with my Uncle Sammie and his new wife who happened to be his fourth wife, Deborah, in Chicago. I could hopefully make a few dollars helping them watch after their twin boys by babysitting.

Sitting on top of a picnic table outside of the high school, I watched Ashner and his football buddies down on the football field practicing. He had asked for me to wait up for him to get out of practice so that he could take me home from school today. There were several people in the bleachers watching the boys practiced, but I still preferred my solitude and opted to sit away from the field in peace. I was so engrossed in watching Ashner run up and down the field that I didn't notice a group of girls both black and white, mostly all cheerleaders approaching me until they were standing directly in front of me blocking my view of the field and of Ashner.

A white girl who bore a striking resemblance to me with her fire engine red hair and blue eyes, spoke first. "So, you're the bitch that stole Ashner away from Teresa?"

Her tone and choice of words took me aback for a minute. "Excuse me?"

"You heard me, skank."

"Why are you calling me out of my name and what does my dating Ashner have anything to do wit' you?"

"It's simple. Teresa's one of us. She's a cheerleader honey and you... You aren't nothing. Just some high yella trash. What the star of the football team sees in you over her, I can't possibly see." Looking from side to side at her fellow cheerleaders, she continued, "Right, girls?"

"Right!" The group of girls responded back in unison.

"I don't appreciate what you just said to me," I replied calmly. There wasn't any way that I was going to allow Teresa's minions to get under my skin. I couldn't believe that instead of approaching me herself she had to have her friends come to talk down on me for her.

"And what're you gonna do about it, bitch?" A tall Negro cheerleader, who I recognized from junior high school, named Bertha questioned with her hands placed firmly on her hips. Her cheerleader uniform looked odd on her disproportioned body. She was very chest heavy but didn't have any thighs or butt at all.

Gathering up my books, I slid off of the picnic table and eased my way on around the simple-minded girls. "For starters, practice is almost over, and I am goin' to go down on that field, give my boyfriend and big kiss and then head home with my *boyfriend.* If Teresa has a problem with that, tell her to call me or better yet come talk to me in person, she knows where I stay." With a flip of my hair over my shoulders, I threw them a small wave while departing. "Bye girls."

Although I kept the outwardly appearance of being calm in front of those ignorant girls, inside I was fuming. I couldn't believe that Teresa had the audacity to ask her friends to confront me on her behalf. And another thing that I couldn't get out of my mind was how much that one white girl looked like me. *Are we related? Is she a Baxter?*

As I walked towards the football field I tried to keep my mind off of what had just transpired between me and those girls, but I couldn't. Never in my life had I been so irritated by a bunch of hormonal females. I always kept to myself at school unless I was with Zannie Mae or more recently with Ashner. Every so often I could be seen chatting it up with a fellow classmate or studying with someone in the library, but in all honesty, I enjoyed being alone because it kept me out of trouble. Sister had stayed in trouble constantly when she was in high school for hanging around the wrong type of girls and I had vowed never to cause Big Ma any heartache in that area. Even though Big Ma was now resting well in Heaven, I still had no earthly desire to have any run-ins with school authorities like my big sister did when she was enrolled in school.

When I neared the football field, I saw Teresa sitting on the bleachers with a smug look on her face surrounded by a couple of other Negro girls I used to be friends with in grade school. I still found it crazy that when Zannie Mae came to our school and became my friend in fourth grade, everyone else wanted to be friends with me, too. The closer I got to where they were, the more they started whispering and pointing my way, laughing. I pretended that I didn't even see them and searched for Ashner on the field. He was gathering up his football equipment before heading down to the Boys' locker room to change.

"Look at that girls," I heard Teresa's voice rise as I continued to walk past the bleachers. "There goes that damn half-breed that Ashner seems to like so much." Teresa's two friends started snickering as if she had just allowed the funniest joke in the world to pass her lips.

"I don't see what he even sees in her ugly self," Ramona, one of the girls pitched in. "He must like his women almost white, but don't worry, T, she ain't got a thang on you."

"Right, Ramona," Ashley, the other girl chimed in, "He'll be back wit' Teresa in no time once he gets tired of her little flat chested self. She looks like a little tail girl. No titties and no booty. Such a waste of his time. Plus, she ain't even cute to look at wit' her funny lookin' self."

"Yeah, once my baby, Ashner, starts missing my good stuff, he'll be back. Her little scared, virgin ass can't handle a real man like him, the way I can," Teresa announced smugly.

When I heard her last statement, I froze in my tracks. Surely, Ashner and Teresa hadn't made love? No, he wasn't like that. For as far back as I could remember, he had never once tried to get me to get busy with him. He hadn't as much as tried to kiss me until the day I had told him I loved him a month ago. Clutching my stack of school books to my chest, I lifted my head up high and commenced to walking again. Ashner saw me approaching the field and ran up to greet me, smiling. When he drew closer, his smile faded as he noticed the discontentment upon my face.

"Baby, what's wrong?" he said, leaning in to kiss me on the cheek as he does every time he sees me after a long period of not being in each other's company. I pulled my face away and his lips met nothing but the cool afternoon air.

"Cora?"

"I'll talk about it wit' you in the truck." Holding my hand out, I asked, "Can I get the keys?"

Ashner looked taken aback by my words and tone. Reaching down into his knapsack, he pulled out the keys to his truck and handed them over to me without a word. Taking the keys from him, I left Ashner standing on the field alone looking after me. I knew I was being a brat, but Teresa's words had gotten underneath my skin. She had given him the one thing I knew I wouldn't be able to. There was no way that I would be able to lay down with him in that way and risk getting in the family way. My future meant way more to me than that. I honestly don't even think children were in my future. I had spent too much of my younger years looking after Isaiah and the idea of having a child frightened me.

By the time Ashner had made it to the truck, I had resolved in my mind to break things off with him. It would be for the best. Then he could go around with girls like Teresa and the other cheerleaders who were popular for not only their looks, but the things they did in the back of pickup trucks, apparently.

Ashner opened the driver's side door, climbed in and shut the door softly behind him. Without a word, he cranked the truck and peeled out of the school's parking lot and headed down a road that led into the neighboring county. Once we were about 20 minutes away from our hometown, he pulled over to the side of the road and killed the engine. Turning in his seat, he faced me, concern plastered over his handsome face. I hated that I was upsetting him, but I couldn't compete with Teresa. She was the type of girl he needed, not me. Not some scared, mixed up and confused virgin. I had heard the girls around school whispering in the bathrooms plenty of times saying that all guys wanted to get between girls' legs at our age. It was just the thing to do when you came of age and from watching my older sister in the past, I knew what they were saying was true.

"What's goin' on wit' you, baby?" Rubbing the back of his neck, his brown eyes focused in on me. "I mean, you were fine earlier today, but now you're actin' and weird and things. And you honestly looked spooked right now."

I couldn't bear the keep eye contact with him, so I looked downward and started chipping away at the pink nail polish on my nails. Norie had wanted me to paint her nails the other night, so we took some of Sister's nail polish and played in it. "I think…" I started quietly, then stopped. My throat started closing up with unshed tears. The thought of living life without him was breaking my heart, but it had to be done.

"What, Cora?"

"I think… That we need to break up," I finished, just barely above a whisper.

The silence in the truck was beyond deafening. My anxiety was reaching a new level of desperation to escape this moment and I started chipping away at the nail polish on my thumbnail with more fervor. Ashner reached over the seat and placed a solid hand on top of mine, halting my manic chipping.

"You don't mean that, baby."

I let out a breath that I didn't even realize I was holding in and said, "I do…"

"Look at me, Cora."

I wouldn't look at him, I couldn't. My heart was breaking in two and my mind was telling me that I was dead wrong to leave him, but I couldn't stay with him and keep him from being with someone who could give him what he wanted.

"Cora, baby… What happened? Did Teresa and her goons say something to you? I saw them giggling and carrying on after you left me alone on the field. Just tell me what they said so I can fix this. I can't lose you, baby. I can't and won't lose us. You're the best thing that has ever happened to me."

With tears threatening to fall from the corners of my eyes, I turned my head to look at him. He still held his hand firmly on top of mine, warming mine against the slight chill in the truck due to the November autumn weather. "How come you didn't tell me that you and Teresa… That you… Oh, God!" I burst into tears at the idea of the love of my life, the only guy I had ever held feelings for sharing such an intimate experience with someone else, especially if that someone else was Teresa.

"Baby, what did Teresa say to you?"

Anger at the thought of them together mounted up like eagles within me and I snatched my hands from underneath his. "How could you have slept with her?!" Nostrils flaring, I pushed the latch on the passenger's side door and jumped down out of the truck. Slamming the door, I walked blindly down the vacant road with sadness coating my face in a sea of salty tears. Pulling Ashner's letterman jacket closer around my body to shield me from the crisp chill in the wind, I continued to stomp down the road. I had no idea where I was or where I was going, but I had to get far away from him.

I could hear the sound of Ashner slamming the truck door off in the distance as I continued my trek madly down the road.

"Cora!" He called out to me, but I didn't stop and only quickened my pace. "Cora! Wait!"

Wiping away angry tears, I pressed my way on down the road and came upon a blue painted store off the side of the road. Fear gripped at my heart when I saw two burly, red-necked men look up at the sound of my footsteps. The biggest one of them who had brunette hair that was long and scraggly looking, rubbed the hair stubble of his beard on his chubby face. Smirking, he spit out a stream of tobacco juice onto the ground and nudged his companion, who was a dirty blonde headed guy with piercing gray eyes. A younger looking, dark haired white boy looked on in curiosity at me. He appeared to be my age or slightly older and I couldn't tell if he was one of them or one of the white people that actually liked blacks. He raised an orange soda bottle to his lips and drank from it, taking in the sight before him.

"Well, what do we have here, Chuck?" The scraggly hair man said before sucking his teeth. "Looks like we got us a no good wanna be white gal comin' our way."

Chuck kicked off some dried mud on one of his construction boots with the back of the other one and took a swig of beer from the bottle he was holding. "Looks to be that way, Jake. What we gonna do 'bout this damn zebra that done escaped the zoo?"

I froze in my tracks, fearful to make a move. I knew that lots of racist white people didn't like people like me who were both Negro and White. They hated to see the races mix and believed that their race was the one and only pure race. Ashner ran up behind me and I squealed. Placing his hand over my mouth to stifle my cry, he eyed the men down.

"We don't want any trouble. We just lost our way for a second. We'll be on our way now." Ashner lowered his hand from my mouth and whispered in my ear, "Don't say a word. Just slowly walk backwards with me."

My entire body was shaking, but I mustered up enough strength to nod in response. I slowly willed my feet to cooperate with my mind and started walking backwards with him as he had requested.

"Naw, nigger, it doesn't work like that," Jake said as he took a few steps closer towards where we were. "This here is a whites' only establishment and y'all have just trespassed. You know what we do to trespassers like yourselves?"

"Just ignore them, Cora, let's go." Ashner grabbed my hand and yelled, "Run!"

Adrenaline kicked into overdrive and I stumbled after him as we ran back up the road towards his truck. My dress shoes slipped and slid on the muddy parts of the outsides of the paved road.

"Get back here!" The angry voice of one of the men called after us.

"Keep running, baby. Keep running!" Ashner coached me and I held onto his hand for dear life as I attempted to keep up with him. My heart beat against my chest as if it were about to burst. My breaths felt as if they were being caught in my windpipe and my throat was starting to ache. Off ahead in the distance, I could see Ashner's truck sitting on the side of the road where we left it. We were almost there. Almost to safety. Once we reached the truck we could get far away from these men and their backwards thinking ways.

I heard the sound of heavy boots hitting the pavement behind us. I looked back and saw that Jake and Chuck were gaining on us. The younger guy that had been standing outside with them was nowhere to be seen. Chuck stopped and picked up a huge rock out of the neighboring ditch and threw it at us. Before I could warn Ashner, the rock made contact with the back side of his head and he cried out in pain, before stumbling to the ground.

"Ashner!"

Falling to my knees, I hovered over him. Blood was pouring out from the back of his head, spilling onto the ground beneath his body. Pulling his upper body into my lap, I gently caressed the side of his face. "Baby, are you o-kay?" I choked out.

Behind me, whoops of joy came from the men. "Look at that Jake, I got that nigger good!"

Cradling Ashner in my arms, I watched in fear as the men approached us. "Leave us be! We haven't done a thing to you!" Tears fell from my face onto Ashner's. His eyes were closed, but his chest was rising and falling, informing me that he was still breathing and was still alive.

"Yes, you have, you half-breed wench! I hate wanna be whites like you!" Jake said as he and Chuck approached us.

The blare of a car horn startled the men and stopped them dead in their tracks before they could take another step towards us. An older, white haired man, who was the size of the two men in stature, stepped out of a white car and slammed the door. The young guy who had been standing around with Jake and Chuck, slipped out of the passenger's side of the car and stood there watching us with his hands placed on the car door.

"Jacob! Charles! What in God's name do you think that you are doing out here?!" The older man fumed, his white face growing redder with every word he spoke. "Danny here came inside and got me and told me that you were pestering two kids. What do you have to say for yourselves?"

The evil smirks that the two men were wearing upon their faces just seconds earlier, disappeared and they looked like two small children right then.

"We weren't doin' anything, Daddy. Just messin' wit' them, that's all," Chuck said.

The older man peered behind Jake and Chuck and saw me holding onto Ashner. "Oh, my God! What did you boys do?!" Rushing over to me, the he pushed Chuck out of the way and took a handkerchief from his back pants pocket and stooped down to my level. Pressing the cloth against the back of Ashner's head caused Ashner to moan.

The older man turned his head up towards to where his sons were standing, eyes flashing, he said, "This is not how your mother and I raised you! For God's sakes you were raised in the church and you know that everyone is a child of God no matter the color of their skin! Is this how you would want to be treated?"

Turning towards me, he said, "My name is Mr. Howard. I am so sorry, child. I apologize on the behalf of my ignorant sons. How'd this happen? What did they do?"

"They threw a rock at us while chasing us down the road, sir," I replied quietly. "Please help my boyfriend."

Mr. Howard scooped Ashner's body up into his arms as if he weighed next to nothing. "Is this here y'all's truck?"

"Yessir, it is."

"Open the tailgate so I can lay him down in the back. I'll drive y'all to the hospital."

I did as Mr. Howard commanded and climbed into the back of the truck with Ashner. Taking off Ashner's jacket, I covered his body with it and held him closely to me.

"Jacob, you take my car back on down to the store with Charles. I'll deal with the two of you when I get back home and don't think for a second that I'm not telling your mother because I am." Looking at Danny, he gestured towards the truck. "Danny, boy, you're coming with me. I don't trust you to be around your brothers right now."

Danny slithered around his older brother, Jake, and walked briskly towards the truck and climbed into the truck bed with me. Once the door the tailgate was lifted, Mr. Howard put the truck in gear and sped off down the road back into town.

"Everything's goin' to be alright, now, baby," I said to Ashner as I held his head in my lap. He groaned in response and I fought the urge to cry some more. The tears from earlier had dried up, but I couldn't help but beat myself up for getting us in this mess. It was all my fault.

"I hope your friend is going to be okay," Danny said, breaking my thoughts. I had almost forgotten that he was back here with us.

Looking at him, I nodded. The wind blew wildly through his dark, medium length locks as trees whirred past him in the background. His cheeks and nose were becoming rosy from the chilly temperature outside and I was quite sure that my complexion matched his right now. His brown eyes were soft as he spoke again, "I'm sorry about my brothers." Shaking his head, he clenched his fists at his sides. "I hate that I'm even related to those cowards. That's what they are you know. Cowards. They hate everything and anyone that doesn't look like them."

"Oh..."

Danny frowned thoughtfully. "Dad was right, you know, when he said that he and mother didn't raise us up like that." Pointing towards the front of the truck where we could see Mr. Howard through the back window of the cab steering us down the road, he continued, "Dad's a preacher. He has always taught us right from wrong and to treat everyone the same, no matter their race, but somehow my brothers don't agree with him."

Raising an eyebrow, I asked, "But you do?"

"Of course! I'm not anything like my brothers. I'm the one who had Dad to come follow you. I didn't want my brothers to do anything to hurt you." Looking down at Ashner laying in my lap, he said, "But it looks like I was too late."

"Your brothers must do this sort of thing all the time?"

"I've seen them do worse."

Before I could ask him what the worse was, the truck came to a still in the emergency zone of the local hospital. Nurses ran out of the hospital with a gurney and placed Ashner on it and quickly ushered him inside. Mr. Howard and Danny walked up to the emergency entrance with me and stopped just outside of the doors.

"Here you go, young lady," Mr. Howard said with a small smile as he handed over the truck keys to me.

Taking the keys from him, I looked up at him in bewilderment. "You aren't coming in wit' me?"

Shaking his head, Mr. Howard clapped his son on the shoulder. "Nope, little lady, Danny and I need to get headed back home. Once again, I'm terribly sorry about what my boys did today. It was wrong and uncalled for." Reaching into his trouser pocket, he pulled out a worn brown wallet. Opening it, he took out some paper bills and gave it to me without counting them. "This should cover that young fella's treatment."

"How are y'all gonna get home?"

Mr. Howard smiled. "Don't worry about us, we'll find our way." Looking at his son, he said, "Come on boy, let's get to trekking."

Danny gave me a slight smile and wave before walking off down the sidewalk with his dad. Turning around, I pushed through the emergency doors and entered the hospital. I would never forget what Mr. Howard and his son had done for me today. It was the first time in my life that the other half of me had ever shown me true kindness. Until then, I never knew that whites could ever look at me with anything but disgust.

Chapter 11

The rock that was thrown at Ashner had knocked him unconscious for a bit. He had a pretty bad knot on the back of his head and a terrible headache, but other than that, the doctor said that he would be fine. I called his parents and my mama to let them know what happened and where we were. They were devastated that we had just experienced such an ordeal and said they would be down to pick us up shortly.

With a heavy heart, I sat in the chair next to Ashner's hospital bed and held his hand. I couldn't believe how stupid I had been. I could've gotten us both killed and for what? All because I was mad about something he had done with Teresa before we were even together? Guilt overwhelmed me, and I buried my head on the cover laying on top of Ashner's legs and wept.

I felt Ashner's hand run through my curls and heard his voice calling out to me. "Cora, baby, stop crying."

With my eyes full of tears, I lifted my head to look at him. I was a horrible girlfriend. How could I have allowed this to happen to someone that I loved? "I... I'm sorry, Ashner. Oh, God, I'm sorry, baby!"

"It's okay, Cora. You ain't make those men come after us or do what they did. I'm just happy you're okay. They ain't touch you or nothin', did they?"

Shaking my head, I wiped my tears away with the back of my hand. "This is all my fault. I shouldn't have ever gotten out of the truck and walked off! I didn't even know where we were."

Ashner's beautiful brown eyes focused in on me full of love. "Stop blaming yourself. I'm fine and you're fine. That's all that matters."

"No, it's not. Nothin' is gonna happen to those men for what they did to you and you know it. If their daddy hadn't of come along they could've killed us both and no one would even have done anything. Just like wit' my Uncle Joe!"

"Baby, that's just the way of the world right now, but it won't always be this way."

And he was right. If I had anything to do with it, the world was going to change. I would stand up for my Negro brothers and sisters just like so many before me had. Today had scared me to death, but I wasn't dead, yet. I was going to let the Lord use me to make a change in this world just like Big Ma had asked me to on her death bed.

"I don't deserve you," I whispered.

Ashner chuckled, then groaned slightly at the pain caused by laughing. "Maybe not, but you're stuck with me, baby."

Standing to my feet, I bent over and gave him a sweet kiss on the lips. Cupping his face in my hand, I said, "I love you, Ashner Jones."

"I know you do. I love you, too, Cora Harris and one day, Imma prove to you just how much that I do."

Reaching for my free hand, Ashner looked at me with seriousness in his eyes. "I want you to know that I never messed around with Teresa like that. Not her or any other girl. I wanted to save that part of me for someone special and that someone is you... Whenever you're ready."

Hearing that Ashner and Teresa had never messed around before only made me feel worse about myself and what I had gotten us into. How he could still love me and want to be with me after what I did was nothing short of a miracle.

Ashner remained out of school for the following week recuperating from his head injury. When classmates asked me about what happened that day after school, I refused to talk about it. It really wasn't anyone's business and I especially didn't appreciate people who rarely even looked my way or spoke to me all of sudden deciding they could butt into my personal affairs.

One girl who I found particularly annoying now, even more than Teresa if you could imagine that, was the white girl who decided to be Teresa's spokesperson that one day after school. Every time she saw me she would go out of her way to be loud and obnoxious and point out how poorly I was dressed compared to the popular cheerleaders or how much I was shaped like a little girl and how she felt that I would never compare to how great of a girl Teresa was. Although she was getting on my last nerve, I still couldn't quite get pass the fact that she favored me so much. We had the same vibrant blue-green eyes and curly red hair, but she had freckles sprinkled across the bridge of her nose the same as Sister did. If she wasn't such a witch to me last week, I would've probably asked her if she was related to Billy Baxter by any chance.

The mystery surrounding my father still bothered me. The only things that I knew about Billy was that he had knocked Mama up twice and supposedly had a chain of kids living in this county and the county over. He was also rumored to be racist, but how could that even be possible when Mama was said to be so in love with him when she was a mere teenaged girl? If he was indeed such a racist white man, how did Mama end up pregnant with Sister and then with me an entire five years later? Things just weren't adding up. While I knew a lot of the Baxters' were a prejudiced bunch, how could Mama have fallen in love with him? Was she just blind to the fact that he was prejudiced or just simply didn't care?

Before breakfast on Saturday morning while Mama stood frying mackerel patties at the stove, I decided to ask her about the situation. Norie was in the front room watching the Saturday morning cartoons with Isaiah and sister was still asleep. The fragrant smells of the mackerels frying alongside seasoned cut potatoes wafted through the kitchen tenderly teasing my nostrils. My stomach started to growl ferociously from hunger, so I scooped up one of the homemade biscuits sitting in the cloth towel lined bread basket in front of me and placed it on the plate on the table before me. Slicing the biscuit open, I smiled as steam rose from it. Dipping a butter knife into some strawberry preserves that Mother Joannie Williams from church makes, I lathered it across the inside of one halve of the biscuit before covering it with the other halve. Lifting the buttery goodness to my mouth, I took a huge bite and savored the moment.

Mama looked over at me and laughed. Shaking her head, she wiped her hands on Big Ma's old apron before turning off the eyes on the stove. "You were always the one child of mine that enjoyed food the most. Mama used to call and tell me all about it. I see that no matter how old you're gettin' none of that is changing."

My mouth was full of biscuit, so I gave her an "Mmm hmm" in response.

Mama pulled out a chair from underneath the kitchen table and sat down. "You wanna go wake up Sister and get Junebug and Norie in here for breakfast?"

Looking over at her, I raised a pointer finger in the air asking her to "hold on", then I grabbed a glass of milk and chugged it down. Licking my lips, I said, "Actually, Mama, there's somethin' that I really want to discuss with you if you don't mind."

"Sure, baby, what's on your mind?"

Taking a deep breath, I wondered to myself how I should phrase my question about my dad. I didn't know whether or not the subject of Billy Baxter was a sore one with Mama or not because it surely was with Big Ma when she was living. Big Ma couldn't stand the air that Billy Baxter breathed.

Mama's nervous tick started up as she awaited my question. I had learned that she had gotten it after abusing different types of drugs for so many years. "Well?" She asked with her brown eyes focused in on me.

"This is kinda hard to ask, but, how did you get involved wit' my daddy?"

"Hmm... I was wonderin' when you were gonna ask me that. You have always been an inquisitive child, different than Billie in that way. You've always wanted to know the ins and outs of the world, whereas your sister would rather go through life forgetting the past or ignoring reality as it is. Billie, bless her heart, would never even think to ask me about y'all's father because she would rather pretend that he doesn't exist."

Mama placed a hand flat alongside the tabletop and began lightly tapping it with her forefinger's nail. Sighing, she continued, "Billy and I met when I was just a sophomore in high school. I was walking home from school alone one afternoon and he pulled up beside me in his daddy's pickup truck. Now, baby, I can tell you straight off that I was scared out of my mind to see a white man stopping his truck beside me and when he stepped out of it, my heart was pounding harder than ten African Congo drums. Oh, I remember that day as if it were yesterday it's still so fresh in my mind. Billy slammed that old truck's door and walked over to me looking as handsome of a man I had ever seen. His red hair shone like copper as the sunlight touched it and his blue eyes pierced me right down to my very core. He came up to me and gently touch the side of my face before askin', 'What's a pretty thang like you a doin' walkin' down this road alone?' I stood there on the side of the dirt road clutchin' my school books to my bosom with fear. I was so nervous that I couldn't even answer him. I knew that white men had a history of raping and violating black girls, so I was afraid that this man was about to do the same to me."

My breath quickened inside my throat at the thought of mama being raped. "Did he... Did he... Rape you?"

Mama chuckled, brown eyes shining as she continued to reminisce. "Honey, naw. Billy wasn't anything like that. If he were, do you really think that there would've been a you born after your sister?"

Shrugging my shoulders, I continued to look on at her. The ways of the South were so unpredictable and backwards at times and I didn't really know whether or not Mama could have caught herself in one of those predicaments where she got raped twice by the same man. Things like that were known to happen to Negro women and nothing was hardly ever done by the law about it. I was going to work hard in the future to change that.

"Anyways, once I finally spoke up and told Billy that I usually walked home alone after school once my girlfriends went their separate ways, he decided to take me on home. I don't know why after talking to him for a while that I started feeling comfortable with him, but I did. I climbed up into his truck and away we went. I cautioned him to drop me off just a few feet from our driveway so that Mama and Daddy wouldn't see me being brought home by a white man. I wouldn't have heard the end of it."

Mama smiled warmly and took my hand in hers. When I closed my fingers around hers, her twitching stopped. "Baby, I fell in love with your father instantly after our first conversation. He wasn't like a lot of the white guys I had seen before. He treated me warmly and with respect. The only problem was that blacks and whites weren't supposed to be together in a love like relationship way back then. It's still frowned on in some parts of the United

States right now. From that first afternoon, Billy would meet me while I was walking every day after school. He would bring me flowers and everything."

She tilted her head back and inhaled deeply. "Oh, baby, he would bring me some of the prettiest flowers there was. Roses, lilies, buttercups... He would bring me chocolates and other little trinkets. I felt bad because our family didn't have much money, so I couldn't really give him anything in return, but Billy said none of that mattered, because all he needed from me was love."

"One day after school was different. Billy pulled his truck over to an unused side road and cut the engine. He looked at me with so much love in his eyes. Thinking back, it was probably lust, but in my young mind it was love. He leaned over the seat and grabbed me in an embrace and kissed me so warmly and deeply. It was my first kiss. Oh, and what a magical kiss it was. I felt like silk in his arms and there was a feeling down below that I had never felt before. While we were kissing, a heavy rainfall began to pour and beat down hard upon the truck. The pitter patter of rain on top of the roof made the moment feel even more romantic to me. Billy asked me if I was ready to heat things up a notch and all I could do was nod. I had no idea what I was in for, but all I knew was that it felt right with him at that moment in time. Next thing I knew, I was pregnant with your sister and my Mama and Daddy had a fit."

"So, what happened between y'all?" Things still didn't make sense to me. Everyone around town said Billy Baxter was a racist. Nothing was adding up. "What happened after Sister was born? Why didn't Billy stay around? Didn't he love his daughter?"

Mama's hand started to twitch again, and I gave her hand a squeeze. Rocking back and forth in her seat, she looked just like Isaiah did when he was anxious or uncomfortable. "Billy's daddy was a mean man, Cora. Oh, God, he was a mean old white man. When he found out that his son had not only knocked me up, but was in love with me, he beat Billy until he was black and blue. Billy came to me one evening right here at this very house with both of his eyes swollen almost clean shut. His face had so many bruises and cuts that it made me cry somethin' awful at the very sight of him. He told me that if he didn't stop seeing me that his daddy would do somethin' bad to hurt my family. His daddy threatened to kill all my brothers and sisters and hurt mama and hang daddy. When daddy heard us talking on the porch, he came outside with his shotgun and threatened to shoot Billy if he didn't leave our property."

A single tear started its slow descent down the left side of Mama's face and I reached out with my free hand and swiped it away. Mama's eyes wouldn't reach mine as she continued with her story. Her rocking in the chair intensified and I wanted badly to comfort her. "Billy's daddy was such a mean 'ole white man and he promised that he was gonna make my family pay for turning his son into a Nigger Lover. Oh, God! It was all my fault!" Mama's body started trembling violently and I stood from my seat and wrapped my arms around her.

"Mama, calm down!" I urged her in a high whisper. I didn't want her to alarm Norie or Isaiah in the other room.

"It was all my fault!" Mama's shoulders moved up and down as she started to weep. She was making such a commotion that I didn't even notice when Sister had stepped into the kitchen.

"Stripes, what's wrong wit' Mama?"

Looking up and over to where she was standing by one of the large cherrywood cabinets, I pleaded with my eyes for her to help me. "She was tellin' me the story about how she met daddy and now she's like this. I... I didn't know she would get like this."

Norie came tipping up to the doorway of the kitchen and Sister saw her peeping in. Pointing her finger, Sister said, "Out, now!"

Norie nodded and ran back into the front room.

Sister frowned and walked over to where we were. Mama was still saying that it was her fault. Pushing me out of the way, Sister took Mama's face into her hands. "Calm down, Mama. It's in the past. Whatever it is, leave it there."

Mama shook her head. "It's my fault why my sister died. Why Bertha died. Oh, God, it should've been me. I should've been here watching after her. But, where was I? I was already gone. I ran away and left all my problems here for my family to deal with!"

Oh, my God! Aunt Bertha! My mind flew back to when I was a little girl and Big Ma had her stroke and was delirious screaming about Aunt Bertha being raped and killed.

Mama's tears wouldn't stopped flowing and the entire top of her dress was soaked from them. "If I would've been here Billy's daddy would've killed me instead of her. Billy's daddy killed my baby sister!"

Both Sister and I sucked in our breath at the revelation that our paternal grandfather had raped and killed our aunt when she was only the precious age of nine years old. Tears flooded my face and I hated myself for even asking Mama to tell me about my daddy. This was just too much for me to bear. How could a man, any man do that to an innocent child?

Sister lifted Mama's face and looked into her eyes. With her thumbs, she wiped away Mama's tears and said, "It wasn't yo' fault, Mama. That was that man's doings and none of yours. You can't keep beatin' yo'self up for what Elmer Baxter did! You've done that for far too long. You ran away from yo' chil'ren and family 'cause you was runnin' away from guilt. You turned to drugs and sex wit' all sorts of men 'cause of yo' past, but you can't blame yo'self for what that awful man did."

Mama fell into Sister's stomach and Sister wrapped her arms around her frame, consoling her. "I'm sorry, so sorry. So sorry for leavin' y'all... All of y'all," Mama whispered.

"It's forgiven."

Once Mama had pulled herself together, she excused herself and went to her room. I felt lower than the tiniest earthworm right then. I had no idea the amount of pain that stood behind my family's past. I was only trying to get a better understanding of how my mama could be in love with a white man who was said to be one of the biggest racists in our town. I guess I was wrong about my daddy... But there was more I needed to find out, just not from Mama. There was no way that I would ever put her through that type of trauma again like I did today.

*

"Wow, so your daddy's dad raped one of your aunts and killed her when she was little? That is some heavy cow manure," Zannie Mae said as she painted her toe nails. She was sitting on her bed in her room, leaning back against the headboard.

"I know. I don't even know how to process this. But Mama's story still doesn't tell me how Daddy turned racist. Do you think it was because of his daddy? He made him that way?"

Zannie Mae put the top back on her red polish and twisted the top onto the bottle. "I don't know. I really don't. It doesn't make any sense. Your dad seemed to really love your mama and then how the hell did you get here if he didn't love her?"

I had been pacing the floor of Zannie Mae's room as I told her the encounter with my Mama the other day. Flopping down on her bed, I groaned. "That's what I don't know. We never got that far and I'm definitely not pullin' the scab off of mama's old wounds again."

"Well... Why don't you find Billy and ask him yourself?"

Turning my head sharply, I looked at her as if she had lost her mind. There was no way I was going to try and track that man down. What if he tried to kill me? "Zannie Mae, are you hearing yourself right now? The man is known to be prejudice against blacks. He has never been a part of me and my sister's lives, so I know for a fact that he doesn't want to have anything to do with me."

"I don't know, Cora... Something about all of this isn't adding up. I think people just may have the wrong perception of your father because of all the hateful things that his daddy and other Baxters' have done in this town." Taking sip of a cherry soda from a can that was sitting on her nightstand, she gave me a sad look. "If you don't talk to him, how will you ever find out what he's really all about and why things really didn't work out between him and your mama after you were born?"

I knew what she was saying was right, but how could I even talk to that man, if I found him? Last I heard he had been staying in the bottoms in some trailer, but that was a few years ago. I didn't even know where he was now. And if I found out that he had anything to do with Uncle Joe's death I would be devastated. There was no way that that much evil ran through my blood. No way.

Later on that evening, I went by Ashner's house to check in on him as I had done for the past week since the ordeal we had experienced. He was feeling a lot better and the knot on the back of his head had subsided substantially. I was so glad that he would be back at school on next week, because I had been lonely there without him. I know I still had Zannie Mae by my side, but things just weren't the same without my boyfriend around.

When I told him about how things went with my mama, he didn't agree with Zannie Mae about me going off to trying to find Billy and I didn't blame him. After everything that we had recently been through, Ashner wanted to take all the precautions that he could dealing with the white race. He was even against my dream about becoming an advocate for the Negro people once I graduated. I had decided to not only advocate for Negro women, but Negro men as well once I saw how poorly we had bene treated by those white men a couple of weeks ago. While I understood that Ashner was only trying to look out for my best interest because he loved me, nothing and no one would stand in my way of making a better way for blacks.

The next day at school the red headed white girl caught me all alone in the girls' bathroom. I was fixing my hair at the sink when I saw her walk into the room. Eyeing me down, she made a tsking sound. Instead of ignoring her as I have done in the past, I turned her way.

"Other than Teresa, why do you seem to hate me so much? Even the other cheerleaders have stopped being so mean to me. You're the only one who keeps on wit' all of this childish behavior. What have I ever done to you? I don't even know you and you definitely don't know me."

The girl eased her way into the room until she stood just a few inches from in front of me. Looking into her eyes were like looking into a mirror of my own except that hers seemed so full of evil and even more than that... Pain.

"I do know who you are, Cora Harris. You're the bastard child of a damn Negro woman and my daddy! And I have hated you all my life because of it!"

My mouth dropped at her statement. She was one of Billy Baxter's kids? Was she one of the ones that he had abandoned like Sister had told me about when I was little?

"So, you're my... My sister?"

The girl tilted her head back in mocked laughter. When she brought her head back down, she stared at me coldly, so cold it felt as if death was knocking at my door through her eyes. "I'm not shit to you. I wouldn't claim you as kin to me if we were the last two living souls on this earth."

Crossing my arms over my chest, I eyed her back down. "So, since you're one of Billy's kids, tell me why you hate me so much when I haven't ever done anything to you? It's not like I ever knew you existed and better yet, I don't even know your name."

Flipping her red curls over her shoulder, she placed her hands on her full hips. "Names Shelley, Shelley Baxter. And because of you, my daddy left my mama. I've hated you as far as I could remember because Daddy loved your mama more than he loved mine. He left mama to be with yours and she got pregnant with you, but guess what? Because your mama was so strung out on drugs, she broke daddy's heart and he hasn't been the same since. I was two years old when you were born, but I remember ever bit of seeing mama and daddy arguing. When I grew up mama told me that they had been arguing because daddy had fallen in love with some 'ole homewrecking Negro woman who had not one but two babies by him. I couldn't believe it. Daddy up and left my perfect mother because he couldn't be with yours. So, if you think for one second that you haven't done anything to me, you have just by being born!"

Shelley pushed me in the chest with both hands and I stumbled backwards, almost slipping on the tiled bathroom floor. Reaching out a hand, I caught a hold of the sink and saved myself from falling. "You're nuts! You had no right to touch me! I had nothing at all to do wit' your daddy leaving your mama!"

Narrowing her eyes at me, she took a step closer. "I plan on making your life a living hell, Cora."

Both our heads jerked up at the sound of the bathroom door opening. A teacher entered with a stern look upon her face. "What is the meaning of all of this?"

Shelley jumped back away from me and gave the teacher a smile. "Nothing, Mrs. Rupert, I was just having a friendly conversation with my girlfriend here."

Mrs. Rupert frowned and her plastic framed glasses slid down her nose. Pushing them back up on her face with her pointer finger, she looked on at us. "I thought I heard yelling?"

Shelley giggled, and placed a hand on her chest. "Oh, heavens no, Mrs. Rupert. If anything, that was my awful singing and we both know that I can't hold a tune."

Mrs. Rupert seemed to buy Shelley's lie, because she began to laugh along with her. "Oh, my dear, you are quite right. Well, young ladies, class is in session. Hurry right on along and go to your respective rooms."

"Yes ma'am," we both responded in unison. I skirted around Shelley and left the bathroom first. When Shelley entered the hall, she walked briskly to catch up to me. I smelled her sickeningly sweet overpowering perfume before she even reached me.

"This is far from over."

I stopped in my tracks and looked at her. "No, it is. I won't be bullied by you or anybody else at this school. I don't care what you think about me, but you won't ever be placing another finger on my body or I'm going to cut it off. That's a promise." Brushing up against her shoulder hard with mine, I stalked off and headed to class fuming.

I always knew that I would meet one of Billy's kids one day, but I had no idea it would be at my school or that they would hate me just for being born. For being part black, yeah, I could understand that due to the times we live in, but just based solely on my existence was beyond ridiculous. When Sister came home from work that evening, I filled her in on my encounter with our "sister".

When I entered our bedroom, Sister was sitting on the edge of her bed taking her stockings off. Slowly stretching her arms over her head, she yawned then reached down and rubbed one of her feet. "Oh, dear, Lawd... My dogs are killin' meh, Stripes."

"Hard day at work, huh?" I asked as I walked over to the opposite side of the room and sat down on my bed.

Nodding, Sister looked over at me with tired blue-green eyes. "I'm exhausted. I'm so thankful that Mama and Junebug are keepin' Norie occupied right now, 'cause I need a little rest."

"Before you lay down and take a nap, I was wonderin' if I could share somethin' wit' you?"

Sister scooted back on the bed until her back met the bedroom wall. Leaning up against it, she said, "Sure, lay it on meh."

"Well, an interesting thing happened to me today at school."

"Is that right?" Sister replied sleepily, her eyes growing heavy.

"Yeah, I met one of Billy Baxter's daughters."

Sister's eyes shot back open, alerted by what I had just told her. Sitting up straight on the bed, she cocked her head. "Say what now?"

"Ya' heard me. I met one of his kids today."

"Who? Which one?"

"A girl who is just a couple of years older than me. She's a cheerleader. Shelley Baxter."

Sister's eyes narrowed as if she were trying to place if she knew Shelley or not. "I've never even heard of that girl befo'. Honestly, I've never even met any of Billy's kids, so I wouldn't even kno' of one if they were standin' right next to me."

"Oh, you would recognize her if you saw her. She looks just like me, ceptin' she's white. She has your freckles and our blue eyes and red curly hair. Her body is all filled out like yours, too. She's not a twig like me."

Sister shook her head and smiled. "There ya' go wit' that twig stuff again. I wouldn't worry 'bout fillin' out. Yo' body will get there soon enough, but back to this girl. You sure she's Billy's kid? I mean, just 'cause she has some of our features don't mean a thang."

"Yeah, I'm positive. She even said that she's hated me since I was born because daddy left her mama for our mama. That's how I got here. He ran off from them to be wit' Mama, but Mama was so messed up on drugs that she broke his heart, and I'm guessin' mama ran back off up North when she got pregnant wit' me."

Sister shrugged, "I guess... It really doesn't even matter now, babe girl. Why are you so hell bent on findin' out 'bout the past? You're here and I'm here and that's all that matters. Billy Baxter is a no good redneck who happened to knock our mama up not once, but twice, then left us. That's all the story wrote and that's all you need ta' kno'."

Pulling back the top cover on the bed, Sister maneuvered her body underneath it and lay down. "I suggest you stay away from that Baxter girl, she's no sister of yours, but I am. That gal ain't gone want anythang ta' do wit' ya' black behind. Trust me." Rolling over, she closed her eyes and the next thing I heard from her was light snoring drifting towards me from across the room.

That night when I was lying in bed reading one of my favorite books about four siblings who discover a hidden magical world beyond the inside of their temporary guardian's wardrobe, Mama entered my room. I loved reading this particular story because it made me believe that anything could be possible in the world and dared me to dream of a life beyond the one that I currently lived.

"Cora, baby," Mama said in a hushed voice.

I looked up from my book and laid it on my lap. Mama was standing in the doorway with her hair wrapped up inside of a bonnet and she had a faded blue robe on with the frayed and worn belt tied tightly around her small frame. On her feet, she wore tattered black house shoes and I reminded myself to buy her a new pair for Christmas with the money I had saved that Aunt Trish had given me last year for my birthday.

"Yes ma'am?"

Wiggling her pointer finger, she said, "Come out to the front room with me... There's somethin' I want to show you."

Curious as to what Mama wanted to share with me, I pushed my book off to the side of the bed so that it rested on top of the covers and quickly jumped out the bed. Entering the front room, I saw Mama sitting on the couch with an old brown box sitting beside her. The light from the only lamp she had turned on, dimly lit the room.

"What's going on, Mama?"

Scooting over on the couch, she patted the now empty space on it and gestured for me to sit down next to her. Taking a seat beside her, I looked at her curiously as she lifted the brown box and placed it on her lap. I couldn't really tell what was inside of the box, but I had a feeling that whatever it was could potentially give me some more insight to her past. Mama was silent awhile before speaking.

"Cora... I'm sorry about how I broke down in front of you a little while back. I've just been holdin' in so many emotions pertaining to my sister's death that I've never really dealt wit' it all before. I used to take drugs to try to hide from my guilt and to ease the pain of her dying, so I never really allowed myself to grieve. God, Bertha died some what? Twenty-one years ago and until you started asking all those questions about your daddy, I never really released all that I had been holdin' on the inside of me until that day."

Looking at me, she gave me a small smile. Unshed tears glistened in her eyes and she blinked rapidly to drive them away. Sniffling, she wiped underneath her nose with a handkerchief that she had pulled from the pocket of the robe that she was wearing. Taking a deep breath, she continued, "Inside of this box holds a lot of answers to the questions that you may have about what kind of man Billy was. If you ever gain enough courage, I think it might be best that you try to find him and talk to him for yourself. Don't believe all of the lies that people around here say about him. He wasn't nothin' like and I would like to believe that he still isn't anything like his daddy and those other bad Baxters that he's kin to. Some people are guilty of things just by association. You can't help what family you are born into."

Handing the box over to me, she stood, then leaned over and planted a soft kiss upon my forehead. "Goodnight, sweet baby." Leaving the room, she headed towards the bedroom that once was Big ma's.

In the still quietness of the house, I sat with that box sitting upon my lap for about five minutes before I mustered up enough courage to peer inside. Lifting a towel that was covering the contents inside, I tossed it over on the side of me and it landed on the couch with a soft thud. Inside of the box was a stack of letters bound by a faded and stained pink ribbon, a couple of pictures, a dried rose, some small trinkets and a ring box.

Reaching inside of the box, I pulled out one of the pictures and the faces of a younger version of mama and a white man that I could only assume to be Billy Baxter, stared up at me. The couple were standing in front of a car parked on the street outside of some sort of store. Billy had his arm wrapped around Mama's waist and they were both smiling at the camera. I couldn't make out from the picture where they were, but wherever it was, it definitely wasn't here. Flipping the picture over, on the back a stamp inked onto the paper read: Los Angeles, CA 1948. It was taken two years after Sister was born.

Placing the photograph back into the box, I pulled out the stack of letters and sat the box to the side of me. Unraveling the ribbon, I pulled out the first envelope addressed to Mama when she was living in Chicago. Opening the envelope, I pulled out a yellowed sheet of folded paper and unfolded it. My eyes scanned over the words from my father to my mother so many years ago.

Glory Jean   *June 7th, 1952*

> *God, woman, don't you know just how much I miss you? I'm absolutely miserable without you and I don't know what I'm going to do. I can't keep living a lie. I just can't. It's killing me daily not being there for you and the girls. Our daughters, our precious babies made from our love. There's not a thing wrong with what we did. We fell in love, damnit! Two souls are allowed to do that. I hate the way*

some people in this world think and how they look at us when we're together, but none of that matters to me. What matters to me is that I gain access to your heart again. Come home, baby. I'll help you get off of that stuff for good this time. I'll make sure that no one else in my family ever hurts you or another member of your family for as long as I live! This I swear to you, Glory Jean. Listen, I plan on leaving Alice. I can't continue staying married to her knowing that I am fully in love with you. It's not fair to her or Shelley. She resents me, I know. The way she looks at me now is beyond unbearable and I can't keep breaking her heart. I never should have married her, but it's what my daddy wanted. He thought that if I married her it would free my mind of you, but he was wrong. All it did was make my heart ache for you more. For your touch, your kiss, your scent... Baby, please come home.

Every time I see Billie I want to go up to her and hug her and let her know that her daddy loves her, but I can't. I'm not strong enough to do this without you. Billie frowns at me every time she sees me. I can't stand the thought that she hates me, too. If only I would've held her a little tighter when you brought her to see me last year. I should've told her that I loved her then, but I was too chicken. How could I explain to our little girl why I hadn't been in her life for the five years she had been on this earth? How could I explain to her that I come from a family that is hell bent on hating anyone that doesn't look like they do? Glory Jean, I need you and I need them. I'm missing out on precious moments with my daughters all because of the times we live in. All because of stupid prejudices and ways that don't rightly make any sense to me. I wish your Mama would let me just take a glance at Cora. God, I bet that baby is as beautiful as you are. I hate to think that she isn't going to ever know who I am. Neither of the girls are. And what kills me most is that none of my children will ever get to grow up together. Alice will probably tell Shelley all kinds of hateful things about our girls and no matter what I try to say or do, it will probably all fall on deaf ears. I love Shelley just as much as I love Billie and Cora, but I'm not going to get a chance to be a father to none of them if I don't have you. Please come home. Help me rise out of this dark pit that I've fallen into. I love you.

Yours, Billy

Clutching the letter in my hands, I held back tears. My daddy loved us? He really wasn't racist like the rest of his family? A million thoughts ran through my mind as I tried to process what I had read. Sister had met our dad when she was little? How come she never mentioned it to me? I'm sure she hadn't forgotten such a momentous encounter like that one. If I would've met Billy when I was little I would never have forgotten it.

Folding the letter back up, I returned it to its envelope. Maybe Mama was right. I should try to reach out to Billy, but I didn't even know where to start. Shelley hated my guts, but she probably wouldn't know where he was and even if she did, I doubted seriously that she would even part her lips to tell me.

Picking up another letter, I silently thanked Mama for wanting to shed some light on Billy. For years now, it has been bothering me that I knew next to nothing about the man and I still hated the fact that Big Ma had lied to me for so long by telling me that my father was dead. If I ever did meet with him, I was going to ask him why he didn't try harder to be in our lives? Couldn't he have found mama and came and got me and Sister so that we could've been one big happy family? We could've left Tennessee and went up North somewhere away from the deeply rooted prejudices of the South. I know that there is racism everywhere, but we could've lived somewhere that was more tolerant of biracial relationships and families.

I could hear soft snoring echoing throughout the house and I knew that everyone else was asleep but me. I had a feeling I was going to be up for a long time tonight. I needed to discover who Billy Baxter was, but more importantly who I was and how this knowledge would shape who I would come to be.

Chapter 12

When Ashner made it back to school everyone was so thrilled to see him, especially Teresa. She made it a point to come over to our lunch table and lean over it which allowed a peek inside of her dress shirt where the tops of her breasts were exposed. I couldn't believe the amount of disrespect that she was displaying right before my eyes flirting with my boyfriend, but I had had just about enough of her. Zannie Mae sat next to the table with me and had been talking to her boyfriend before Teresa walked up to our table. She had been deeply involved in a conversation with him, but now her face was fire engine red as she shot daggers at Teresa. Even a blind man could see how desperate for attention and wrong Teresa was.

When Teresa giggled loudly and placed a hand lightly on Ashner's shoulder, Zannie Mae started to stand up and confront her, but I put out a hand to stop her. Shaking my head, I looked into her eyes and said, "No, let me handle this." Zannie Mae nodded and sat back down in her seat.

Rising from my seat, I walked over to the other side of the lunch table and snatched Teresa's hand off of Ashner's shoulder. Her head snapped back and she looked as if I had just struck her down with lightning. Snarling at me, she placed her hands on her hips. "I know you just didn't touch me!"

"You have no right to be over here flirting wit' Ashner right in front of my face. Have you no shame?"

Ashner grabbed me by the hand and looked up at me from his seat. "Baby, she was just welcoming me back to school. Teresa knows that I don't like her and only has eyes for you. She's not my type of girl and no matter how much flirting she calls herself trying to do, nothing will ever change that."

Teresa's face fell at his words and it looked as if she were about to cry. She had the same look on her face that she had when we were little girls and her pet cat Whiskers died. "But Ash…"

Ashner ignored her and stood slowly from his seat. Still holding my hand, he looked deeply in my eyes with such passion that it made me feel as if we were the only two people in the room. "I was going to save this for a more special occasion, but I want the entire school to know how much I love you so that there won't be any more problems or hearsay or rumors from anybody because everyone is gonna get this straight from the horse's mouth."

Dropping down to the cafeteria's floor on one knee, Ashner reached into his letterman's jacket pocket and pulled out a gold ring with a tiny diamond in the middle of it. The lunch room had been deathly quiet while watching our ordeal, but a collective gasp erupted at that moment. "Cora Leanne Harris, I have loved you since I first laid eyes on you when we were kids. I was just too foolish to say anything to you back then. I used to sneak and glance at you in class and got teased mercilessly by my friends because of it. When I look at you, I see my future. I see my whole life, and nothing would make me happier if you'd become my wife. Will you marry me and become my Mrs. Jones?"

I had not been expecting this. Like not in my wildest dreams. Just a few short months ago I had been scared out of my mind to date him and in denial of my feelings for him. Was I ready to be a wife? I mean, I was just a few days short of turning 17. What about my plans for the future? Would Ashner be willing to leave Tennessee and follow me while I go off to school? I had just recently decided that I would study law and become a Civil Rights Lawyer. I needed to go away to school to become that.

My hand was trembling inside of his. Looking into his eyes, I could feel that he would never intentionally hurt me or leave me and that whatever path God placed us on, we would walk it together. "Yes. Yes, I will," I said biting my bottom lip with a smile.

Ashner let out a whoop as he slipped the ring onto my ring finger and the entire cafeteria erupted into cheers. Teresa sauntered away from us dejectedly as Ashner stood to his feet and grabbed me into a tight embrace. Leaning his head down, he whispered into my ear words that calmed my fears, "Wherever you go, I will follow. I know God has big plans for you to change this world and I'm gonna be right by your side when you do. I'm sorry about before, too... Whatever you want to do in life, I'll support you fully."

The rest of the day flew by like a breeze. I couldn't quite believe that I was now engaged. I knew that Mama and Sister would be excited for me. Ashner and I decided that we would get married next year right after our high school graduation. We wouldn't have kids until after I graduated college and made a career for myself. Ashner said he was going to go off to school, too and take up studying business. He wanted to learn all that he could so that he would be able to start up his own horse training business one day.

Over the course of the next few weeks, I took on a part-time job working around the square at the local drug store. I swept the floors, stocked the shelves and helped customers out when they needed to find something. Since it was the holiday season, the store was always busy with people running in and out. One Friday evening before it was my time to clock out, the little bell over the door to the drug store ringed as the door opened and an older white man who had to be in his early forties entered the store. Dusty red hair with splatches of gray in it peeked out from underneath his winter hat. Coughing slightly, he browsed the aisles for a minute before I walked up to him.

"You need some help?"

The man took his attention from the cough lozenges that he had been looking and turned my way. The first thing that I noticed about him were his blue-green eyes. Behind those eyes held a world full of pain and I was instantly drawn to him. He held my gaze for a moment before saying anything.

"Um... Um, yes," he coughed. Pointing to the shelf, he asked, "Which one of these works the best for a cough? I've been coughing up a storm for the past three days now and it's likely 'bout to make me bonkers."

I reached around him and picked up a blue bag containing cough lozenges and handed it to him. "These seem to work the best for me when I'm sick." When my hand grazed his, I jumped back. My heart starting racing inside of my chest and I caught his gaze again. Studying his face which bore small wrinkles at the corners of his eyes, my eyes traveled downward, and I saw a sprinkle of freckles upon the bridge of his nose that I hadn't noticed moments before.

The man nodded and smiled his thanks before walking towards the front of the store to pay for his item. I couldn't shake the feeling that that man was exactly who I thought him to be. He paid for the cough lozenges and left out of the store without so much a backwards glance. I came out of my stupor and ran to the back of the store and grabbed my coat and threw it on. Wrapping a scarf around my head, I called out to my boss as I walked briskly to the front of the store, "I'm clocking out, Mr. Gaines! I'll see you in the morning!"

"Alright, Cora. Have a good evening," came his response.

Pushing the drug store's door open, I tumbled out onto the sidewalk. The crisp winter's night air hit me like a sledgehammer as it whipped around my body. Looking up and down the street, I searched for a sign of the man who had just left the store but found none. My shoulders drooped with disappointment at the revelation that I'd probably just encountered my father for the first time in my life and had missed out on the one chance I would be given to know him.

Ashner's truck pulled up to the curb where I was standing, and he hopped out of it. Walking over towards me, he pulled me to the truck and opened the door. "Baby, what are you doing standing out here in the cold like this? I thought I told you to wait inside until I got here?"

I sat down in the passenger's seat and he shut the truck's door. Running back over to his side, he opened the driver's door and hopped inside. Rubbing his hands together, he said, "Good Lord, it's cold out there!"

Noticing that I hadn't said anything to him yet, he looked over at me. "Baby, you look like you done seen a ghost. What's wrong and why were you outside instead of being inside of the store waiting for me?"

Looking through the front window of the truck, I stared straight ahead. "I think I just saw my daddy."

Ashner started looking around and leaned forward in his seat and looked out the truck's window, too. "Baby, I don't see anybody. It's far too cold for people to just be standing out and about like that tonight."

I looked over at my handsome fiancé and smiled. "No, baby, not out here. I think my daddy visited the drug store tonight."

Ashner's eyebrows shot up upon his forehead. "Really? What did he say? Did he know you were his daughter?"

I dropped my head and groaned. "No. He just asked me what cough drops were the best and I told him, then he paid for them and split. I ran out of the store as fast as I could to find him, but by the time I'd made it outside, he was gone."

"Aw, baby, I'm sorry." Ashner started the truck and pulled off. "You know, maybe he'll show back up at the store again," he said as we rounded the square.

I looked out of the passenger's side window and sighed. My heart was so heavy. I can't believe I had let the opportunity to meet the man that could be my father slip away from me. "I don't know, love. I'm only going to be working at the store for another week..." Pausing, I sat up straight in my seat as I saw a man wearing the same coat and hat that the man had on just moments before in the store walking down the street.

"Stop the truck!"

Confused, Ashner looked at me and said, "What?"

Pointing frantically out the window, I screamed, "Stop the truck! That's him! That's him!"

The truck came screeching to a halt on the street, causing the man to stop walking and look up alarmed. I hopped out of the truck with Ashner hot on my trail and ran over to the man. He put his hands up out in front of him and said, "Look, I... I don't want any trouble. I don't have much cash on me."

Frowning in confusion, I stared at him. "Wait, what?" Realizing that he must've thought we were trying to rob him, I shook my head. "We aren't trying to mug you. I... Um, you're the guy from in the drug store earlier, right?"

The man nodded slowly.

"So, um, I was wonderin' if you knew me?"

The man looked from me back to Ashner then back to me again before speaking. The streetlight above us was shining down on his face highlighting the blue of his eyes. "Yes... I know who you are, Cora. I've always known."

My heart seemingly stopped beating in my chest. Was he for real? Was this happening? Could I actually be looking my father in his eyes right now? "Are you... Are you..." I couldn't get the question out because it seemed impossible to me for him to be who I thought he was, but it was as if my soul already knew.

The man nodded. "Yes, I'm your father. I'm Billy Baxter in the flesh."

My mouth dropped open and I reached out my hand and placed it on Ashner's arm to steady myself, so I wouldn't fall. Ashner reached down and took my hand in his and squeezed it tightly. The warmth of his fingers over mine were about the only thing that felt real right then. I had pictured this moment so many times in my mind before, but I never knew how I would feel when I finally met Billy Baxter. Would I feel scared? Angry? Happy? But right now, all I wanted to do was hug him... So, I did.

Letting go of Ashner's hand, I tossed my arms around Billy and hugged him. He stood in shock for a moment before encircling his arms around my body. When we broke apart he looked down at me with tears welling up in his eyes. "Do you know how long I've wanted to do that?" He reached up and swiped a tear that was falling from one of his eyes away. "I thought you wouldn't ever want to meet me or accept me."

"Truth be told, I didn't know how I would feel if I ever met you. I've... Well, I've heard all sorts of things about you."

Billy's cheeks flushed redder as he blushed than they already were from the cold of the wind outside. "I'm sure not all good things."

I shook my head and smiled, embarrassed because we both knew exactly what the not so good things that had been said about him were.

Ashner cleared his throat as he adjusted the collar on his olive green peacoat. "I hate to break up this while lovely yet unexpected reunion, but um, it's as cold as an Eskimo riding a polar bear out here."

Billy chuckled, and I laughed at my fiancé's description of how cold it was outside, but I had to agree. "My fiancé is right. Um, Billy, if you don't have anything to do, would you like to ride back to the house with us? I would love for you to see my sister and I want to get a chance to get to know you better."

Billy's eyes twinkled. "I would like that a lot."

We sat like three sardines in Ashner's truck as we drove towards home. I purposely hadn't mentioned Mama because I didn't know if Billy had even heard that she moved back to town five years ago and wanted it to be a surprise for both of them to see each other after so many years had passed.

When we pulled up into the yard, Ashner cut the engine and said, "Y'all ready?"

"Ready as I'll ever be, I'm guessing," Billy said with a nervous smile.

We got out of the truck and walked across the grass leading up to the porch. Never in a million years would I have thought this day would come. My daddy was going to be in the same house as me, Sister and Mama. It was an amazing, yet nerve wrecking feeling.

The house was warm and inviting when we stepped inside. The lamps were on in the front room and Isaiah was sitting in his spot on the floor in front of the TV. Norie was sitting down next to him combing the hair on one of her dollies. I could smell the wonderful fragrance of fried chicken, greens and cornbread wafting through the air and I knew that Mama must've just finished cooking supper. When Ashner shut the front door behind us, Norie looked up wide eyed at the stranger in the room.

Standing to her feet, she discarded her doll on the floor and walked over to where we were and stood right in front of Billy. With her head tilted upwards, her blue eyes shone with curiosity. "Who are you, mister?"

Billy laughed and extended his hand out to her for Norie to shake. Norie glanced in my direction to make sure that it was okay. After I nodded my head, she took his hand and shook it saying, "How do you do?"

"Very fine, thank you," came Billy's response. "My name is Billy. What's yours?"

Norie placed her hands on her small hips and replied proudly, "Nora after my Auntie Cora right there, but everyone calls me Norie."

"It's a pleasure to meet you, Norie."

"Ya' kno', you and my mommy have the same name."

"Is that right?"

"Uh huh," Norie replied nodding enthusiastically.

At that moment, Sister stepped into the room coming out of the kitchen looking down at a magazine in her hands. "What's goin' on in here? Norie I thought I asked you and Junebug to keep it down. I ain't wanna hear any talkin' while I was tryin' ta' read..." When she looked up and saw Billy standing in the room with us, the magazine flew out of her hands and fell to the floor.

"What in the hell is he doin' here?!"

Walking over to where she was standing, I put my hands out in front of me. "Now, don't go gettin' all heated, Sister. I met Billy tonight and asked him to come back here wit' us."

Sister's eyes were ablaze as she stared daggers into the soul of our father. Cutting her eyes at me, she gritted her teeth. "Like I said, what in the hell is that man doin' in our house?!"

"I wanted him to see you, Sister," I said quietly. "It's been years since you last saw him. You were a little girl and I just thought that..."

"How'd ya' kno' I saw him when I was little? Who told you? Mama?" Stepping aside from me, she stomped over to where Norie was still standing in front of Billy and grabbed her by the hand.

"Ow, Mommy!" Norie cried as she tried to pry her hand out of her mother's.

"I don't want ta' see this asshole ever in my lifetime. This man is as dead to me as his bigoted, no good daddy! It'll be a cold day in hell before I ever acknowledge this man's presence on earth!" Pointing a finger at me, she eyed me coldly. "How dare you bring him around mah baby!"

"Sister..."

"Don't you, Sister, meh! I hate Billy Baxter!"

Mama came running into the front room from out of the kitchen. Perspiration from standing in front of a hot stove cooking decorated her forehead in tiny beads. Wiping her hands on her apron, she exclaimed, "What in the world is goin' on in here wit' y'all keepin' up all this fuss?"

Her eyes scanned the room until they feel upon Billy and rested there. A hand flew up to her chest as her mouth dropped open. "Billy? Jesus Christ! Billy is that you?"

Billy took his winter hat off and nodded with a smile as big as Mt. Everest upon his face. Coming closer to her, he replied, "Yes ma'am, Glory Jean, it's me."

"Oh, my Lord, Billy!"

Billy scooped Mama up into a warm embrace and kissed her passionately on the lips.

"Ewww," Norie said as she covered her eyes with her free hand.

Sister let go of her daughter's hand and pushed Billy off of Mama.

"Billie Christina what has gotten into you?!" Mama asked.

Sister didn't respond but hauled off and socked Billy right square in the jaw with her fist. Norie started crying and I rushed over to pick her up. Isaiah started rocking back and forth on the floor and humming loudly in an attempt to drown out the commotion.

"Sister!" Ashner yelled as he grabbed her around the waist and tried to keep her from throwing anymore blows. He picked her up off of the floor and she wildly kicked her legs with one of the kicks landing right in the middle of Billy's stomach. He fell back and over the arm of a chair and sunk down into it with an "oomph".

"Billy!" Mama cried aloud as she kneeled down on the floor in front of him. Caressing his face softly, she asked, "Are you okay?"

Meanwhile Sister was still throwing a tantrum, cursing and carrying on as she tried to free herself of Ashner's strong grasp.

"Put me down, Ashner or I swear ta' God Imma bite ya' arm and take a chunk out of it the entire size of the state of Tennessee!"

"I'm not lettin' you go until I know that you won't haul off and hit anybody else in this room."

Sister's face was splotchy from her irritation of the situation at hand. Blowing out some air hard, she replied, "Fine! I won't touch that yella-livered ass old coot again! Now, put meh down!"

Ashner reluctantly placed Sister back down and the moment her feet touched the floor she walked over to me and pulled Norie out of my arms. "Give meh mah baby!" Eyeing me coldly, she said, "I can't believe you welcomed that there trash into our home! That no good, couldn't even stand up to his pappy, coward over there! He's the reason Mama got on drugs in tha' first place 'cause she couldn't deal wit' how his daddy killed her sister and you wanted to bring him home to meet me for what?! To make ya'self feel like you's accomplished somethin'? Well, guess what buttercup? The only thang you succeeded in ta'night is pissin' meh off by tryna stir up the past! Billy Baxter is dead ta' meh and will stay dead!" Brushing pass me she went to our room holding a wailing Norie in her arms.

"Billie, wait!" Billy coughed out from the chair. He was now sitting upright and Mama was dabbing blood off of his mouth with a towel. Looking at Mama, he said, "Glory Jean, I didn't mean to start any trouble. I just wanted to see her. Outside of seeing her from a distance over the years, I haven't ever gotten a chance to just talk to her. I wanted to tell her that I was sorry." Glancing over at me, he said, "You, too, Cora. I am so sorry."

With Norie gone, I had now walked over to where Isaiah was sitting and was patting him gently on the back to help him calm down. From experience I knew that it would take several minutes before he returned to normal. He was still humming to soothe himself, just not as loudly as before.

"It's okay, Billy," I replied with a lump in my throat. "While you are here, I do have some questions for you though and maybe it will help Sister to hear the answers to these. Even though she's mad right now, I know she's still listening to what's going on in here."

Ashner came over and took a seat behind me on the couch and I inhaled deeply trying to muster up enough courage to ask my father some very difficult questions. "It's okay, baby, just take your time and ask him," Ashner encouraged me softly.

Nodding, I began my interrogation. "Billy, why didn't you just run off with Mama after she had gotten pregnant wit' Sister? Why did you stay down here and pretend to be racist like the rest of your family when you are anything but? How could you allow this town to view you like that? How could you just stay here and do nothin' when Mama was hurtin' about how she lost her little sister? Why did you marry someone else and have a child wit' them knowin' full well that you could never really in truly love her? Just why? Do you know how much hurt and pain the actions of yours caused all of us?"

Billy sat there ingesting my questions as they rolled off of my lips one by one. I watched as pain welled up inside of his already tired eyes. "The answer to those questions is a simple one, Cora. I was weak. My daddy ran my life the way he wanted it to go. It didn't matter that I was grown by the time I had met your Mama. Daddy wasn't having any of his children messing around outside of their race. I hate the fact that no matter how old I got, I never was strong enough to stand up to that man. When he died right after you were born I tried my hardest to get Glory Jean to come back home. I divorced my wife and left her and our daughter, Shelley, to fend for themselves. I regret leaving Shelley, but I felt that if I couldn't be a father to you and Billie, then I wasn't fit to be a father at all."

Shaking his head, Billy continued, "Your sister was right. I am a coward. I took the easy way out and hurt so many people and that is something that I will regret for the rest of my life, but I can't go back and change what I did all of those years ago. I can only work on right now. I'm still looked at as being racist by association to some people who don't know me just because I'm a Baxter, so, that's why I try to stay out of people's way. But, there's one thing that I want you to know, Cora, the world is changing and there's nothing wrong with finding out the good parts of your white bloodline. You can learn to love that part of yourself, too. Everything isn't always going to be black and white."

Mama spoke up next as she patted Billy's hand lightly from the spot on the floor where she was sitting next to the chair. Glancing up at him with a guilt-ridden face, she reached up and touched the outline of his jaw. "Cora, it's not all of your daddy's fault and you probably gathered that from readin' the letters I gave you that your daddy wrote me all those years ago. I have lived with the regret of my decision not to make a life with your father for many years now. If I hadn't of chosen to let drugs be the love of my life instead of Billy things would've turned out better for all of us. Mama wouldn't have had to raise all of you. Sister wouldn't have grown up so angry wit' so much hatred in her young heart and Cora," turning towards me, her brown eyes were full of sadness. "You wouldn't have spent so much of your life not knowing who you truly are. You spent so much of your childhood thinkin' your father was dead and not truly being free to live as a little girl should have. Instead of playing with dolls and coloring, you were busy raising your little brother as if he were your own. We can't blame Billy for all of this. I shared a part, too."

Billy lifted Mama's hand to his lips and gently pressed a kiss on the back of it. "Can we start over again, Glory Jean. If you'd have me? I don't care what people in this town may think of me, of us, I just want to be by your side for the rest of my life." Looking over at me, he said, "And in our daughter's lives if they will have me."

I didn't know about Sister, but my heart was sat on forgiveness. This was what all of those Bible Studies and Sunday School meetings Big Ma had dragged me to as a child were all about. If our family could heal from the destruction that racism had caused as it teared us apart, it could lead us one step closer towards healing as a people, as a nation and as the human race.

"Of course, Daddy," I replied with a genuine smile and a full heart. It felt wonderful to know that everything I had grown up knowing about Billy Baxter wasn't true. He had made a mistake, but he was human just like the rest of us are and should be forgiven as well.

*

Over the next two months, Mama and Billy began courting one another again, taking things slowly, one day at a time. My heart swelled at the sight of seeing her all in love with my father. It was like watching two young kids discover love all for the first time. Sister wasn't pleased with Billy being in our lives at first, but she slowly warmed up to him where she could stand to be in the room with him longer than five minutes without wanting to punch him in the face.

It was a late Sunday afternoon when I received a phone call that would change my life forever. As I was giving Norie a bath in the old large metal wash basin that we used to wash our clothes in, I heard the phone ringing in the front room. Sister had taken Isaiah into town to go shopping and we were the only ones at home.

"Stay put," I directed my niece as I wiped my wet hands on my pants, stood quickly and raced into the other room to catch the phone before whoever on the other line hung up.

Picking up the receiver, I breathlessly answered the phone, "Hello?"

A female voice on the other end of the line that I didn't recognize questioned, "Is Billie or Cora Harris at home?"

"I'm Cora, may I ask who's calling?"

"This is Nurse Betsy Blue from the county hospital. I'm sorry to be contacting you but I have a bit of bad news..."

Betsy began explaining to me that there had been an incident at the diner where Mama and Billy had gone out on a date for a late lunch after church services were over. A crazed white woman wielding a gun had come inside and headed right towards my parents table and opened fire on them. Instantly killing Billy and severely injuring Mama. Betsy went on to tell me that Mama was in surgery right now and that the doctors were trying to do everything in their power to save her life.

The receiver slipped out of my hand and hit the floor with a thud as I fell to my knees. "Oh, God! Nooooo! God, no!" Tears flooded my face like Niagara Falls as I clutched at my heart. "Please, God, no!"

"Auntie Corieeeee! Auntie Corieeeee!"

I could barely hear Norie calling out to me from the kitchen through the loud beating of my heart echoing in my ears. How could this have happened? I had family gotten the family that I'd always wanted. Why was this happening now? God, please save my mama, I silently prayed.

"Auntie Corieeeee!"

Standing to my feet, I made a weak attempt at wiping the tears away from my face, but it was of no use, they kept falling. I rushed back into the kitchen and pulled Norie up out of the suds. Drying her off with a towel, I wrapped it around her small body, picked her up and held her tightly to me.

"Auntie, why you cryin'?" she asked, softly in concern.

I couldn't bear the thought of explaining to a five-year-old the seriousness of what was going on, so, I just continued to sob. "We need to find your Mama, baby, and Isaiah." Carrying her to our room, I placed her down on the floor. "Find something warm to put on, okay?"

Norie stared up at me with her huge blue eyes and nodded in response. Her sun spun golden curls flopped into her eyes and she brushed them away with her hand. Leaving her in the room, I ran in the front room and picked up the phone and dialed Ashner. His mother answered on the first ring. I explained to her what was going on and she said that they would be on their way over to pick us up.

Mr. Jones passed Sister's car on the road as we were heading into town. He flashed his lights at her and she pulled over. He jumped out of the car and ran over to hers and quickly explained to her the situation. Running back over to the car, he jumped back in and sped off with Sister trailing us. Ashner held me in his arms in efforts to comfort me as we sat in the backseat. Norie was wide eyed, but quiet as she sat in my lap watching the world beyond the windows of the car pass on by.

When we arrived at the hospital, Mrs. Jones took Norie and Isaiah as Sister, Ashner and I ran inside together. Sister was frantic as she rushed down the hospital corridor at full speed leaving us trailing behind.

"Where's mah mama? Where's mah mama?" She desperately cried out. She ran over to the information desk and banged upon it hard with her hand. Addressing the nurse sitting behind it, she yelled, "Where's mah damn mama?" Tears slid down her chin and plopped onto the desk.

"Ma'am just calm down, so I can help you."

Ashner and I ran up to the desk and he placed a hand on Sister's shoulder as he explained to the nurse who we were looking for. The nurse found Mama's chart and paged another nurse to come and get us.

"I should've been a better daughter ta' her," Sister cried and I took her into my arms. Resting her head on my shoulder, her body shook with grief. "What if I don't get another chance wit' her? To tell her that I love her? God, in all the years that she's been back, I haven't even told her that I love her." Pulling back away from me, Sister looked me in my eyes. "It's too late ain't it? It's too late?"

I didn't have an answer for her, because I wanted to believe in my heart that Mama would be alright, but something in my spirit was telling me that she was gone. When the paged nurse made her way out to us, the operating room's doctor was right behind her. Blood was splattered all over his scrubs and I nearly doubled over at the sight of it. That's my mama's blood on him.

The doctor explained to us that they had done all they could to save Mama, but the bullet had pierced a main artery causing her to lose a substantial amount of blood. There was nothing more that they could do. Mama was gone. Sister burst out crying hysterically as I held her tightly in my arms.

"Mamaaaa! Mamaaaa!"

Ashner wrapped his arms around the both of us and steered us towards the waiting room area where we could sit down. Sister pushed his hand away and broke away from my grasp. Running back towards the doctor and nurse, she pleaded with them. "Please let meh see mah mama! Please, let meh see her. I need ta' tell her that I loves her. She needs ta' know that I've always loved her! Please!"

My heart was breaking even more at hearing my sister cry out in grief. Ashner and I walked back over to where she was standing and once again tried to steer her back towards the waiting room. With her head bowed down, this time she allowed us to. I couldn't believe how much my life had changed in just a short few months, but never in my dreams would I have figured this nightmare would happen. *With Mama gone now, how are we going to carry on? Who's going to watch after Isaiah now?*

Epilogue

Two and a Half Years Later

August 1971

We all took Mama's death pretty hard and it took months before we could gain some sort of normalcy within our lives again. The woman who had taken Billy's and Mama's lives, was his ex-wife, Alice. She had been in a fit of rage when she found out that Billy was back dating the very woman who had caused the end of her marriage and she decided that the only way she could gain some closure on the dissolution of her marriage was to kill her ex-husband and his "mistress".

Alice was detained at a women's correctional facility and would be spending the rest of her life there for the murders of my parents. Shelley ended up being so warped with grief at our father dying by the hands of her mother that she committed suicide a month later. She was discovered in her aunt's bathtub submerged in water after taking a combination of pills she had stolen from the medicine cabinet. My heart ached for the loss of a sister that I never got a proper chance to know due to the circumstances behind our existence.

I continued living with Sister, Norie and Isaiah at our country home for the months following Mama's death until Ashner and I graduated. We were married in July of 1968 on his birthday and are now residing in Washington D.C. where we are both enrolled in college. I am still planning on studying law and he's already taking up his business courses. Isaiah is staying with Ashner's parents until Ashner and I are ready to move back to Tennessee. The plan will be for my little brother to live with us, once we are settled down.

Sister is doing well for herself. She is a supervisor at the boutique on the square and she is married to a nice black man named Charlie Biggs who is about seven years older than she is. They are expecting their first baby together. I hope that it's a little boy. Norie is excited about being a big sister and says she can't wait for the baby to get here.

Although we never found out who was behind my Uncle Joe's death, I haven't forgotten about it. I'm going to make it my duty to reopen his case as soon as I become a Civil Rights lawyer. Not only will I take a stand for African Americans, but I will take a stand for all races who are being mistreated and discriminated against. I will be the voice for the voiceless and the face for the faceless. I will make my Big Ma proud and let the Lord use me as she commanded me all those years ago on her deathbed.

It's my mission to make this world we live in a better place for all. I want little biracial children coming up after me to know that you can love both parts of your race equally. I won't people who face oppression to know that we can overcome injustices and hardships if we practice forgiveness and love one another for who they are and not just for what we can physically see on the outside. I can't wait to see what the future holds for me and my people, but I know that whatever it is, it will smell as sweet as honeysuckles on a Tennessee breeze.

Meet the Author

Other Novels by LeTresa Payne include: Daughter Cry No More, Secrets Within Her, Prayer Warriors, Her Lethal Desire, Motions, and Emotions. All titles are available on Amazon and Kindle at www.amazon.com/author/letresapayne